# LORD
### *of*
# BONES

## DEATH BOUND DUET: BOOK 1

AIDEN PIERCE
R.K. PIERCE

Cover Design: GraphicsbyGeka

Editing: The Fiction Fix

# A WORD OF WARNING

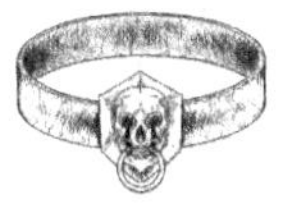

Some content within this book may be disturbing or triggering for some readers. Reader discretion is advised.

Subjects include gore, violence, murder, kidnapping, discussions of suicide, mentions of parental loss, breath play, erotic degradation and humiliation, praise, primal play/chasing, dub-con, non-con (not between MCs), psychological abuse, manipulation, bondage, impact play, pain play, wax play, somnophilia and other graphic sexual content.

If you have any questions pertaining to this warning, please don't hesitate to contact the authors, Aiden Pierce and R.K. Pierce.

*"Your eyes can be so cruel,*

*Just as I can be so cruel."*

*David Bowie*

# PLAYLIST

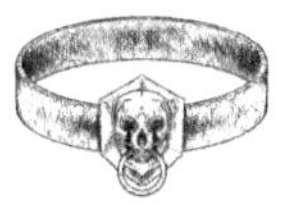

"Within You" – David Bowie

"Can't Help Falling in Love – DARK" – Tommee Profit, Brooke

"Wicked Game" – Ursine Vulpine, Annaca

"Devil Devil" – MILCK

"As The World Falls Down" – David Bowie

# CHAPTER ONE

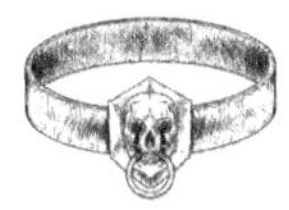

## RAYVEN

DEAD MEN TOLD NO tales, but they *did* fill my bank account. The ones worth a damn anyway.

It wasn't easy. I'd sunk so much time and energy into perfecting my craft, not to mention the physical exertion it took to exhume the corpses.

Grave robber, grave digger, tomb raider... There were many names for my chosen career path, but I preferred *asset repossessor*. It had a nice ring to it.

It wasn't honest work, but I didn't give two fucks about that. It paid decently, and that was good enough for me. The heirlooms, jewels, and dollars I collected covered my necessities, but it was never enough to scratch the insatiable itch for more.

Still, my favorite part wasn't even the money. No, it was the high that came with every job. That's what drove me at the end of the day. I was addicted to the hours of late-night research, the careful plotting, staking out the cemetery, and my favorite part of all: actually pulling it off.

And tonight promised to be my biggest payday ever.

Nothing I'd uncovered over the years could hold a candle to the riches rumored to be hidden in the Petherick family tomb. Even the name oozed opulence and grandeur. It was everything I'd been waiting for, the big break that would change my life completely, and after weeks of plotting and planning, the time had finally come.

As I stared up at the impressive mausoleum, my pulse quickened. The family name was chiseled into the stone above the steel door, along with some indecipherable details. It had been a bitch to get to this point, from hiding the car half a mile away in the closest patch of trees to scaling not one, but *two* wrought iron fences. I had a nasty scar on my thigh from my first time climbing one of those things.

Now that I was finally here, my mind ran rampant with what awaited behind the sealed entrance, my fingertips tingling in anticipation.

This right here? The moment of silence before cracking into some rich asshole's final resting place? It was my drug. The money was great, but the rush I got from disturbing the eternal rest of those who looked down on people like me in their waking life? That was better than gold.

The building was tall and wide, a sharp steeple stretching up from the stone roof. There were no flowers or decorations adorning it, aside from the detailed images chiseled into the walls, but they were too compacted with dirt and dust to make out clearly. It was raised on a dais in the middle of the cemetery, three marble steps leading up to it, making it the focal point of the dilapidated graveyard.

Even after centuries of weathering the elements, whispers of grandeur remained, but there was mystery surrounding the mausoleum. Despite extensive internet searches and even delving into public records at City Hall, I still had no idea exactly which member—or members—of the Petherick family were buried here.

Whatever was inside had been hidden for centuries, and I was minutes away from unearthing it.

Little sparks of electricity danced through my bloodstream. I could hardly contain my excitement.

"Are you sure you want to do this?" Mark asked in my ear, keeping his voice low. I'd been so focused on the excitement buzzing through me, entranced by the towering mausoleum, I'd almost forgotten he was there.

He was quiet on the job, but I liked it that way. His voice got on my nerves after a while. That probably should have been my sign to break up with the guy. We'd been dating for over a year, if you could call lame dates and disappointing dick "dating". I wasn't feeling it, but...he was, so I was putting off ending things.

While we'd been sleeping together for a year, we'd been working and living together for almost five. I didn't want him to get mad and refuse to work with me anymore, especially when I needed help. While he was a bit on the nervous side when it came to the whole filthy criminal thing, he was a good asset. These graves weren't going to dig themselves, and being just over five feet made it difficult for me to swing a shovel for hours on end.

Mark was the muscle of this outfit, and I was...Well, I was everything else.

Tonight was like most nights–we knew the drill. Get in, take as much as we could fit in the duffle bag clutched in my hand, get out without being seen.

With this job, though, the stakes were higher. Tonight, we were hitting the Petherick tomb, and they weren't just rich bureaucrats or trust fund babies. No, they were royalty, and they came from one of the richest families to ever grace this continent.

These people were so upper crust, there was a crazy myth about the entire family being descended from gods, a direct bloodline to supernatural deities. I called bullshit. What I *did* believe were the rumors about them being filthy fucking rich, and greedy rich people of their caliber loved being buried with their earthly riches.

"Of course I want to do this," I snapped back, slinging the backpack off my shoulder and letting it fall with a *thud* to the ground. I knelt beside it, tearing open the zipper and rummaging through it for my tools. "We have rent to make, remember? Don't tell me you're chickening out, babe." I didn't bother biting back the annoyance in my tone. This wouldn't be the first time he'd backed out of a job.

He forced a laugh, but I could hear what he didn't say. There was something off about this, something that had his skin crawling. I felt it too.

It wasn't unusual for Mark to get a bit nervous before a job, but usually, he got over himself once we arrived on site. Since we'd parked the car and made our way to the middle of this private graveyard, he'd only gotten more nervous.

"It's gonna be okay. This place is out in the middle of nowhere. No one's gonna catch us," I assured him. "This is gonna be cake. This place is supposed to be untouched; no one's had the balls to hit it yet. Just think of the payday waiting for us inside."

My mind teeming with delicious possibilities, I pulled on a headlamp and passed one to Mark.

"Why don't you make yourself useful and get to work on the door?" I asked sweetly, batting my eyelashes up at him, even though it was too dark for him to see.

Mark's broad shoulders and athlete's physique made him perfect for wielding a shovel or a crowbar, though he did get a little queasy depending on the age of the graves. Dead bodies never bothered me. I actually found bones quite beautiful.

While I had a knack for stomaching gruesome sites, Mark had a proclivity for homemade explosives that had come in handy on more than one occasion.

"Of course, doll," he said, swinging his crowbar up so it land-ed on his shoulder. "As you wish."

My eyes trailed him as he marched up the stairs to the mau-soleum door and inspected it for a brief moment, running his fingers along the seam where metal met stone. If he decid-ed he couldn't break in with the crowbar, we'd resort to the homemade explosives at the bottom of my bag, though that was always our last resort due to the noise. Besides, Mark wouldn't miss a chance to look manly wielding a solid rod of steel.

I pulled on a respirator mask, along with long rubber gloves–you could never be too careful when dealing with dead bodies–and joined Mark at the mausoleum entrance.

He prodded the seam with his crowbar once before jamming the steel into the tiny crevice. To my surprise, it didn't move.

"It's sealed pretty well for being so old," he muttered, swing-ing again.

This time, the crowbar wedged, and he threw his body into it, trying to pry the door open. It didn't budge much.

"Impressive." I whistled, glancing over my shoulder at the backpack on the ground. "You want me to get the dynamite?"

"Not yet," he grunted, throwing his weight into the crowbar once more. "I'm just getting warmed up."

It was slow going, but with deep, vibrating groans and squeaks, the door finally opened a few inches. A gust of stale air hit me, like the building suddenly exhaled after centuries of holding its breath, and Mark handed me the crowbar. He grabbed the edge of the door, wrenching and prying until it opened enough for us to slip inside.

He was panting, sweat dripping down from his hairline, but his mouth ticked up in a smirk when he stepped aside and gestured to the entrance with a sweep of his hand.

"Told you," he breathed, taking back his crowbar. "After you."

"You're too kind." I rolled my eyes with a half-smile and stepped toward the doorway, slipping in sideways to avoid the rusty metal snagging my clothes.

It was pitch black, the sliver of light from the entrance not permeating past an inch or two inside, and ice cold. Considering the crisp fall air outside the building, I wasn't expecting it to be so frigid, but goosebumps raced up my arms, and I instinctively looked for my breath to escape in white puffs. It didn't, but I attributed that to the mask I wore.

My teeth began to chatter.

"Shit," Mark hissed as he slipped inside behind me. "Why the hell is it so cold?"

"It's a crypt, babe," I said with a laugh, though there was no humor in my voice.

He was right. The blast of air that blew through the door was abnormally chilly.

It probably should have been an indicator that something was different about this grave, but I didn't pay it much attention. Swinging my head left and right, I let the light from my headlamp dance through the darkness, illuminating the mausoleum's interior.

Small alcoves were carved into the walls to make floor-to-ceiling shelves, and they were all laden with things–boxes, vases, trinkets, things that shimmered and shone when the light hit them. My stomach did a sickening backflip.

"Holy shit," I whispered, my voice barely audible to my own ears.

I loved crypts. I mean, so did every goth girl in theory, but my appreciation erred on the side of obsession. Something about the silence, the dust in the air, the undisturbed spiderwebs. I even liked bones. Hell, I especially liked bones. I liked to stare at them and imagine the person they'd once belonged to.

The crypts I broke into usually belonged to people who hadn't been so great when they'd been alive. So, I liked to imagine the sunny part of their lives, like the beams of light that broke through the tiny windows of a crypt, disturbing the murk. In my experience, even the darkest crypts had small traces of light. The same usually went for the people they belonged to.

It was hard to imagine the family laid to rest within the walls of this place. It was the most opulent mausoleum I'd ever been in. It was lined in white marble, pretty coffins perched on individual ledges, all with their own plaque framed in gold.

I took a few steps deeper into the building, farther into the impossible blackness, and my gaze landed on three marble vaults laid evenly along the middle of the space. They were identical and unadorned, aside from name plaques at the foot of each one, and *fuck* my curiosity was piqued. I'd searched so much to figure out who was laid to rest in the Petherick tomb, and this was my chance to find out.

Tempted as I was to run for the shelves and start grabbing everything I could get my hands on, I slowly approached the first vault and paused beside it to read the name plaque: *Elias 1713-1745.*

Next in line was Nathaniel, and Mark stepped up to the third and final vault, bending to peer over the name placard.

"Catherine."

At the sound of the name, a hollow knock sounded, reverberating through the mausoleum, making my blood run as cold as the air around us. Mark and I met each other's gaze across the dark space, and I swallowed hard, trying to shake off the uneasy feeling.

I hadn't felt so uncomfortable at a grave site in over five years, but a tickle of dread laced its way up my spine, making me eager to get the hell out of there.

"This place gives me the creeps, and not the good kind. Start grabbing so we can get out of here," I said urgently, turning away from the stone vaults and toward the first wall of shelves.

As expected, there was so much stored away here. I could only imagine how much these things would fetch on the black market. What kind of secrets did this family seal up with their dead? What kind of precious stones and metals hadn't seen the light of day in over three hundred years?

There was enough here to catch up on my rent for an entire year, probably more.

I could pay off my car, I could get my own place. I wouldn't have to live with Mark anymore.

This was the payout I'd been searching so long for, and I could hardly control myself as I grabbed a wooden box off a shelf and popped the lid open. Inside was a silver tiara that made my pulse quicken, and with a huge grin, I threw it in the bag. The rest of the shelf was laden with more elegant jewelry, all stunning. Regal. *Fucking expensive.*

This was exactly the jackpot I'd been hoping for.

My head went light—from the high that came with a successful raid, or the thick air that seemed to stuff itself down my throat like a chloroform-soaked rag, I wasn't sure.

"We might have to break this up into two trips. I can't fucking breathe in here," I rasped, gasping for air. "Move faster so we can get the hell out of here."

I grabbed everything I could get my hands on, dollar signs racking up before my eyes. This raid was everything I'd ever dreamed it would be. I should have been ecstatic, but as we stepped out of the mausoleum, dread washed over me.

*Something was terribly wrong.*

# CHAPTER TWO

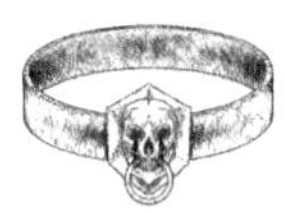

## BELIAL

To live is to die.

It was a fact of nature, a hymn that echoed across the heavens, their lyrics inscribed upon the bones of God himself.

All things that drew breath would eventually age and rot. Then, they became mine.

There was no fighting it. It was a cosmic law. All living things were destined to become mine in time.

With Catherine, I couldn't wait for her heart to give out.

I'd kidnapped her from the land of the living, dragged her down to the darkest pits of my realm. I had defied nature itself.

Even death has his vices. How could I be blamed?

The breath from her lungs had been like a breeze, sifting through the hair of a freshly-freed inmate. The healthy flush of her cheeks had made my fleshless skull ache with longing.

The moment I set eyes on her, I longed to hear the echo of her laughter through my cold crypt of a palace.

I'd lusted for her vitality. My cock had stirred to life for the first time in centuries at the thought of owning her before her life ran its course.

I wanted to own so much more than her corpse.

In the beginning I'd planned for her to be a pampered pet, something to bring life to my castle, but in the end, she'd been nothing but a prisoner.

The never-ending, labyrinthine hallways of my palace had driven her to madness. When she failed to escape, she tried to leave me in the only way she could.

Every night, she took her own life. At first, she'd done it quick, clean, with a letter opener in her room. On the second night, she'd hung herself from the balcony of her tower using her bed sheets.

Every day, she'd wake up unscathed, like the previous night had never happened. As the days mounted, so had her desperation, and her suicides became more...creative.

She'd drowned herself in the Styx behind the palace, fed herself to the carnivorous oak in the garden, intentionally gotten herself crushed between the walls of the moving chambers within my castle, thrown herself onto the swords of the haunted suits of armor that patrolled my halls.

The list went on.

Those were the only ones I distinctly remembered; the rest blended together. The only thing that stood out was the sight of her mangled body just before I revived her. I should have felt more than nothingness each time those lifeless eyes stared up at me, a pool of dark red blood spreading beneath her.

Maybe if I had, I would have kept it up longer. Eventually, I tired of the constant cycle. So, one day when I found her, I decided it would be the last.

I'd brought her body back to the surface to be buried in her family crypt. I would have buried her on the grounds of my palace, but the poor girl had worked so tirelessly to free herself of me and my realm.

She would prefer the company of maggots and grave robbers over my own anyway.

The maggots I could deal with. It was the grave robbers I'd have to occasionally exterminate like the vermin they were that irritated me.

Grave robbers were the lowliest of beasts. I'd punished such filth countless times before. Between their pathetic sobs and pleas for me to spare them, they always regurgitated the same old shit—that stealing from the dead was no crime, for the dead had no use for worldly possessions.

But it wasn't the dead from whom they stole.

It was *me*.

As the Lord of Bones, I was the master of the dead, the keeper of graves. I owned every part of the deceased until they passed from my realm into the next, if I allowed them to pass at all.

I couldn't protect every grave, nor did I care to. However, I would rise from my throne to guard any corpse that had so much as a trace of Catherine's bloodline.

*I owed her that much.*

Most humans, as stupid as they were, had enough sense not to fuck with the Petherick family mausoleum. There'd been rumors that the god of death stole Catherine away to the underworld and that her father, a rich lord at the time, paid me off in exchange for eternal life.

Unlike most rumors, all those had been true. I did grant Catherine's father eternal life. What I hadn't promised him was that I wouldn't bury him anyway. Now, he lay in a box somewhere—I didn't even remember where—far beneath the surface where no one would hear him scream.

Regardless, her family talked, and the rumors eventually turned to superstition. Most mortals stayed away, but humans were curious, greedy vermin. There was always one every half century or so who dared to get too close, dared to disturb the Petherick's elaborate resting place.

The last man who dared break into Catherine's tomb now made up a lovely chandelier that hung over my dining room table. At least, what was left of him.

When I felt that tingle in my horns, I knew the magical wards I'd placed inside the crypt had been breached once again. An intruder. *A thief.*

What piece of furniture would I make out of this poor bastard? A wine rack, perhaps?

This was the first time I'd been to the surface in over a century; I'd almost forgotten what it was like: the scent of greenery, the caress of fresh air against my bones, the gentle breeze through my eye sockets.

There was no time to enjoy it, though. It felt wrong to revel in the moonlight when I came here for an execution.

Normally, I didn't deal death. Usually, I'd wait for its natural course, but not this day, not with this scum. If they'd so much as breathed on Catherine's crypt, I'd cut out their hearts and suffer their blood like mediocre wine.

They would pay for disturbing what was mine.

I portaled into the mausoleum invisibly, my cloak's hem blowing up years of dust in a swirling cloud around my boots. The place grew colder with my presence—cold enough for anything with a heartbeat to catch its death.

When the temperature dropped, I expected them to run, but these thieves were persistent. They shivered, their breath hanging in puffs around them as they moved through Catherine's family crypt, stuffing their bag full of relics and trinkets. Some of them were magical in nature, as I'd laid them to rest with Catherine. These humans wouldn't be leaving with them.

I started forward, freezing in my tracks when I got a better look at them.

One of them was female.

Intrigue hooked in my gut. In all my years, this was the first time I'd ever crossed paths with a female grave robber. Most human women had better instincts than that.

Her skin was vampire pale, as if she lived in my realm rather than this one, and she was so tiny. She'd be so easy to break if I wasn't careful. The clothing she wore made her look even smaller. *God's Below*. What was she wearing?

Her form was wrapped in a dark jacket, the front zipper low enough to reveal a V-necked shirt and ample cleavage. Her skirt was sinfully short, exposing much of her stocking-wrapped thighs. The stockings themselves didn't seem to have much point; they certainly weren't for preserving modesty, with their net-like pattern that somehow seemed more brazen than if she was bare-legged.

I should have found her appearance disgraceful. Instead, it only stirred a dark part of me—a part I thought had died long ago—to life.

I found the male infinitely less interesting.

Was he her mate? Did he force her here? Not by the excitement sparkling in her eyes as she stuffed her bag full of treasures.

Would I punish her the same way as I had all the men before her? I could, but...no. That would be a waste. This one was too pretty to be made into furniture. And her scent. *Bleeding Hells.* It was far too pleasing to make her into anything so mundane as a wine rack. Her aroma of cloves and bitter cherries had my mind going wild with possibilities for her punishment.

I could tie her naked to my bed, and keep her there for all eternity, for the mere purpose of scenting my sheets. My own living potpourri. She could have other uses, tied to my bed...

My thoughts turned dark as death, and I pushed them away.

No. What was I thinking? I couldn't take another living being to my realm. I swore I never would again, not after Catherine. It would be best to kill her alongside her mate, quick and easy. She wouldn't suffer.

I watched as the girl shoved the stone lid of Catherine's sarcophagus and managed a few inches of clearance, enough to wiggle her hand inside. Her nose scrunched up on her face as she pawed around the corpse. Her mate seemed to gag and turned away. Clearly, the female had the stronger nerves out of the pair. Good. She'd need them.

I shouldn't have been studying her the way I was. What did it matter, if I was going to kill her? I couldn't help it. I needed to imagine the look of shock that would pass behind her chocolate brown eyes as I plunged my hand through her chest to claim her heart. I wanted to know what that raven black hair pulled up into a ponytail would look like down, matted with blood.

Why couldn't I picture it? A beat later, my question was answered. The girl's eyes lit up as she found something of interest among Catherine's remains. With a sharp tug, there was the sound of snapping bone and the crackle of centuries old flesh. She held up a ruby amulet that caught the beam of light pouring in through the mausoleum's singular window. It had been ages since I'd seen it.

The amulet was of a silver skull, with two, tear-shaped garnets fastened below the skull's eye sockets, made to look as though it was weeping blood.

"Nice," the little thief murmured before tossing the ancient relic into her sack of filched goods, like it was nothing but a common trinket.

Unadulterated fury thrummed through my being. The amulet's chain could only be broken by its creator, so when the thief tugged it off Catherine, she'd snapped her neck in two.

All resolve to spare this little human from my boundless cruelty withered in an instant. She'd desecrated Catherine's body. She didn't deserve a quick death—she didn't deserve to die at all.

Whatever punishment I deemed worthy of her crime, I'd draw it out.

In my clutches, this little thief would suffer. To start, I'd make her watch me disembowel her soft, nervous mate.

I slowly approached them. As I passed the various coffins, my heavy footsteps roused the bones of the dead, and they stirred to life, moaning and banging on their lids in hopes of catching the attention of their lord and master.

The thieves stopped their task of stuffing their bag, their eyes going wide. They wouldn't see me unless I wished it. For now, I'd remain hidden, rouse their fear until they were pissing themselves with terror.

"What the fuck was that?" the male asked, his voice shaking.

Another step toward them, then another, until the air in the mausoleum was deathly cold. The female swung her eyes in my direction. She must have caught a glimpse of my shadow, something frightening enough to make her scream.

"Let's get out of here," she yelled, and they bolted outside. *Ha.* As if the night could protect them.

There was no escaping death when it came to call.

I followed behind them, pausing at the mausoleum's entrance and watching them run for a moment. The male was faster, leaving his woman behind to fend for herself as she carried the bag of stolen goods over her shoulder. She'd abandoned her mask at the base of the mausoleum, and her dark hair was whipping behind her as she ran away.

My gaze flicked back to the male, who was putting more space between him and Catherine's tomb with every second that passed. What kind of pathetic excuse for a male left their mate behind?

Surely, he sensed the danger? Coward.

Normally I didn't revel in such brutality, but I'd take pleasure in stripping the bones from the flesh of this miserable welp.

I was in front of him in a blink, sure to remain hidden as I took hold of his throat and hoisted him into the air. His eyes bugged out, desperately searching the darkness for his assailant, only to find none. His feet thrashed the air, his hand coming up to pull futilely at my fingers.

I grew bored of the male's reaction within seconds, so I turned my attention to the female, only to find her staggering backward, the look of horror on her face making my cock stir.

With one claw still firm around the male's neck, I sunk my free hand into his hair and gave his head a sharp tug. I snapped his neck—making us even—and pulled his head clean off. A torrent of blood painted the grass, and a sickening plop echoed through the graveyard as I threw the male thief's head to the ground.

I plunged my claw into the body's gaping neck and got a good grip on the spine before tugging it out with a sharp flourish of my wrist. With the spine clutched in my fist, I trudged over to the female.

All she could see was the floating spinal cord of her dead lover slowly approaching her. This was the part where she should have run, but she didn't. Perhaps she was in shock, or maybe a part of her knew running was pointless.

It was only when I was towering over her, my black boots inches from her feet—they were *so* small in comparison—that I revealed myself.

I leered down at her, the moon at my back painting a shadow of my horns over her trembling form. Her soft, feminine features were painted in heavy, black as night makeup, and she had a ring looped through her nose like a bull's. Had I not been so set on causing her pain, on inflicting misery upon her until she begged for the sweet release of death, I might have admired her delicate beauty.

Instead, it only fanned the flames of anger burning through me.

Holding up the spine so blood dripped over her chest and soaked into the dark material of her jacket, I let loose a guttural chuckle. "It seems your mate had a spine after all."

"Who are you? *What* are you?"

I parted my jaws, allowing a growl to roll up from my throat as I painted a lick over my incisors. "Death incarnate, seeking penance for your deed."

Just as I hoped, she began to tremble at my feet, even though she tried her hardest to keep her voice steady and firm. "D-deed? What deed?"

"Vandalism. Trespassing. Robbery. Now, you are to suffer and bleed."

Her delicate throat twitched with a tantalizing swallow. I began to salivate, and with no lips to catch the fluid, droplets of spit joined the blood soaking her chest. When the warmth hit her, making her shirt cling to her breasts, she tried to crawl away.

I threw the spine to the grass and stooped down, grabbing her by the ankle and dragging her back toward me. She screamed, her fingers raking tracks into the dirt.

"Struggle all you want, little thief. You've committed a crime against death itself, and until you atone for your sins, there's no escape."

"Are you going to kill me like you killed Mark?" The acid in her tone took me by surprise. She was terrified, but what mortal wouldn't be after watching their mate be torn to shreds? Still, there was no missing the spark of defiance behind her eyes, the hatred.

The *life.*

Just like that, my obsession to possess life had me in a choke-hold once again.

Eventually, she would become mine. They all did, but I needed to own more than her bones several decades from now when her heart gave out.

I'd take her for myself *now*, with her heart still beating.

I'd make her my slave.

I'd be her lord and master.

And I would ruin her for stealing from death himself.

# CHAPTER THREE

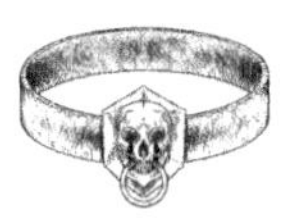

## RAYVEN

THE SPECTER OF DEATH stood over me, glaring down at me from empty eye sockets. A moon-colored animal skull, long and slender, sat perched on his shoulders, antlers stretching out on both sides and reaching toward the midnight sky.

He was dressed entirely in black, but his clothes weren't torn and tattered like I'd expect a night-crawling monster to wear. No, the form-fitting clothes he wore beneath his floor-length cloak were elegant, damn near regal, albeit old and moth-eaten. They were an odd juxtaposition to the fleshless head with a forked, black tongue and large, sharp teeth.

Odd and *intriguing*.

I was too terrified to scream or run, but I couldn't deny the curiosity clouding my thoughts.

This beast said he was death incarnate, but what did that mean? Was he the grim reaper come to drag me to the bowels of Hell? Or was I face to face with the literal devil, here to make me pay for my sins?

"I-I'm sorry." I crawled backwards an inch, desperate to put space between me and this creature, but he stepped forward to close the distance again. "Please, just let me go. You can keep all the trinkets..."

The beast laughed, a deep, guttural noise that made my stomach flip, and he slowly shook his head back and forth.

"Oh, little thief," he said, chuckling menacingly. "A mere apology isn't enough to atone for your transgressions."

The rest of the blood drained from my face, a new wave of fear lancing through me.

"Then what do you want?" I pleaded, crawling backward another inch, unable to tear my eyes from the skull looming over me. "Name it. Money? Gold? I'll give you whatever you want."

He paused, turning still as stone, and hope flickered in my chest. Was he really considering it? Would he accept some form of payment in exchange for my life? I waited with bated breath, goosebumps racing over my skin, and my heart sank when he spoke again.

"What I want is your blood."

I moved to scramble away, but he swooped down again and grabbed my ankle before turning to march across the graveyard, dragging me along behind him like a doll. Finally, I found my voice, and a scream tore from my throat as I kicked at his pale fingers with my free foot.

"Let. Me. Go."

The specter merely chuckled again, and my frantic fingers gripped at the ground, finding nothing but blades of grass that tore in half easily. I attempted to roll onto my stomach, digging my fingers into the dry earth, trying to find purchase, only to scrub my fingertips raw.

He paused by the sack of treasure I'd dropped and knelt beside it, his grip still tight around my ankle, I thought he would grab the entire thing and bring it along, but he rummaged around inside it with his free hand and retrieved the necklace I'd ripped from the marble tomb. He slipped it inside his cloak and stood again, dragging me along without missing a beat.

I screamed, the shrill noise racing out across the empty grave-yard, even though I knew no one would hear me.

Even if they did, what would they do? Fight him? The thought was laughable. He killed Mark in the blink of an eye, removing his spine entirely. Would knives or guns have any effect on this thing?

*Was he even alive?*

Judging by the pale, blue-tinted flesh of his fingers wrapped around my ankle and the fleshless talking skull head, I guessed not. This beast was as dead as Mark was, only somehow he could still walk and talk.

He was as dead as I would be shortly, after he made me suffer whatever horrible consequences he had in store for me.

The thought of torture renewed my fight, and I grabbed at a passing headstone in an attempt to slow the creature down. My fingers gripped the edge of the faded stone, knuckles pale white from my desperate grip, but it only stalled the monster for a moment. He yanked my ankle hard once, causing pain to shoot up my calf, and my grip slipped free, leaving several layers of skin from my fingertips behind.

"Fuck," I growled through gritted teeth, wincing against the pain.

"You're feisty," the beast said without looking back over his shoulder. His sights were set on the mausoleum, his slow, steady footsteps leading us closer and closer to the entrance.

Was he going to bury me inside the tomb I'd disturbed and leave me there to die? Was he going to shut me inside the mausoleum and watch as I slowly ran out of oxygen?

I had no idea what he was planning, but I didn't want to find out.

"Please," I begged a final time, hating the desperation in my voice. "Let me go."

Finally, he stopped and craned his neck to stare down at me with his emotionless gaze. Every time I looked into the empty sockets where his eyes should be, a wave of discomfort washed through me. It was so unordinary, so *wrong*, but all I could do was stare.

"Little thief, if there is one thing I can assure you, it's that I'm *never* letting you go."

He waved his hand in front of him, producing a tear in the air. It started as a thin, black rip that widened into a portal wide enough for him to pass through. For *us* to pass through.

Wherever the hell he was headed, he was taking me with him.

Rolling onto my side, I was able to catch a better glimpse of Hell—or what I expected to be a fiery world of damnation—but what I found surprised me. Sleek, black walls, adorned with glittering silver fixtures. Gothic archways and glossy floors.

My brow furrowed as I tried to take it in, but then the monster was marching forward once more, dragging me toward the portal he'd conjured.

*Fuck.*

I craned my neck to look at the graveyard a final time, my bag of treasures discarded amongst the headstones, Mark's headless body a crumpled heap in the distance. In a matter of minutes, every shred of my reality had been torn apart, the tattered strings of it drifting away as I slipped through the portal. It closed behind us without a sound.

The specter moved silently down a hallway, his feet clacking methodically against the tile floor as he continued to drag me behind him like a sack of dirty laundry.

The first thing I was immediately certain of: this place was grand, more extravagant than anything I'd ever seen. Were there manors in Hell? Castles? Chandeliers composed entirely of bones hung interspersed overhead, lit with dim light that barely penetrated the dark hallway.

Elegant doorways were spaced evenly along both walls, adorned with glossy black trim and silver door knockers. It was everything you'd expect an elegant, creepy mansion to have.

The second thing I realized was that the stone flooring hurt a hell of a lot more than grass had, and my skin felt like it was being ripped apart as the monster mopped the floor with me. I reached for the hem of my shirt, trying to pull it down to cover my exposed skin, but it was nearly impossible.

"Let me go! I'll scream!"

"Then scream," he rumbled in his Hell-deep baritone. "Only the dead will hear you, and trust me when I tell you, no corpse will dare oppose me. Certainly not for some grimy little grave thief."

With a huff, I thrashed about to jerk my ankle–which ached intensely in his iron-clad grip–away from him, but his fingers tightened against my skin. I whimpered, a pitiful sound that I immediately regretted, and the monster laughed.

"Keep struggling, and I'll drag you by your hair instead." It wasn't a threat, but a promise–one I fully expected him to keep.

"Why don't you just let me walk?" I whined, still tugging my shirt down, only for it to slide up my back again a second later. "It's not like I'm going to run away. Where the hell would I go?"

"You wish me to show you the same respect you denied to my belongings?" he mused, his voice dropping an octave. "I don't think so."

"You're such a dick." The words flew out of my mouth before I could stop them, but I meant what I said. The devil himself or not, this monster was a giant asshole. I almost wished he would have killed me instead of dragging me around like a sack of potatoes.

"And you're a thief." He raised his shoulders in a shrug. "Disgusting and irredeemable."

I opened my mouth to let another smart-ass comment fly, but we stopped abruptly, the monster's gaze fixated on a door to our right. With his free hand, he rummaged inside his cloak and produced a singular key, which he fit into the handle. It unlocked with a click, and he dragged me through the doorway without another word.

The room was large and more brightly lit than the hallway, but everything was made of the same, dark material. Black walls, a black ceiling, and an enormous bone chandelier hanging over a dark, four-poster bed. Crimson carpet covered the entirety of the floor, matching the linens draped over the bed.

Finally, he released my ankle, and my leg dropped to the floor. It had fallen asleep at some point, and it felt like a thousand ants were biting their way across my skin as the blood circulation returned to my limb.

"On your feet, little thief," the monster snapped, turning and glaring down at me, waiting expectantly for me to move.

I knew I should have obeyed. Whatever he asked, I should have done without a beat of hesitation if I valued my life, but I was annoyed. *Angry.* I didn't want to listen to a word this fucking monster said, and so I laid defiantly on the floor, a scowl plastered across my face.

"Oh, *now* you want to let me walk?" I gritted out, crossing my arms over my chest. "You'll have to make me."

He chuckled once, though it was devoid of any humor. It made an icy wave of fear roll up my spine and seize my chest.

"Very well."

In a swift motion, the beast swooped down and grabbed me by the throat, hoisting me to my feet with ease as his cold fingers pressed unforgivingly into the soft flesh of my neck.

"You'd do well to remember your place here," he said menacingly, dragging me closer to his skeletal face until I flinched. "You belong to me; therefore, you will do as I say. Unless you wish to die a much slower, more gruesome death than your friend."

He walked me backward slowly, the edges of my vision fading to black as he continued to squeeze my throat. When my legs hit the edge of the bed, he shoved me down onto it, and my stomach turned nervously.

Was he going to force himself on me? Fuck me with some weird cock of death?

I swallowed hard against his hand on my throat before he released me, leaving me gasping for air. He shifted, but not enough for me to skirt around him and make a break for the door. Even if he'd walked away, I doubt I would have run.

I didn't know enough about this place yet; I didn't know what was in store for me. Running now would have meant certain death.

When he moved again, there was a thick circlet of steel in his hand, and he unclasped it before shoving it around my throat. It clicked together, locking behind my neck, and my heart pitched toward the floor when I realized what he was doing.

He was collaring me like a goddamned animal.

"And just so you don't get the urge to run away," he said, his hands working just out of my periphery. The *clink clink* of a chain moving before being hooked to the collar turned my blood to ice.

"Are you kidding me?" I gaped, shocked and confused. "You're just going to keep me chained up in here... *forever?*"

He glared down at me with his emotionless face, his empty sockets making my skin crawl with unease. For the first time, I could see a faint blue glow flickering deep inside them.

"If you're lucky." He ran a single, skeletal finger along my jawline, stopping at my chin and tilting my head up a little higher.

If there was something more he wanted to say, he changed his mind, and he turned silently on his heel to head for the door.

"Wait!" I cried, already jumping to my feet to run after him. "You can't leave me like this!"

I wanted him to turn back around, to argue with me some more. I wanted to whittle away at his mysterious armor and find out what his plans were for me. Not that it would have helped much; I wasn't sure knowing every detail of your impending torture would make things easier or more difficult to process, but I didn't want to be left alone.

He slipped through the doorway without another word, snapping the door closed behind him with finality. The chain around my neck jerked taut a few feet from the door, and despite my best efforts, my fingertips couldn't quite reach the handle.

"Fuck!" I yelled into the empty room, tugging with all my strength on the chain that seemed welded to the headboard. "Fuck! Fuck! Fuck!"

After fighting in vain for several minutes, I slumped to the floor, exhausted. My hands were scrubbed raw from the ordeal of being captured, and my back ached from being dragged across the ground. My ankle was still sore from the monster's deathly grip, and my throat was bruised from having his fingers pressed against it. To top it off, there was a pounding headache blooming to life behind my eyes.

I was stuck, trapped, without anyone or anything to help or give me peace of mind.

As the shock began to wear off, my hands started to tremble. My bottom lip wobbled, but I bit down on it to keep it in place. I'd seen some pretty fucked up things in my years of asset repossession, but this had to take the cake.

I'd been kidnapped by death himself, dragged into another realm altogether, and now I was chained up in a glamorous jail cell.

*How did I fuck up this bad?*

Everything I thought I knew had gone out the window, and I wasn't sure of anything anymore. This all felt more like a fever dream than reality.

One thing was certain: I couldn't lose my mind in this room if I was going to get out of here.

I was going to escape, one way or another.

# CHAPTER FOUR

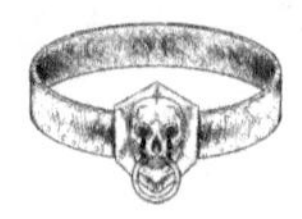

## Rayven

THE FLOOR WAS COLD and unforgiving, despite being covered in the thin rug, and it took every bit of energy I had left to drag myself onto the bed. It was plush and perfectly dressed, but it was just as cold as the floor. Icy like the rest of the hauntingly beautiful castle. Harsh and unwelcoming.

I was exhausted, in need of a long, uninterrupted nap, but it was impossible to sleep.

At the same time, I wasn't entirely sure I wasn't dreaming. What else could this be? Not reality. Otherwise, I'd have to acknowledge that Mark was dead. *Gone.* Pulled to pieces right before my eyes by a hulking creature of death and bone.

I'd been dragged off to this other world, with a collar locked tight around my neck. The metal bit into my skin, making my throat ache. After what felt like an eternity, I finally settled for sitting on the edge of the mattress while my mind ran rampant.

No. This wasn't a nightmare.

This was Hell.

Mark was really dead. Had he been getting on my nerves? Yeah, but there was no part of my brain cruel enough to invent the bloodshed I'd witnessed in the graveyard.

A sickly sensation slithered over my skin, making me shiver and wrap my arms tightly around myself. The gravity of my situation was starting to sink in. Mark had been alive one minute, then nothing but a puddle of blood and lifeless flesh the next, murdered by the same mysterious beast that had dragged me here. That strange, dark, callous creature...

The memory of him had my thoughts reeling, unanswered questions mounting.

What *was* he? A devil? A god? A cursed deity in charge of guarding graveyards? If that was the case, why had I never seen him before? I'd been in hundreds of graveyards, robbed countless graves. Why had the beast picked tonight of all nights to show up?

Perhaps the rumors about the Petherick family were true. Maybe the family really was descended from gods and this monster, the beast who'd kidnapped me, was connected to them somehow.

Honestly, it didn't make a difference who or what he was. He was still an asshole. A cruel asshole who'd killed Mark, dragged me through a portal, and chained me up.

My temper flared, my cheeks heating. I refused to stay locked up like an animal, despite the creature's threat to keep me here forever.

I might not have excelled at much, but if there was one thing I was really fucking good at, it was breaking into things. And if I was good at breaking in, breaking out would be a breeze.

Step one would be getting the stupid collar off. Then, I could see about breaking out of the room. After that... I'd have to wing it.

My fingers crawled their way around the collar, slowly studying the metal's design. It was fairly simple, a thick steel circle with a single, tiny keyhole in the back. The chain he'd attached to it should have been able to clip on and off–how else would he have gotten it latched–but the metal was seamless. I squeezed, pulled, and prodded at the spot where the chain connected to the back of my neck, but it didn't budge.

*Son of a bitch.*

This wasn't going to work. I had to pick the lock if I wanted to detach myself from the bed, and if I wanted any chance at success, I couldn't do it from this angle.

Experimentally, I tried to move the collar side to side. It was snug, hugging my skin tightly, but I was slowly able to get it turned completely, the keyhole now on my throat. Now, I needed something to pick the lock with.

I'd picked dozens of locks over the years, but this was a whole new ball game. I'd always had my tools, a flashlight, and a rough idea about the inner workings of the lock at the very least. This contraption was totally foreign, and with it around my neck, it was at an angle I wasn't used to.

But I wouldn't let it faze my determination.

I had to focus on my task at hand, or the weight of my situation would come crashing back down. I couldn't freeze up now. I had to escape before that monster came back.

As odd as the lock was, it was old. Old locks weren't complicated. A bobby pin would do the trick.

I reached for my ponytail, snatching a bobby pin out of my dark, tangled hair, and set to work fitting it into the keyhole. I twisted and jiggled it, trying to turn over the mechanism inside, but despite struggling for several minutes, it didn't unlock.

"Damn it," I muttered under my breath, taking a deep breath to calm my nerves before attempting one more time.

To my despair, it still didn't work.

Frustrating, but not the end of the world.

I just needed something heavy duty, something more than a bobby pin, to flip the antique piece inside.

Scanning the room for anything useful, I lasered in on the details I'd missed when I was first dragged inside. Two doors led off to the right–probably to a bathroom and a closet, if I had to guess–but they were too far away for me to reach. A glossy black grandfather clock sat in one corner, but there were no numbers on its face, only hands that spun around slowly. On the opposite side of the bed from where I stood, an ornate desk sat in the corner.

So many things for me to investigate, all just out of my reach.

I groaned in annoyance, but my eyes kept crawling back to the desk, wondering what sort of useful things might be concealed in the drawers. There had to be something I could use to pick the lock—it was just a matter of getting over there. The chain pulled taut, the metal collar biting into my neck.

*All I needed was a few extra feet of reach...*

Dragging my gaze away from the desk, I glared at the enormous four-poster bed, wondering how hard it would be to move. It looked solid, carved out of real wood, so I knew it would be heavy, but I was no stranger to moving heavy shit. Caskets, tombstones, sacks full of recovered belongings. I might have been short and petite, but I wasn't weak, not by a long shot.

With adrenaline igniting in my veins, I stepped up to the side of the bed and pushed on one of the banisters experimentally. It didn't budge.

Fuck. If this plan didn't work, what would I do next? I shuddered to think of the frightfully short list of options. Nope. This had to be the answer.

I braced myself next to the bed, squatting low and shoving against the enormous bed. To my relief, it shifted, the sound of it dragging across the rug echoing through the room. Unfortunately, it didn't move much.

I tried again, digging deep and shoving as hard as I could manage. My arms strained, my toes aching as my boots dug into the floor, but I kept going. Gritting, swearing, and sweating, I managed to move the giant four-poster a couple of feet. When

I couldn't move it anymore, I scrambled across the bed to the other side, reaching for the top middle drawer of the desk.

I groaned, fighting the disappointment weighing down my shoulders, and tried again, stretching as far as I could while the unforgiving metal of the collar cut into the tender skin of my neck.

With a cry, I was able to grab the handle and wrench open the drawer, relief flooding my limbs when it was full of miscellaneous items. I searched frantically through papers, scraps of fabric, and random knick-knacks before my fingers brushed against a letter opener. A letter opener! A weapon and a half-decent lockpick. I could have cried.

Snatching it from the drawer, I hardly admired the slender, white bone handle and thin blade before turning it on the collar and jamming the metal into the keyhole. I silently prayed to any and every deity listening as I twisted and turned the blade, my heart nearly stopping when the lock clicked. My hope soared. With trembling fingers, I pulled off the collar and threw it down, the metal clanking hard against the floor.

I choked down several deep breaths of air, flooded with the relief of being free, but I didn't hesitate before running across the room for the door. There was no telling how long the creature would wait before returning, and I planned to be long gone before he came back.

I made quick work of the door, almost disappointed that the lock wasn't harder to pick, and eased it open to peer into the empty corridor. It was silent, the dark macabre aesthetic giving it an eerie feeling that had goosebumps racing down my arms.

Gripping the handle of the letter opener like a miniature sword, I swallowed hard against my heart beating in my throat and slipped through the doorway, keeping my eyes peeled for any sign of movement.

I had a feeling the monster who'd captured me wouldn't be too pleased if he discovered I'd escaped, but I was almost insulted that he didn't think I'd be able to. I was one of the greatest grave robbers I'd ever heard of, and he thought a couple of simple locks would keep me bound indefinitely? I scoffed.

He'd have to try much harder next time—if he was able to catch me.

Keeping my footsteps light–as light as I could with the shit-kicker boots I was wearing–I hurried down the hall, my eyes poring over all the enchanting details. Ornate fixtures, random-ly placed suits of armor, and black, detailed crown molding that lined every inch of every wall. Elaborate staircases, horrifically beautiful paintings in thick frames, and a mesmerizing, dark atmosphere worthy of any gothic horror film topped it all off.

It was the most stunning thing I'd ever seen. I hated how much I loved it.

I had no idea which way I was headed, or even which way would lead me to an exit. This whole place was disorienting to all the senses, so I tried to keep track of the turns I made in case I had to double back. *Left at the suit of armor, right at the painting of the woman in the tiara, left down a set of stairs.* There were so many hallways and stairs, it was a futile effort to try and remember them all, but I tried nevertheless, all while seemingly getting myself more lost in the castle.

*Left at the suit of armor, right at the painting of the woman in the tiara, left down a set of...*

I froze at the top of the stairs, the prickling sensation of familiarity skirting up my spine.

"What the..." My voice trailed off as I turned around to face the painting of a demure woman, her black hair cascading behind her back. Her face was hauntingly beautiful, thin and angular, with dark, eternally sad eyes. The silver tiara on her head seemed familiar, but maybe that was just because this wasn't my first time seeing the painting.

My stomach pitched toward the floor. There was no way I was going in circles. *No freaking way.* I'd gone down at least four sets of stairs. How could I have ended up at the exact same place again?

Pulse quickening as my mind began to spin out of control, I hurried down the stairs, taking them two at a time. Instead of taking a right at the bottom like I had the time before, I went straight, hurrying into an unfamiliar hallway, the letter opener clutched firmly in my grip. I took a left, then a right, purposely attempting to get myself lost amongst the endless hallways that all seemed to look different, yet exactly the same.

The only thing creepier than the repetitive scenery was the impossible silence of the castle. My short, choppy breaths were the only thing breaking the silence, along with the soft clop of my footsteps against the polished floor.

Where was the creature who'd brought me here? Was he hiding? Biding his time? Watching me?

There was no trace of him, but I couldn't shake the sensation that I was being watched, and that whatever studied me could see through more than walls, that they could peer straight inside me and see my anxiety mounting.

Taunting me. Taking pleasure in my suffering.

I made a left at yet another suit of armor and stopped short when I found myself face to face with the same painting yet again, the sad woman watching me with a look of pity in her eyes. As if she could see my future. My stomach bottomed out as I stared up at her, my mind tumbling out of control.

*There's no way I'm back here again, unless...*

Unless this entire castle was some kind of magic maze, purposely spitting me out back where I'd started.

Fuck. Fuck. Fuck! How the hell would I ever get out?

Behind me, something rustled, making me jump, and I whirled around, brandishing the letter opener as a weapon. I expected to see the monster, his giant skull face towering over me as he prepared to kill me, but there was no one. Instead, one of the walls was shifting, sliding slowly as it swallowed the hallway beyond it.

My mouth fell open in horror as the hallway narrowed, eventually closing off completely, and I found myself staring at a bare stretch of wall, like the hallway had never been there at all.

My lungs seized as panic lanced through me, and I stared at the wall in disbelief. My suspicion had been correct.

This place was filled with magic that animated the walls, a labyrinth of stone brought to life by dark energy.

And I was the helpless mouse lost in the middle of it.

# CHAPTER FIVE

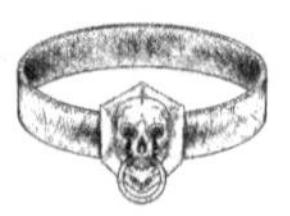

## BELIAL

"Disappointing..." My skeletal figure skimmed the row of soul tombs for what had to be the dozenth time, my displeasure leaching into my bones and turning my marrow acidic. "I've spent eons as this realm's master, countless centuries sorting through souls, and these are the only witches we have in the library?"

I turned away from the bookshelf to see Cecil, the overseer of the Soul Library, cowering behind me. He was tall and skeleton-thin, with withered flesh wrapped in a moth-eaten, brocade waistcoat, a yellowed cravat knotted tight at his throat. He wore glasses, which sat askew on his face. One of the lenses had cracked, which only made him all the more off-putting.

Cecil didn't have any eyes. The maggots had long since eaten them. What grew in their place was—well, what was always in abundance in my realm: bone. Specifically, teeth. His eye sockets were lined with dozens of uneven teeth.

He'd been handsome once, if I remembered correctly. Time here had warped him, as it had warped all of us. At least he had a purpose now as my Soul Keeper.

Even with Cecil's height, he looked small engulfed in the shadow of my beast form. For such a frightening-looking creature, he was a nervous thing.

"I-If I may be so bold to say, you don't tend to keep souls for yourself, My Lord." In addition to a slight stutter, his three sets of teeth tended to *chatter*. "Most of these books are empty."

I turned away from Cecil, peering down the long aisles between the towering bookcases that seemed to go on forever. So much space, yet it was true. I wasn't in the habit of harboring souls. I allowed most of them to pass on to the lower layers of Hell, if I remembered to usher them on at all.

Admittedly, since Catherine's death, my duties had fallen to the wayside. There was a long backlog of souls waiting to pass into the next realm. If I wanted to keep them, their souls would be cataloged into a book in my library. If not, I'd usher them to the second layer. Those who awaited Judgement would wander my halls and eventually settle in whatever items they could find around the estate.

The souls I bothered to catalog were supposed to be notable, skillful people. Souls to make into my servants when the need arose.

"This won't do. I need a witch, Cecil."

"We might have one in the queue somewhere. I think she's currently inhabiting a coat rack."

"If she's inhabiting a coat rack, that means she's been in the queue for how long?"

"At least a hundred years, My Lord."

"Then she's beneath my notice for the time being. Certainly not up to the job I have in mind."

"M-my L-lord, what exactly is this job?"

"Our newest guest needs an attendant, someone to see to her basic needs. Mostly to keep her alive…"

"Alive?" Cecil blinked, his toothy eye-sockets looking normal for a split second. "Another human in the castle?"

The librarian's apprehension bled into the air, thick enough to choke on. I couldn't blame him. Catherine's stay here had been traumatic for us all. Limbo was depressing enough for the souls who called my realm home. The last thing they needed was another lost mortal throwing itself onto every sharp edge or off whatever balcony it stumbled across in a vain attempt to escape my labyrinth.

"This won't be like before. I mean to make this one suffer. I will control her pain, her punishment. Every drop of her blood that's spilled will be at my behest."

Cecil blinked again and pushed his glasses up the bridge of his nose with a slender finger. "Forgive me if this is impertinent, My Lord. If it's a witch you seek, why not resummon Holga?"

I bristled at the name. Holga hadn't been just any old servant. She was a witch who'd burned at the stake a good century before

Catherine had even been born. Stubborn. Full of life. I thought she'd make a good friend, a good support for my intended queen.

As it turned out, Holga had been too good of a friend. She'd poisoned her against me, made her fear me.

In truth, I'd already thought of assigning Holga to this task. As much as I hated the woman, she had a knack for inspiring fear, especially toward me.

This time, I wanted the human to fear me. There was just one tiny problem.

"I ushered Holga to the second layer. Who knows which of my brothers owns her soul now. Her water-logged carcass is floating face down in the nine-circle's lake for all we know. Even if Asmodeus kept her, he wouldn't send her back."

"Why not ask him, My Lord?"

I groaned, massaging my temple, as if rubbing the bare bone would do anything to ease the headache I always got when I thought of my siblings.

I'd rather pull out my own horns than speak to any of them, *especially* Asmodeus.

I turned, casting one last glance around the library, knowing there wasn't a soul in here up to the job of watching over my little thief. Only Holga would do.

Squaring my shoulders, I nodded at Cecil, and he gave me a series of flustered bows before striding out of the library. The walls and their many panels rotated for me, showing me the way to my study.

The moment I stepped inside, the walls started to flip and shift back, making the room larger than it had been before. I usually frequented this room in my smaller form, but if I was going to talk to Asmodeus, it needed to be in my more intimidating one.

I threw my cloak across my desk and approached the mirror on the other side of the room. It was large enough so that the glass reflected all of me, horns and all.

"Show me my brother," I told the mirror, unable to keep the bite out of my tone. I glared into the mirror's surface, waiting for the image to take shape. One moment, I was staring at my study, and the next, Asmodeus' bedroom.

I fucking loathed that he kept the mirror we all used to communicate in his bedroom, but what else could be expected of the Lord of Lechery? I wouldn't have minded, if it wasn't for the fact that Asmodeus was one cruel bastard.

I hated my brother with every bone in both of my bodies.

Before the blurry images started to sharpen, noises met my ears. The squeaking of a bed. The screaming of a woman. The grunts of the monster defiling her.

Asmodeus' body was brawny, with shoulders thick enough to support his three heads. On the left was the head of a bull, on the right, the head of a ram. In the center was a human head topped with several inches of flowing, flaxen hair. As he moaned, all his mouths opened, oozing a sound that would have my skin crawling, had I any.

The poor woman on his bed was covered in bruises. He slapped her across the face as he fucked into the cradle of her sweaty, cum-streaked thighs, and her screams died down into mewling whimpers.

"I'm busy, Belphegor," the monster snarled, waving a dismissive claw at the mirror without bothering to look up.

I folded my arms over my chest and steeled myself for the conversation about to unfold. "I'm not Belphegor."

All three of Asmodeus' heads jerked up at the sound of my voice. A brief look of surprise flashed over his middle face, only to be replaced with a smug smirk a beat later. "Lord Belial. How long has it been? I was starting to wonder if that mold-infested wasteland you call a realm had finally corrupted your mind."

I said nothing, refusing to let him get to me so soon.

The three-headed beast sat back on his heels, looking down at the woman in his bed with a sadistic smile twisting his lips. "Look at this soul. So pretty. At least she was before I got my hands on her."

He held up a hand, his index finger extended, and a moment later, a razor-sharp claw pushed out of his fingertip. He moved quickly, slashing the woman's throat with a flick of his wrist. There was a gurgling sound, and her naked body jerked. Then, she fell still.

Too bad she was already dead. He could revive her and abuse her as many times as he saw fit.

Pushing her off the bed with a sickening thunk, the demon lord rose from his bed and grabbed for a red velvet robe. I assumed he would put it on, but instead, he used it to wipe the blood off his dick—he'd been fucking the girl for some time.

After a few seconds of suffocating silence, he tossed the robe over a chair beside his hearth and slowly approached the mirror. The hooves of his cloven feet clacked against the stone floor, and I tensed as his eyes found mine through the mirror. "One of the dozen souls you sent last month, and the *only* one with her body still attached."

I shrugged off his accusatory tone. "Bodies should remain in the mortal plane. That one must have slipped through."

"Fuck you, Belial. *Twelve damned souls.* The corridors of your castle must be awfully cramped. You can't hoard them forever."

"I'm not hoarding them. I've fallen behind."

As much as I hated my brothers—Asmodeus most of all—they could always read me like a book. "All these years after losing your precious human pet, you're still sulking?"

"I didn't contact you to chat. Two, almost three, centuries ago, I sent you the soul of a witch. You should remember, because it's the only one I've ever hand delivered to you. I need it back."

"Let me get this straight. Your obsession with that human turned Limbo into a waiting room for the damned. You've sent me all of a dozen fucking souls in the last month, when you should be sending me *thousands*, and now you actually expect me to send one back? Your brain really has been eaten by maggots, hasn't it?"

"If you're stalling because you hurt the witch—"

"So what if I did? You gave her to me, meaning you didn't give two fucks about her, brother. Wasn't she your human pet's attendant? The one who tried to help her escape? Why would you want her back?"

If I could smile in this form, I would have. "That witch brings suffering to whoever she touches. I'm finally in need of such a skill."

My brother's bull head shook with disapproval while the other two held steady, their glares burning into my bone. "Souls are supposed to be filtered down the layers of Hell, not up. It's against the natural order. The old ways state—"

"Do not recite the old ways to me, *brother*. I helped write them."

"Lucky for you, I never passed the soul on. You can have her back...but you have to do something for me."

*Blood and darkness.* I should have expected as much. A selfish cunt like Asmodeus would never do anything unless he got something out of it. Knowing him, he'd want more female souls, their bodies attached for him to torture.

I'd have to be more careful about stripping all souls of their vessels when they passed into his realm...

"What is it you want? I can send you more souls, but remember, I govern their flesh and bone. Their bodies will stay with me—"

"I want you to throw a party."

I balked, as if I'd been struck. Had I heard him right? Was this his idea of a stupid jest? "I'm waiting for the punchline," I snapped, annoyed that he was wasting my time.

"No punchline. I mean it. All Hallows' Eve is in a few days. Host a masquerade. All the demon lords will attend."

I laughed, the sound cold and mirthless. "You don't want a party. You want to snoop around my castle to see what souls I've failed to deliver to you and our brothers."

The demon lord gave a one-shouldered shrug, brushing off my accusation. "We're just concerned. Souls must pass through Limbo to reach the lower layers. If you don't have your horns on your task, soon, there will be no fresh souls to torture."

"I'm simply behind on my work. There are ledgers I have to organize. My system is outdated, and I need to refresh it. Plus, I have to restock my own catalog of souls before I start sending them out to you."

The center head's expression turned cutting. "Throw the party, Belial. We're coming, so clean your halls. Dust off your wine casks, pull out some musicians and serving wenches from that pathetic little collection you call a Soul Library, and send the invitations. Agree to that, and I'll send you the witch's soul."

I shuddered to think of throwing a social event of any kind, let alone one my brothers were to attend, but this was nothing compared to what Asmodeus could have asked for.

"Fine," I bit out. "You'll have your party."

"Good. One more thing. If I am to hand back the witch's soul, tell me why you want her back after all this time. Have you decided to make her suffer for her betrayal after all these years?"

"I'm going to use her to make another suffer."

"Really?" His brows hiked into his blonde hairline. "Maybe you are feeling more like your old self after all. Give me the night to sort through my old store of souls. I'll send her up."

I turned away from the mirror to make my leave when Asmodeus called out to me. "Belial, once you're done torturing this soul, send her down to me so I can have a turn."

I stopped abruptly. Sending souls to Asmodeus always filled me with a sense of loathing. Suggesting I send my newest toy to him? That possessive part of me I thought I'd buried with Catherine flickered to life. I slowly turned back to the mirror, enjoying the way Asmodeus flinched at what he saw in my eyes.

"No, you're never sinking your claws into this one. She'll never leave my realm. Even when the Hells crumble, when all other souls pass on, she'll remain mine. Forever."

*Forever.* Such a long time. Yet, when it came to my little thief, I had a feeling it wouldn't be long at all.

# CHAPTER SIX

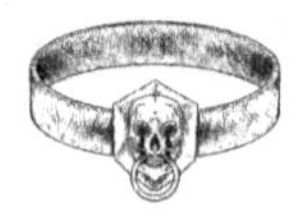

## RAYVEN

No matter how many turns I took, or how long I wandered through the corridors, everything was the same. The same dusty furniture, the faded paintings, the threadbare rugs, the same peeling wallpaper. *It was all the same.*

This place was alive, silently mocking me as the walls slowly shifted, leading me right back to where I started at that damn painting. After what felt like hours, I finally gave up and collapsed into a sitting chair opposite the painting.

I stared up at the woman, taking in details I hadn't bothered noticing before. Her pale face was pinched with pain, like someone had forced her to pose for the portrait, her silver tiara shimmering in her dark hair. With the letter opener still firmly clutched in one hand, I reached into my jacket pocket with the other and extracted my phone.

The battery would die soon—not that it mattered. There was no service here. Sighing, I shoved the cell back into my pocket and lifted my gaze to the woman in the portrait. "Did he kidnap you too?"

My stomach dropped when I registered the glittering skull amulet around her neck. It was the same one I'd stolen from that crypt. And the tiara on her head had looked so familiar before, now I knew why.

It had been her grave I'd robbed.

"The Lord has always had a terrible thirst for dark-haired maidens, especially ones with warm flesh on their bones."

Jumping at the voice, I swiveled my head in search of its owner. I glanced up and down the corridor to find no one. "Down here, love."

I looked down at the side table next to my chair to find a porcelain teapot in the shape of a fat toad, sitting on a stack of dusty books. No, there was no way a teapot had just spoken to me. I shook my head with a nervous laugh. "I'm going crazy."

The toad blinked, one eye first, then the other. "Already? My, that's fast, even for these halls."

I nearly fell out of my chair. "U-um, you're a talking teapot."

"Am I? That's funny. Last I checked, I was a baker." A bit of dust blew from her spout with a huff. "Or was I a candlestick maker? You know, I can't recall."

I leaned toward the teapot, intense curiosity pushing out my next words. "What is this place? Is this..." I almost didn't want to say it. "Hell?"

"It's the land between, the realm of lost souls, awaiting their audience with the Lord of Judgement."

"The Lord?"

"The King of Limbo. Death incarnate. The Lord of Bones. He has many names, yes. Many. You can run away, like the Mistress, but he'll always bring you back."

I found my gaze drifting back to the sullen woman in the portrait. "Who was she, exactly?"

"The queen who never was. The beauty cursed with the love of a beast."

I pushed to my feet, my legs going weak. All of this was a lot to unpack. "H-how do I get out of here? How do I go back home?"

The teapot's lid rattled, and she blew out another cloud of dust. "Oh dear. You don't. There is no escape from this place, not unless the Lord wishes it. You best return to your room. He won't be pleased to find you here."

"He's coming," several voices whispered from various nearby objects at once, their urgent tone making the hairs on the back of my neck stand up.

"Don't bother running. He'll find and capture you either way..." a candlestick holder on the table warned. "There is no escaping the demon lords. They will use you up until they grow tired of you and pass you on to the next."

I ran. I didn't care if they said it was pointless. No matter how scary this place was, or how far-fetched my escape was shaping up to be, I wasn't going down without a fight.

If I was destined to be the Lord of Bones' prisoner, I would be the most hellish one he'd ever had.

"There's no escape," another ghostly voice said, this one coming from a mirror fixed to the wall. I paused, turning to look at my reflection—except it wasn't mine. The girl from the painting stared back at me, with sunken eyes and death-pale skin. An old, festering gash covered her throat, dark blood crusted on the neckline of her once-white dress.

I broke out into a full sprint, the thick soles of my boots pounding against the polished floor. No matter what turns I took, I always ended up at that fucking painting.

"Climb out the window."

I froze in place. This time, it was a woman who spoke. I looked down at the letter opener in my hand. "There's an overgrown hedge that should let you climb down..."

Her voice was as dainty as the blade. It was just like the furniture. Were these lost souls, inhabiting random objects around the castle? As soon as the question formed in my mind, it was pushed away when my gaze found an open window at the end of the hall. I hurried over to the window, running my hand over the sill.

There'd been bars here, judging by the huge holes in the stone where iron grates had been bolted. *Why had he taken them down?*

My focus shifted outside to the bleak sky covered by a dark storm cloud that grumbled in the distance. The palace sat on the edge of a cliff overlooking an ocean as black as ink, and a shiver shot through me as I registered the thick bramble attached to the castle—just like the knife had said.

One misstep, and I'd plummet to my death…

Steeling my nerves, I stuck the knife into my belt and climbed out the window, taking hold of the vines. Below was a balcony. I took my time with my descent, checking my footing with each step.

"Let go."

My blood turned cold at the knife's instructions. "*What?* I'll die!"

The knife said nothing. Whatever soul inhabited it was out of its freaking mind. Shaking my head, I continued on, and when I reached the balcony, I let out the breath I'd been holding.

"Hurry. I feel him coming. Down that hall to your right." The dagger's voice started to quake.

It probably wasn't the best idea to trust it, whatever "it" was. It was insane, that's what it was, but wandering aimlessly around the castle seemed like a worse plan. I ran through the gaping doorway, taking a right and following the knife's directions down several flights of stairs until the air grew damp. "Where are you leading me? Is this the dungeon?"

An uneasy feeling hooked in my belly. This didn't feel right. I had to turn back. I whipped around, just as the door above the stairs—where I'd come in—opened with a groan. The dim light from the floor above painted the stone wall in the arched shape of a door, with a horned silhouette haloed in light.

"He's here," the knife gasped, the feminine voice fraught with fear. "Run!"

I did. I turned and bolted past a wall of barred cells—I ran so fast, I didn't bother looking to see if they were occupied.

"I know you're in here, little thief. I can taste the pound of your heart on my tongue."

His heavy footsteps charged after me, falling in line with my pounding pulse.

"The harder that *sweet* little organ beats, the more excited I get." His voice was barely more than a growl, laced with hunger and fury that had my heart beating faster than it ever had before.

I had to get away from him. I had to ignore the little voice in the back of my brain telling me he was the safest thing in this place. It was a lie. This hell was designed to fuck with my internal compass on every level.

I rounded a corner, my foot stepping down...onto nothing.

"This is it. This is escape," the knife said from my belt.

On the next beat, I was plummeting, and I screamed as the hole I fell down swallowed me. The chute was narrow, cold, lined with stone, and something *else*. Something evil.

Hands. Countless hands were somehow affixed to the solid stone, grasping at me as I fell and slowing my descent towards whatever pit awaited me below. So many hands on me, touching me in places they had no right to touch. The hands passed me down the line of appendages, purposefully going slow now so they all had time to grope me.

I threw my head back to see the mouth of the hole above, bile burning the back of my throat. The little square of light was so small now.

I was falling deep into the darkness, maybe into a lower level of Hell. Was this what the knife meant by escape? I wouldn't be leaving Hell, but I would be escaping the Lord of Bones.

I squeezed my eyes shut, wishing I'd drop faster. I wanted this to be over.

The hands were greedy, their cold and clammy skin stroking over mine and leaving goosebumps in the wake of their touch. The deeper I fell, the crueler the hands became.

They pulled on my clothes, ripping the fabric from my body, leaving me exposed.

They were stripping away more than my clothes.

My cell phone fell out of my pocket and dropped down the chute. I waited for it to hit the bottom, but no sound came.

I sobbed at the possibility of this going on forever.

I'd managed to grab the knife before they'd torn everything away, but the blade was useless, even as I managed to slash at some of the appendages. These hands were already dead. Unlike me, they couldn't feel pain.

I would never forget this moment. The intense loneliness, knowing no one was coming to save me. The feeling of countless cold, dead fingers curling around my wrists and ankles, prying my legs open, sliding up the interior of my thighs. They pinched at my nipples and tugged on my hair, pulling on me until I thought I might split wide open.

A cry wrenched from my throat when a palm rubbed over my center. I tried to squirm away, but I couldn't move. Two dozen hands held me still as a thick finger wriggled its way inside me.

"No! Stop!"

The arms started to pull viciously on my limbs. My muscles screamed. There was so much tension I felt like my skin would snap.

"You lied," I screamed at the knife still clutched in my fist. "You said this was the way out."

"Death is the only escape. He might bring you back, he might not. If he grows bored… at least he'll leave you alone to rot in peace."

I felt so stupid. I'd really thought a fucking letter opener could help me. Now, I'd pay for that desperate mistake.

All lingering doubts about this being real were crushed in an instant.

I really was in Hell.

My mind went blank, darkness threatening to carry me away. I didn't fight it. I drifted into a state of half-consciousness, with only the vague awareness that I was being pushed back up the chute.

I opened my eyes and lifted my face just in time to see the Lord of Bones crouched over the chute's opening, reaching for me. The next moment, his claws were digging into my scalp, and he wrenched me out of the hole by the hair.

"Let go of me," I seethed through clenched teeth. To my surprise, he listened and dropped me. I crumpled to my knees beside the pit and looked around to take in the surroundings I'd been too distracted to notice before.

The walls were lined with prison cells, packed with rotting bodies. They were all reaching through the rusted bars of their cells, moaning and grabbing for me.

"What do they want?" I sobbed. "Why won't they leave me alone?"

The Lord of Bones loomed over me, his intense demeanor choking all the warmth and breathable air from the atmosphere. "You have something they don't. A beating heart and warm, perfect flesh." Countless eyes were on me, but the only ones I became aware of were his, burning into my bare flesh like brands.

"They covet your blood. Your pretty pink cheeks. Your soft lips. They want you." His voice dropped into a rasp. I had a feeling he wasn't talking about the lost souls anymore.

I lifted my chin and glared at him through the filthy strands of my black hair. "Why? Why would you keep something like this in your *home?*" My voice was shaking now, with a dangerous cocktail of terror and rage.

"This is hardly my home," the bone monster growled. "You've wandered into the darkest depths of my dungeon, where the most unworthy souls in my charge rot."

"Then why did you bother to save me? Why didn't you leave me in that hole to die?"

"Oh no, little thief. These souls are unworthy of my *attention.* You? You are going to get so much more of me than all these pathetic souls combined. You get my undivided attention as your personal sovereign of suffering."

"Why is this happening to me?"

"Haven't you figured it out by now, little thief? This is purgatory. When you slink through the shadows, you're bound to be eaten by the monsters within them."

"Eaten? You mean assaulted."

His eyes glowed hot, the light in them flaring, and I felt their fire as his attention slithered down my body to rest on my thighs. Bruises where the hands had forced them apart were beginning to form.

"What did they do to you?"

A lump formed in my throat at the dark bend in his voice. When I didn't answer, he swooped down and gripped me by the shoulders, shaking me. Liquid fire tore through my veins at his touch.

"Did they enter you?" The flames in his eye sockets glowed with malice, and his deep as Hell growl had the corpses shrinking back into their cells. "Did they touch what's mine?"

# CHAPTER SEVEN

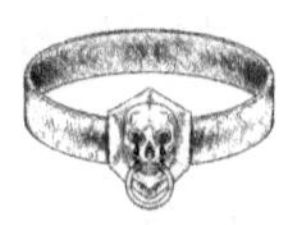

## BELIAL

UNHOLY, SINFUL SOUNDS CLAWED up from my throat as I recited a string of dark magic—the black mass, an execution spell that would make every unworthy soul here die within seconds.

I prided myself on being better than my brothers, but maybe I wasn't better than them after all. Not if the sight of a few bruises had me wiping out dozens of souls as if they'd never existed at all. I couldn't bring myself to care.

The only soul that mattered in the entire God forsaken dungeon was *hers*.

All around us, the corpses slumped to the ground, dropping like gassed flies. The thief's eyes widened as she watched them die before she peered into the oubliette to find the limbs limp and unmoving. "What happened to them?"

"I gave them their final Judgement. They'd been waiting for some time."

Her eyes flicked to mine, the black stains from her makeup leaving dark trails down her cheeks.

She was weeping.

*Bleeding Hells.* Seeing her puffy cheeks coated in tears did dark things to me, but I hated knowing I was not the cause of them.

"Why did you kill them?" she asked, her tone rife with disbelief.

"They touched you. Defiled you." I gritted my many teeth. "Just as I will make you suffer for defiling my Catherine, I will make anything and anyone suffer for defiling you. I protect those who belong to me."

"Catherine...That's the woman from the portrait, isn't it? You were in love with her, that's why I'm being punished. Because I took her necklace?"

Anger possessed me like a demon at her words. Was she really downplaying her crimes?

"You snapped her neck! You'll be lucky if I don't snap yours in return." I shouldn't have made any quick movements for her—not after she'd been violated by those forgotten souls—but my claw flew out to grab her.

She was prepared, jumping back and brandishing a knife so small, I hadn't noticed it before. "Don't touch me you fucking bastard."

I was barely listening to her now. My attention was on the little blade clutched in her trembling hand. "Where did you get that?"

"In my room... but fine. Take it. It tried to have me killed anyway."

I snatched her wrist, my iron grip making her cry out in surprise. I wrenched the blade out of her hand, and felt the despair of the soul within.

How had I been so stupid? I'd been so careful not to leave any sharp items in Catherine's room, yet I left this knife—of all things—for my little thief to stumble upon?

Fury and loathing churned inside me like a storm. This was my fault.

When Catherine had been alive, I'd done my best to "child-proof" the castle to keep her from killing herself. I'd placed bars over the windows, nailed down the various trap doors scattered around the palace. After she'd died for the last time, I'd removed it all in a sad attempt to brighten the place.

*I could put it all back*. No. I knew from experience that it wouldn't stop my thief from trying to escape me. Something told me she was more innovative and stubborn than Catherine.

This time would be different.

I'd keep a closer eye on her.

I'd chain her to me, if that's what it took to keep her close, to keep her safe from the perils of my castle.

Because when the time came for it, I wanted to be the only thing in her nightmares. I'd be the sole cause of her agony.

I'd be her only woe and torment. As the god of this plane, I'd be her sole salvation.

I shoved the knife into my cloak. "Remember this. In the dark hours of the night, after I've crawled under that delectable skin of yours, invaded your every cell, peeled back your layers, and branded myself onto every bone of your body, know that you brought this on yourself."

With a flourish of my hand, the skull amulet I'd given Catherine all those years ago appeared in mid-air. I took it, running a finger delicately over the familiar pendant, and walked over to the nearest cell. Reaching through the bars, I grabbed a collar around one of the corpse's necks and yanked, ripping it through the dead body's neck, shaking off any scraps of withered skin still attached.

Fixing the amulet to the front of the collar with a bit of dark magic, I returned to the human still standing in the middle of the hall. She hadn't made another break for it. Smart on her part. Maybe she was learning her place after all.

Stopping in front of her, I stared down into her dark, wide eyes and held up the bejeweled circlet of metal.

"You robbed the wrong body, little thief. You didn't just steal a necklace. You stole her whole curse."

Her dark lashes batted, knocking a tear loose. As I watched it streak down her cheek, it took everything in me to keep myself from dragging her little body against mine and running my tongue over her face so I could taste her misery upon my tongue.

Instead, I slipped the collar around her neck and locked it into place. She might have escaped the first one easily enough, but this one she would wear until her body turned to dust. If I ever let it.

It was a symbol of ownership, a daily reminder that she would belong to me forevermore.

"What curse is that?" she whispered.

I laughed, the sound deep and grating. "*Me.*"

I SHOULD HAVE PUNISHED my little thief for her attempted escape. I should have made her bleed, extracted every drop of fear I could until she was a beautiful, whimpering mess.

Yet, something held me back.

There was no urgency for me to inflict torture. I had every second of eternity for that.

Was it the whisper of a conscience stirred to life by Catherine's memory that swayed my actions? Or the bruises on the little thief's thighs burned into my brain?

Had I been any of my brothers, she wouldn't have received a reprieve. She would have been tortured to the brink of insanity, most likely killed like the woman I watched Asmodeus murder.

Instead, I chained her up again. This time, in a much more secure room, one that would be impossible for her to break free from. I wouldn't make the mistake of underestimating her again.

I'd stood at the door for several minutes, admiring the way her pale flesh looked against the silky black sheets, reveling in the sweetness of her racing heartbeat before heading to the Library of Souls. Content as I was to listen to the little thief's plight, the eager desperation in her tone as she begged me to set her free, there was an urgent matter of business to attend to.

*Holga.*

As promised, Asmodeus had sent her soul back to me, and it was time to bestow her newest responsibility upon her. Not to mention, I'd like to see what haggard state my brother had left her in, if there was much left of her at all.

She was waiting for me in the wide entryway of the library, wearing the same floor-length dress she'd died in centuries ago. Only now, it was shredded in some places, revealing bare bones underneath. Flowing silver hair fell from her skull, patchy in some places, but still gleaming in the dull lighting. Her empty sockets stared in my direction as I approached, and I could feel the contempt seeping from her bones.

She wasn't happy to see me, but she couldn't deny that being here in my castle was better than being in the lower levels of Hell. It looked like Asmodeus had stripped every inch of skin from her corpse, leaving her nothing but a walking, talking skeleton.

"Holga," I said, stopping a few feet away from her and nodding my acknowledgement.

"Lord Belial." Her voice was sharp and strained. "Why have you summoned me again after all this time? Didn't you get to make me suffer enough the first time I was in this realm?"

Snarky, the way she always had been. If I hadn't needed her help so badly, I might have sent her straight back to Asmodeus and come up with another plan, but I couldn't. My little thief needed an attendant, and only Holga would do.

"I have a job for you," I continued, ignoring her impertinence.

Her head tilted to the side, her empty sockets staring at me, void of any expression. The last time I'd seen her, she'd looked more like Cecil, but it was clear Asmodeus had enjoyed tearing into her once she'd arrived. He'd shredded her of any hint of life, leaving her hollow and empty aside from her soul. I'm surprised she had much of a body left at all.

"A job? Like the last one you left me in charge of, taking care of that poor human girl you locked up like a dog?"

A twinge of regret formed at the mention of Catherine, but I shook it off. Thoughts of her were becoming more difficult to recall and even harder to dwell on as my little thief occupied more and more of my mind.

"Yes and no," I said. "You'll be tending to another human."

She scoffed, an odd noise for a skeleton to make, and if she'd had any eyes, I imagined she'd roll them toward the ceiling. "You brought me back to babysit, Belial?"

"Not babysit, but tend to, yes. To help keep her alive, tend to her basic needs, but you won't have to coddle her," I explained. "I don't plan to keep this one safe from me."

"I won't do it. I won't stand by and watch as you destroy yet another poor girl. Not for a second time."

"Disobeying the Lord?" Cecil hissed from behind a shelf somewhere behind me. "She's got a lot of balls..."

"Everyone has more balls than you, Soul Keeper," Holga raised her voice, acid dripping from every syllable. Nearly three hundred years and these two still hated one another.

"Enough, witch," I growled, making her fall silent. "You will do as I say, or I'll send you back to my brother. From the look of you, he was far less kind to you than I. Serve me well, and I'll free your soul."

At that, the witch's demeanor shifted in an instant. "You mean... No, you couldn't possibly be suggesting..."

"You will finally find eternal peace. It's not a gift I offer many."

There was a pause before Holga dipped into a low curtsey, her skeleton fingers clutching at her tattered skirts. "As you wish, Lord Belial. Where can I find her?"

"Upstairs, at the far end of the east wing. You'll find her chained to a bed," I said, amused. "She must not leave that room, do you understand?"

Holga nodded obediently.

"Perfect. There's just one more thing," I said, reaching into the inside pocket of my cloak and retrieving a cool, round sphere from within. I showed her the plum, large and ripe, before handing it to her. "She's probably starving. Give her this to eat."

The skeletal woman stared at the fruit, suspicion oozing from her. "What did you do to it?"

"That is not your concern. Give it to her."

She hesitated, debating her fate. After a beat, she took the fruit from me, as I expected. As much as her kind nature had stuck with her after death, she wouldn't want to return to my brother's charge.

She'd value her peace over everything else.

"Of course. Yes, sir." With a slight bow, she moved away down the hall, the fabric of her dress sweeping along on the stone behind her.

# CHAPTER EIGHT

## Rayven

I EXPENDED THE REST of my energy screaming and fighting against my new restraints, tugging until my wrists were bruised by the shackles. My throat grew sore, my voice cracked, and I eventually slipped into unconsciousness from sheer exhaustion, unable to keep my eyes open any longer.

When I came to–it could have been minutes or hours later–the sound of footsteps made my breath hitch. Was the Lord of Bones back to punish me? Hot tears stung my eyes.

Did I really deserve this kind of treatment? I'd stolen a stupid amulet, one that was now fused to the metal collar around my neck. Taking her head off in the process had been an accident.

When the doorknob twisted and the door swung open slow-ly, the blood froze in my veins, and time stood still as I waited for my visitor to reveal themself. Thankfully, it wasn't the skull-faced monster who stepped into the room.

It was a woman, a skeleton of a statuesque figure, with ripped Victorian clothes and flowing silver hair. She carried a covered silver tray in her bony hands. Her empty eye sockets were similar to the Lord of Bones, but where he had pale skin covering the rest of his body, she had none.

Closing the door behind her, she walked silently to the edge of the bed before letting her gaze lower to meet mine. I wasn't sure how I could tell, but this woman didn't radiate the same cruel energy my captor did, despite her terrifying appearance.

She was softer, gentler.

"Who are you?" My throat ached as the words clawed their way out. I'd probably overdone it screaming earlier, but I'd been so angry, I couldn't help it. Now, I was too tired to put up a fight.

"My name is Holga," she answered, her voice tender. "I'm your attendant."

My brows lowered over my eyes as I struggled to understand what she meant. "Attendant? You mean, like, my servant? Prisoners normally don't get servants."

"Seeing whose bed you're chained to, you're not a normal prisoner, are you?"

Every sinew in my belly tightened. "Wait, I thought this was to be my new room? Whose bed is this?"

Could this be the Lord of Bones' bedroom? A flush of heat washed over me at the thought. *No.* This room wasn't fancy enough to be the Lord's chambers. Sure, it was huge, but it lacked all the grandeur of the first room I'd been in. This one was depressing with its dark fabrics, faded wallpaper, and dusty tapestries.

So, whose bedroom was this, if not the Lord's? Maybe a high-ranking member of the court.

Was I supposed to be some kind of gift to them? I shivered at the thought.

"This realm isn't kind to the living," the woman said, avoiding answering my question. "I'm here to help keep your delicate heart beating. To start, you must eat."

She gestured to the tray in her hands.

I had no idea how much time had passed since my last meal, but my stomach growled at the smell of food. I was almost afraid to know what passed for food down here, in the realm of the dead, but I'd eat whatever was on that tray.

"What do they call you, dear?" she asked, stepping closer.

"Rayven."

"Lady Rayven," she repeated slowly. "I'd say it's a pleasure, but... well, this isn't the best of circumstances to meet under, is it?"

Holga sat the tray down on the bedside table, and with a snap of her fingers, the shackles around my wrists popped open to set me free. I gasped, surprised to be released, and rubbed the feeling back into my hands. Then, I watched her reach inside her torn dress and–impossibly–produce a half-empty bottle of wine.

"No need for those rusty old things," she said, waving a hand in the air. The manacles floated over to the bedside table and settled next to the tray. "I bet that's better, isn't it?"

I nodded, still taken aback. "Can you undo the chain on the collar so I can at least walk around and stretch my legs?" I tried to keep my tone innocent, and my expression blank.

The second I had a chance, I'd make another run for it.

"I'm afraid I can't," she answered. "My power is not enough to override the dark magic infused in the collar, but it will extend enough for you to roam freely in this room. There's a shelf of books over there." She gestured to the other end of the room, where a giant, built-in shelf held an assortment of ancient, leather-bound books. "You can read beside the hearth. Take your mind off what's to come."

"And what's to come, exactly?"

"Much suffering," she muttered, more to herself than to me.

I cocked an eyebrow at her, wondering how long this poor woman had been here, and how much suffering of her own she'd endured.

"What *are* you?" I asked after a beat.

"A witch, " she said matter-of-factly. "Although my magic isn't as strong as it was when I was alive. I can still manage simple spells." She turned to head toward a door on the opposite end of the room. "First things first, let's get you clean. Then, you can eat."

As hungry as I was, I was even more desperate for a bath. Between the blood and dirt staining my body, and the grimy feeling left on my skin by the hands in the oubliette, I wanted to scrub my skin until it was raw.

Holga opened the sleek black door and revealed a sliver of an elegant bathroom with a clawfoot tub in the center.

"Come, dear," she said, waving me along behind her. "I'll run the bath."

I hesitated, staring after her and wondering how she expected me to reach that far with the chain around my neck. It was slack, sure, but not nearly long enough to reach the bathroom. Skeptically, I got to my feet and made my way slowly across the floor, waiting for the moment the chain would catch and prevent me from going any further.

However, just as Holga had said, the chain kept going, stretching out of the headboard with every step. I stopped in the doorway of the bathroom and turned to look back, amazed at the length of chain keeping me tethered.

Then, I turned back to Holga, who was retrieving a towel from a polished black cabinet next to the sink as the bath continued to fill.

"How long have you been here at the castle?" It was an awkward attempt at small talk, but maybe, if I prodded just enough, Holga could answer some of my burning questions, the ones the Lord of Bones had left branded on my brain with no explanation.

"Many, many years."

She moved to cut off the tap, and my eyes settled on the steam swirling up from the bath water. I could already imagine how incredible the warmth would feel against my chilled skin, and it took everything in me not to run and dive in right then.

"Get in while the water's hot," she urged, and I took several cautious steps forward. The chain never jerked taut, and with a sigh of relief, I slipped into the bath.

The water was heaven on my sore muscles, working them loose and drawing out the ache. Slowly, the chill in my bones ebbed away. It was incredible. I slipped down into the tub until my shoulders were submerged.

"Do you take care of many captives?" I asked, trying again to pry for answers.

She shook her head and handed me a rag with a bar of plum-scented soap. I immediately went to work scrubbing my limbs, washing every inch of me like it would somehow wash away the mix of emotions making my chest tight. It was suffocating despair from being trapped and helpless, despite attempting to keep my hopes up. Things were looking bleak.

"How many others do you tend to?" So far, I hadn't seen any other humans—any living ones anyway—but surely, I wasn't the only person alive in this entire realm. There had to be more captives hidden somewhere in the labyrinth...

"Just one before you," Holga answered impatiently. "Hurry so we can dress you."

"Was it Catherine?"

The witch went still. Her hollow eye sockets bore into me, her glare making the hairs on my nape rise. "Don't speak that name here. Now up. Up!"

With a huff, I dipped my head under the water and set to work scrubbing the blood and dirt from my hair, wishing I had conditioner to run through the brittle ends. When I was as clean as possible–a part of me still felt dirty after the oubliette–I stood and turned toward Holga, who was waiting with a towel in hand.

Wrapped in the towel, I made my way back to the bed, the chain shrinking back into the wall like it was on some kind of magical pulley. Holga marched over to the wardrobe against the far wall and pulled open the doors, flipping through the garments hanging there. She pulled out a thin white nightgown with a tie around the waist and brought it back before urging me to my feet.

It was a wrap-around dress, easy to pull on and off so it didn't interfere with the chain around my neck.

"Have that in black? White's not exactly my color."

If the witch could blink, I had a feeling she'd be doing it now. "Black is for those in mourning or for the dead. You are neither."

"Well, my boyfriend was murdered right in front of my eyes by your precious Lord." I flashed her a too-sweet smile. "So it's the perfect occasion for black, yeah?"

Holga shook her head in sympathy. "I am sorry. The Lord likes his human consorts in white."

*"Consort?"* Heat flushed my cheeks, quickly spreading through my limbs like wildfire. "You don't mean...He can't...He's too big. I'm too small. He'll break me."

My brain broke at the thought of fucking the Lord of Bones. He had the fleshless head of some unknown animal, but from what I could tell, he had the body of a man. At least, it appeared that way. Who knew what he was hiding under that cloak.

My mouth went dry trying to unpack the mental image.

"Who knows what the Lord has planned for you, Lady Rayven. He never bedded Catherine. Thank the Darkness for that. Poor thing would never have handled him."

"What?" My eyes widened. It was becoming clear that the monster had been pretty taken with the woman. "He never tried to sleep with her?"

Holga held the gown open for me and I turned, pushing my arms through the sleeves. "Oh, he went to her bed several times, but she refused. She always refused."

I turned this new piece of information over in my mind. He was so huge, the beast could have easily overpowered her. Why hadn't he?

If he came to my bed, would he take no for an answer?

"Better?" Holga asked as she tied the bow around my waist.

The material was thin and almost see-through, but I did feel better with the semblance of modesty.

"It's not black, but it's better than being naked. So thank you." I took a seat again and towel dried my hair before Holga set to working out the tangles.

"Silken locks as dark as a raven's back..." the witch mused.

"I was named after the color, actually."

"Yes. My previous mistress had the same hue." Her voice was soft, with a twinge of something new mixed in. *Pain?*

It seemed that whoever Catherine had been, her presence had affected more than just the ruler of the castle.

It might have only been a bath, but being squeaky clean had raised my spirits and renewed my hope. Escaping might have been off the table for a moment, but the thought still sat heavy in the back of my mind. I'd figure out an escape; I just needed time to work out a better plan.

When Holga finished with my hair, she set the brush aside and removed the lid from the platter on the bedside table. I eyed the plate curiously. There was a piece of bread, something pale that could have been meat, and the darkest, juiciest-looking plum I'd ever seen. There was also a tiny, empty goblet, which Holga soon filled with wine from the bottle. Aside from the plum, it didn't look overly appetizing, but my mouth watered regardless.

"Someone must like plums," I said, remembering the plum-scented soap from the bath.

"The Lord keeps a few fruit trees in the garden. Plums are his favorite." Holga jabbed a skeletal finger at the food. "Now eat."

For a brief moment, I thought I'd be able to eat alone, but when she didn't turn to walk away, I knew she planned to stay until I finished. Not that I minded the company. After being alone for so many hours, it was nice to see someone else aside from the Lord of Bones.

I tentatively reached for the bread and took a small bite out of it. It was bland, but at least it wasn't stale.

"Where does the Lord of Bones stay in the castle?" I asked, still on a mission to get information out of Holga. "Like, where does he hang out the most?"

She tilted her head to the side, her bones cracking and making my stomach turn. "The master is everywhere and nowhere. He knows everything that goes on within these walls."

"That's specific, thank you."

"You're welcome, Lady Rayven," Holga said with a small dip of her head.

I wasn't sure how old the witch was, but I guess she'd been born sometime before sarcasm was invented.

"Does the Lord at least have a name?"

She chuckled once, a dry, raspy noise. "You sure are a curious thing. Way more talkative than the last mistress. You may call him Lord or Master."

Also unhelpful, but her laugh made me think she was warming up to me. Or maybe I was delusional, and this place was slowly eating away in my mind, making me crazy. "Yeah, I'll pass on calling him Master."

In an attempt to spice things up in the bedroom, Mark had once asked me to call him Master, but the guy's idea of being a Dom was a gentle ass spanking and a stained tie around my wrists that he used for the occasional interview—since grave robbing wasn't always his ideal career choice.

My stomach went sour at the thought of Mark, and I had to choke down the rest of my meat and bread without tasting it, for fear it would come up again.

The wine in the goblet was bitter but strong, and I welcomed the temporary relief the alcohol brought.

My eyes settled on the plum, and I thought about saving it for later. After all, who knew when I'd receive another meal. Hopefully it wouldn't be too long, since Holga was there to make sure I had everything I needed. Still, I couldn't be sure. There was nothing I could trust in this realm, especially when it came to my wellbeing.

"I think I'm full," I said. I grabbed the plum off the plate. "I'll save this for later."

"The master said specifically to make sure you ate every-thing," she warned. "So be a good girl and finish it now. Surely, you've learned not to disobey him by now."

I swallowed hard over the lump forming in my throat, and stared down at the fat fruit in my hand. There was nothing sinister about it, but Holga's insistence made me wary.

I took the first bite, sweet juice exploding in my mouth, and Holga nodded approvingly. She stood there, a few feet away, waiting until I'd finished with the fruit. She placed the top back on the tray and snatched it off the table.

"Aren't you going to restrain my wrists again?" My eyes bounced nervously to shackles on the bedside table, my stomach knotting uncomfortably.

"If that's what you desire," she said with another dry chuckle. "You won't get anywhere with that collar on your neck, so there's no need for them."

"No, I'd rather leave them off." I wrung my hands together, thinking about the hours I'd spent chained up to the bed. "I just didn't want you to get in trouble for defying your master."

I'd seen how easily the Lord of Bones could wipe out a room full of souls, and even though I didn't know Holga well, I didn't want him to do the same to her. She'd been kind to me so far, nicer than anything else in this realm had been, and I didn't want to be the reason she died... again.

"No need to worry, dear." She shook her head slowly. "Now you get some rest. I'll be along eventually to check on you."

Before she mentioned rest, I hadn't felt the least bit sleepy–after all, I'd napped before she arrived–but as soon as she said it, I felt my eyelids droop. My limbs were heavy, and the silky-smooth sheets called to me, wanting to claim me again.

"Thanks, Holga," I said, my words slurred. Sleep was quickly taking me under.

"Good evening, Lady Rayven." With a bow, she slipped out of the room, and the door closed softly behind her.

I crawled up the bed, exhaustion sinking down to my core, and laid my head on the pillow. The last thing that crossed my mind before sleep pulled me under was the Lord of Bones standing over me, enraged that another being had dared touch my body, and how his anger sparked a warmth in my chest to combat the icy air inside the castle.

Then, the sweet embrace of darkness swept me away.

# CHAPTER NINE

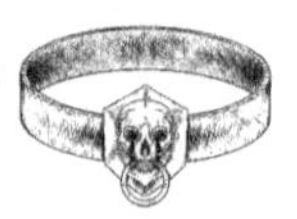

## RAYVEN

I FELL INTO A deep, restless sleep. Even if this was a nightmare, at least it was a reprieve from Hell. Scary dreams had never bothered me before. I'd always loved my nightmares back home.

I was *that* person—the creepy, weird girl. I liked horror movies, scary stories, and the macabre. I spent most of my childhood in cemeteries, but it didn't start out because I liked them. My father died when I was young, and my mom was always away, working three jobs to support us. So I hung out with dad at his grave.

I found the company of the dead peaceful–I always had–but this realm was on a whole new level. It scared me.

I knew I needed to escape. I didn't belong here. I was still *alive*. My presence in this realm defied the natural order of things, but...there was a part of me that didn't want to leave.

The horny little goth girl inside wanted to stay in the realm of the dead and play the pet of the evil bone monster.

Obviously, good ol' survival skills weren't going to let that happen. If I wanted to survive, I could never submit to him that way. I had to keep my distance, had to escape. It was the logical thing to do.

But when the nightmare took hold of me, I welcomed it. This was a safe place to explore that part of myself, to indulge in the nightmares without actually living them, without having to deal with the consequences.

The first thing I became aware of was the collar still around my neck, pulled tight at my nape by the heavy chain fastened to the front.

The second was that I was sitting on something very warm. Something alive. I was in a man's lap. No, a monster's. *The Lord of Bones.* My skin prickled at the realization, at his closeness.

And the third thing I noticed was that a gauze-like dress was draped from my collar, giving off exotic slave-girl vibes. The material was even thinner than my nightgown, leaving nothing to the imagination.

The Lord of Bones sat in a throne made of–fittingly–bones, which stood in the back of a dark, dank throne room. Chunks of stone were pushed off to the perimeter of the hall, where the pillars had begun to crumble with age, and cobwebs hung from every corner.

A procession of souls–corpses in various states of decomposition–stood before the throne. The line was so long, it encircled the room and out the double doors at the end of the hall. I couldn't be sure, but I had a feeling it wound through the entire castle.

The most shocking thing about the room wasn't that I was sitting on the Lord's lap, or the hundreds of souls waiting in the queue. It was the river of crimson water wrapping around the throne. It had a slow current, moving lazily along, and there were thousands of decomposing corpses floating just beneath the surface.

My stomach flipped. Somehow, even though I'd never seen it before, I knew this was the river Styx. These souls were all awaiting their Judgement, and the Styx would carry them on to the next stage of hell. *If*, and only if, the Lord of Bones ushered them on.

The monster in question didn't seem to be paying attention to anything around us. His large fingers stroked my hair with slow, reverent motions. It was just a dream, but his touch did things to me, stirred dormant feelings that I hadn't felt in so long. If I were awake, I'd... Well, I wasn't sure what I'd do. Scream? Run? What good would that do, considering the chain around my neck?

My gaze followed the heavy links, my cheeks heating when I saw it looped around his wrist. He was holding it like a leash, and the end was secured to an iron hook affixed to the base of the throne.

I was the Lord of Bones' little pet, and here in the safety of my dream, I didn't want to escape.

"Next," he summoned the next soul in line without bothering to lift his head.

His voice was so guttural and deep, even in my head. I lifted my eyes to his, only to find his eyes sockets alight with soft blue flame. They flickered when he noticed I was staring.

The King of Limbo looked so terrifying in his throne, with his moth-eaten cloak draped around his broad shoulders. Underneath, all he wore were black pants, leaving his broad chest open to my curious gaze. It was muscular, with pronounced pectorals and rippling abs, but what drew my eye was his pale, almost blue flesh, with streaks of necrosis-like black patterning all down his torso. It almost looked like tattoos.

My mouth began to water. He was a horny goth girl's dream. Mark always made fun of me for the monster romance books I kept in my room. Now that I was faced with one—a very dangerous one who wanted to torture me for accidently decapitating the corpse of his last human pet—my "monster fucker" status came with some hefty implications.

But this was a dream, so what was the harm?

"You're admiring me," he mused, lifting his head from his hand, which was propped on the arm of his throne. He almost sounded surprised.

"I guess I am. You're not the real you, so it's perfectly fine if, you know, the whole 'bone daddy' thing you got going on actually does it for me."

A growl so soft it was almost a purr rolled from his chest. "You've admired your Lord with your eyes. Now, let me worship you with mine."

He slipped his wrist out of the chain loop and gestured to the floor at his feet. "On your knees."

I froze for a beat. My mind said no, but everything else screamed yes. So, with all the souls watching, I slipped off his knee and knelt at his feet before his throne. My heart lurched into hyper-speed as I felt the flames in his eye sockets scorch my flesh.

He slowly leaned forward, his skull head canting to the side as his black, forked tongue painted a lick over his top row of teeth. "Turn around."

I did as I was told, the fire inside me making my skin bead with sweat and my pussy drip. Holy shit. This felt so *real*.

"That's a good little thief. See, I knew you'd make a perfect pet," he praised as I did as I was told and shuffled so I was kneeling with my back to him. "Now, lift your dress and spread yourself for me."

My thighs clenched, slick arousal oozing down my thighs. Jesus, this was making me so wet. Every soul in the throne room had their eyes—at least, those who had them—on me. If this wasn't a dream, I'd probably be just a tad more hesitant about doing this in front of a bunch of rotting souls, but they weren't real. This was just another fantasy in which I could safely indulge.

Reaching around, I slipped the hem of my dress up to reveal my ass and gripped my bare cheeks to spread them.

"Good. Now, bend over until your lips touch the stone. Show your Lord all that he owns."

I did as he instructed and kissed the cold stairs that led up to the throne's platform while holding myself open for the Lord's hungry gaze.

The air was cold against my exposed center, but the Lord of Bones' attention swept over my skin like a fever, keeping me hot and cold all over. It was delicious torture.

"Next," he instructed the soul at the front of the line. "State your name, soul, for your Judgement. And don't you dare look at my pet. Eyes on me, lest you wish to lose them."

The soul obeyed, approaching the first stair. As he spoke, detailing his identity and his life, the Lord of Bones seemed to lose focus as I began to tremble.

"You're enjoying this." He sounded surprised again. "You're shaking from pleasure, not shame."

"The shame brings me pleasure, My Lord."

The monster released a low groan, catching me off guard—especially since this was my dream. "Blood and Darkness. I knew you'd make a perfect pet for me. Now...I'd like you to touch yourself. Make yourself come."

He must have gripped the chain again, as it clanked gently. *Fuck.* I shouldn't have found that sound so hot.

I didn't need to be told twice. I took one hand and reached between my legs, my fingers sliding through my folds. I was so slick with arousal, wetter than I'd ever gotten with Mark. Then again, this was a dream.

Nothing could ever be this good in reality.

I moaned as my fingers picked up speed, massaging my tender flesh in tight little circles. I lost myself to the bliss as all the souls did their damndest not to look at me, for fear they'd lose the precious body parts they had left.

From behind me, there was a rustle of fabric, and the chain rattled again. Then, big, growly breaths began to barrel out from the Lord. Was he...? I was too curious not to look.

Craning my head over my shoulder, I found him tense in his throne, his muscles straining against his flesh. He'd freed himself from his pants and was furiously stroking himself at the sight of me. His huge, claw-tipped hand blocked much of his cock past his pants, but what I could see was that he'd looped the chain around his shaft and was choking himself with it.

I strained to get a better look, but he snarled at me to turn back around.

"This is your fate if you don't escape me," he huffed over the chaos of the clanking chain.

"I know!" I cried. "I will escape you. I will... *ooooh!*" As pure ecstasy washed over me in brutal waves, I crumpled onto the floor, the cool stone heaven against my flushed cheeks.

He finished with an animalistic roar that had dust raining down from the ceiling. Then, after several moments, I heard him push to his feet. "You can try to escape, but you will fail. Then, you'll be mine forever. Is that such a terrible fate? You're not like Catherine. There's a part of you that wants me, a twisted, dark little part that I'll uncover."

A yelp of surprise dropped from my lips as he hauled me up from the floor and dumped me into his throne. His hands gripped my thighs and spread them, guiding my legs so they were propped over the armrests.

Then, he dropped to his knees, the bare bone of his snout mere inches away from my pussy. "Even if I have to break you open and wrench it out, I'll do it." It wasn't a warning. His gravelly timbre carried all the weight of an oath. "Don't make me do that. I can be gentle. If you let me... I can tease it out. Milk it from you."

His black tongue snaked out from his parted jowls. Beads of saliva oozed off it, peppering over my folds. He laughed at the way my flesh twitched at the contact. Then, the monstrous appendage slid over my seam, lapping up my arousal.

His eyes flickered as my flavor seeped into his taste buds. "The freshest cream any soul has ever tasted."

Fuck me. He felt so good against me. Forbidden. Sinful. *Good.*

Unlike anything I'd ever felt before, especially in a dream. My brain was either working on overdrive to drown out the horrors of my reality—creating a version of this monster that I desired–or showing me just how salacious and horrifying my deepest desires were.

Something told me this wasn't all a figment of my imagination, which was only more reason for me to escape this place as soon as possible.

Because if this was a taste of what Hell was going to be like, maybe, just maybe, I wouldn't want to leave.

# CHAPTER TEN

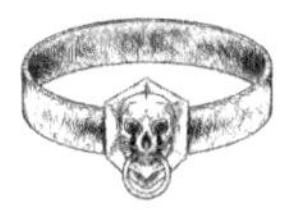

## BELIAL

My little thief was becoming a very serious problem.

*It was happening again.*

I was becoming obsessed with another human woman, letting her consume far too many of my thoughts. I'd been foolish to think history wouldn't repeat itself. Though, this time, it was different.

I'd only wanted Catherine's love.

With my little thief, I wanted everything.

Her pain. Her pleasure. Her fear and loathing. I wanted to wring every drop of blood, cum, and tears from her. I wanted to taste every inch of her, and when I inevitably broke her, I wanted to piece her back together so I could do it all over again.

What I hadn't counted on was for her to *like* it. Catherine had loathed me, in both my forms. In all the years my beauty had spent in this castle, she'd never softened to the idea of loving a beast like me.

But this woman, this audacious, little thing... she was aroused by my monstrous form.

I wouldn't have believed it if it wasn't for the spell I'd cast on the plum. It allowed me to peer into the dream I'd crafted just for her. I saw the way her eyes brightened at the sight of her leash. I felt the uptick of her heartbeat when she looked back and saw my fist around my cock.

I'd expected her to wet herself in fear, not pleasure, but she reveled in every second of the debauchery. It was her excitement, her willingness to give herself to me in her sleep, that had me marching down the empty hallways toward her room in the middle of the night.

*I had to see it for myself.*

Stepping into her room, I didn't bother to tread lightly. She couldn't hear me, and she wouldn't wake until I allowed it. She looked so small, nestled in the center of my large bed. I paused, catching my reflection in the ornate, full-length mirror at the far end of the room.

I liked this form. It was mostly human, with the exception of the twisted antlers sprouting from my skull, draped in silver jewelry. My lithe frame was swaddled in perfectly tailored—if a little moth-eaten—clothing.

If she found my demon form enticing, what would she think of this one? My hands ran over the mask hiding my marred face. Catherine had screamed when she'd seen my scars. She'd reminded me how repulsive she'd found me, enough so that I vowed to never remove my mask again.

My attention drifted to the little human in my bed. Would she feel the same way?

My heart ached at the notion of revealing this face to her, the one I'd had before I became this monster so long ago.

*No.*

When she'd raided Catherine's grave, she'd earned herself my attention.

And when she'd wielded the letter opener bearing Catherine's soul—the very same one she'd taken her life with—my little thief had won my obsession.

But she'd never have my heart, nor my trust.

I'd buried that with Catherine's body.

My brothers had warned me never to give any part of myself to a human. It hadn't been intentional with Catherine. It had just happened. There'd been no stopping it. Watching her wither away, slowly driven to madness and reduced to nothing, had broken something inside me.

*But my little thief...*

There was a part of my new pet that wanted me. She wanted my darkness, my corruption. The thought of my punishments had her heating with excitement, even if they scared her. Hells, her terror seemed to heighten her arousal.

She tossed and turned in her sleep, sweat beading her brow. Then, she started to moan. "My Lord," she whimpered.

My cock thickened in my pants.

*Blood and Darkness.*

I knew exactly what had her so worked up. What I'd give to play out that scene for real. It would be easy enough to chain her to my throne, easier still to have my way with her, but there was no chance she'd be obedient for me in reality. She wouldn't abandon her resolve and willingly spread herself for me, nor would she get on her knees and beg for my cock.

I strode toward the bed and stood at the footboard, my hands gripping the carved wood. The chain fasting her to the wall hung slack between the valley of her breasts and rattled faintly with her motions.

"My Lord, *please...*"

It was with that pathetic little mewl that all my self-restraint disintegrated. No living woman had ever begged to have me. It was just a dream for her, a fantasy. If only she knew she was dredging up my own fantasy from the grave, one I'd sworn to leave buried.

My little grave robber really had a way with digging up the past.

Crossing to the side of the bed, I pushed the lantern-sleeves of my black shirt up and peeled my gloves off. I set them down on the pillow beside hers and crawled onto the bed. The mattress dipped with my weight, but she didn't stir. No matter what, she wouldn't wake until I ended the spell.

My little sleeping beauty. I reached out, my fingertips tracing her plush lips. I toyed with the ring adorning her nose. It was just a simple piece of jewelry, but fuck, why did it make my cock so hard?

My fingers continued their path down her face, tracing the edge of her jaw and skimming her delicate throat. It looked so dainty with the heavy collar around it. My eyes narrowed behind my mask at the sight of the skull amulet glaring back at me.

I grasped the chain and moved it to the side of the bed. I pressed my palm to her sternum, my long fingers pushing into the pillowy mounds of her breasts. Her chest was pale with a tinge of rouge dipping into the neckline of her nightgown. Dead flesh didn't have that.

I swallowed thickly, biting back a primal growl as I honed in on the pound of her heart beating against my hand.

Hells. I wanted her, but if I woke her now, I'd have to build her trust enough to allow me to touch her. *If* she let me touch her at all. There was a sinister part of me that wanted her to fight, to scream for me to stop even as her body begged for more. But I wasn't as cruel or merciless as my brothers, and I couldn't force myself on her. I wanted her to want it deep down.

More than anything, I wanted her to want me.

That's why I couldn't wake her, not yet. I couldn't bear another rejection, not when all I needed was a small taste...

I pulled the covers down, my hand curving over her thigh and pushing the hem of her gown up over her knee. A lump formed in my throat at the old wounds marking her flesh. She had scars, like me. Hers were likely from her trade. Scaling old wrought iron fences, if I had to venture a guess.

She was perfection, even with her scars. *Especially* with her scars.

My hand drifted up toward her apex, closer, closer—until my fingers brushed against her coarse patch of pubic hair. She'd been naked in the dungeon, since all the lost soul fragments had shredded her clothes. In my anger, I'd barely registered these details about her.

I'd make sure to never make that mistake again. I'd commit every inch of her to memory, inside and out. I'd know every part of her, and I planned to start learning right now.

With one hand still cupping her thigh, my other grasped the tie at her waist, gave it a tug, and undid the wrap. I sucked in a breath. Just as I hoped. The pretty patch of hair between her legs was the same hue as that on her head. She was naturally raven-haired.

There was something about a pale-skinned, dark-haired woman that gripped me by the balls.

I lifted my eyes to her hips. Her pretty navel. Her soft, medium-sized breasts and her perfect rose bud nipples. My chest tightened when glints of silver caught my gaze. Two metal bars pierced her nipples, one pushed through each peak.

I'd lived a long time. No, lived wasn't the right word. I'd *existed* a long time. I'd seen souls of all kinds, so I wasn't a stranger to body piercings, but they'd never appealed to me before. Not like this.

How could two little bars make me so painfully hard?

"Fuck," I rasped as I leaned over her to pluck at one.

Her lips parted on a gasp. "Yes, My Lord. More, please. I need more."

Need. Not want. *Need.*

My muscles seized and my jaw tightened as I gaped at her, trying to process the words. It was like my mind couldn't comprehend the fact that this woman was begging for me in her sleep, needing me. The magic was making her dream of me, but her actions within the spell were her own.

Just like that, the darkness inside me took hold. I straddled her upper body so her shoulders were nestled snugly against my thighs, caged between the V of my legs. I jammed my thumb into the laces of my pants and wrenched them loose. On the next ragged breath, I had my cock out.

I was about to spit in my hand to use as lubricant, but I paused. The scent of her arousal permeated the entire room. She was oh so wet. With one hand still choking my shaft, I reached behind me and stroked my fingers through her soaking folds, gathering her wetness.

She whimpered, squirming beneath me. I smoothed her essence over my shaft and began to work my hand up and down, my palm sliding easily as I worked her into my flesh.

I groaned, tipping my masked face to the ceiling.

Her slick on my shaft was like a drug, leaching into my body and shooting straight to my brain. I'd waited too damn long for this. I'd been but a shell of myself, barely existing, a ghost among wayward souls.

Death falling in love with life was a tale as old as fucking time. I'd been warned, so many times. I couldn't help it. This was my weakness. *She* was my weakness.

Just as I felt myself tip over the edge, I dropped my attention back to her and shoved my fingers into her mouth. "Open for me, pet. Take what I give you."

Her lips parted around the digits, and I held the head of my cock over her open mouth.

On the next beat, I was pulsing thick ropes of cum. It streaked her lips, painted her tongue, and beaded her dark lashes.

She was a mess. My little living pet looked so goddamn gorgeous splattered in death's seed.

My timing must have lined up with the dream spell perfectly, because she breathed a heavy sigh and *licked* her lips. "Thank you, My Lord."

"Do not thank me. You will be my ruin, and I will be yours in return."

I pushed my spent cock back into my pants then eased my mask off my face. No one ever saw this face, but I could take it off while she slept. While she was sleeping, we could be something different—something other than the heartbroken monster with a penchant for suffering, and the lonely little human so desperate to return to a home I had doubts was much of a home at all.

I ran my tongue over her face, lapping up the last traces of my seed before kissing her softly with my marred lips. She sighed beneath them, breathy and content.

Securing her nightgown back in place, I tucked her under the covers and put my mask back on. Then, I pulled myself off the bed, grabbed a book from my vast collection, and sat beside the fire, pretending like I'd been there all along.

And with that, my little sleeping beauty woke up.

# CHAPTER ELEVEN

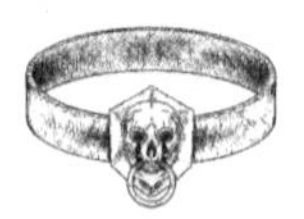

## RAYVEN

A FILM OF SWEAT covered my entire body, and my mouth tasted funny, like I'd eaten something forbidden, like Eve biting into the serpent's apple. My mind went to Holga and the plum. Had she put something in the food?

My head was swimming. It felt like I'd been drugged. *Had she poisoned me?*

I wanted to be mad. I should have been furious, but that dream—fucking Hell. I wanted to go back and experience more of *that* Bone Lord.

"Have sweet dreams?"

At the strange voice, I shot up into a sitting position, my chain pulling on my collar, choking me.

A man sat in the lounge chair beside the roaring fire, reading a book. He wore an old-fashioned black shirt—the kind sexy men wore on old, bodice-ripper book covers—and black, form-fitting pants with heavy leather boots. He could have passed for a pirate, until I dragged my gaze up above his shoulders.

A black mask covered his entire face. It didn't have much detail to it, save for the way it was sculpted to curve over his sharp jawline and arch over an aquiline nose.

I would have assumed that he was human if it wasn't for the immense power rolling off him in waves...and the antlers sprouting from his unkempt black hair. They were draped with silver chains and charms that gleamed in the firelight.

In addition to the horn jewelry, earrings in the shape of daggers dangled from his ears.

"You scared the shit out of me," I rasped, enamored with his strange demeanor.

"I certainly hope not. That's my bed you're in. Though, it seems you've already made a mess of the sheets."

It took me a second to realize what he was talking about. My hand pushed under the covers, feeling the spot between my thighs. I was soaked, in more than sweat. A full-bodied blush swept over my skin like a fever. "How did you..."

"I can scent you from here, little human." He flipped a page in the book. Either he read faster than anyone I'd ever seen, or he was only pretending to pay attention to the printed pages. "You stink like a bitch in heat."

I narrowed my eyes at him while trying my best to pretend his words didn't sink straight to my core. "Who are you?"

"My name is Belial."

"I'm Rayven…"

He finally glanced up from his book. "Rayven," he said, tasting my name in his mouth as if it was something sweet to savor. "Like your hair."

My heart clenched in my chest at the way the melodic lilt of his voice took a dark bend. "Um, yeah. Just like my hair."

My hands idly twisted the covers over my lap. "So, this is your room?"

"It is." His attention returned to his book.

I breathed a sigh of relief. "I was afraid it belonged to the Lord of Bones."

"Luckily for you, it doesn't," he mused. "He would have torn you apart by now. I'm simply a member of his court."

His clothes were worn, but they still seemed a little on the fancy side for being a servant. "So are you some dead noble or something?"

"No. I am a native of this realm. A psychopomp, technically. A kind of demon that ferries souls of the dead from your realm into this one."

My brows shot up with interest. "You're the ferryman, then? Like Charon from Greek mythology?"

"Something like that, yes."

The tension in the room was thick, his dark magic radiating from him like noxious gas, filtering into my lungs and making my head spin. I waited for him to speak, but he continued reading his book.

I got the feeling he was enjoying the suspense, the way it had started to eat at me from the inside like a parasite.

"Why did he put me in here?" I held my breath, waiting for an answer. None came.

The only sounds to fill the silence were the crackle of the fire and the rustle of parchment as he turned another page.

Swallowing down the lump in my throat, I turned my attention to something dark in the corner of my eye. A set of black leather gloves sat on the pillow next to mine. My brow furrowed as I tried to remember if they'd been there before I'd fallen asleep.

I looked back at Belial. "Are these gloves yours?"

I couldn't see his expression, but his surprise was so palpable, I could feel it bleeding into the room's warm atmosphere. His surprise morphed into irritation by a flippant page-turn in his book. "Everything in this room belongs to me."

A deep pang pulled under my gut and buried into my bones at his hard-as-steel voice sheathed in velvet. "Are you trying to say the Lord of Bones has given me to you?"

"You ask too many questions." He snapped the book closed and placed it on the table beside his chair, shoving to his feet and whipping his gaze in my direction. Slowly, he strode toward the bed.

Holy.

Fucking.

Shit.

I hadn't noticed it before because he'd been sitting, but now that he was standing, I saw it. The bulge in his pants was huge. His cock had to be so big, I wouldn't be surprised if it came with its own gravitational pull.

My breath turned sharp and short as I watched him tug at the laces of his shirt. All the breath crystallized in my lungs when he pulled it off over his head and revealed a chiseled torso.

He had an athletic build, with heavily scarred, death-pale skin encasing powerful, lean muscles. Tossing the shirt over the footboard, he kicked off his boots and started for me.

"W-wait." I scooted backward up the mattress until my back hit the headboard. "What are you doing?"

"Preparing for bed."

My mouth went dry at the thought of sleeping next to this stranger. Holga might as well have rolled me up in toilet paper for how much the nightgown concealed. It would be so easy for this man to tug it off, to strip me bare.

My brain was a whirlwind of thoughts. The Lord of Bones seemed so possessive of me, yet now, he was handing me off to some random member of his court? Why?

"You're going to sleep here?"

"It *is* my bed." There was no missing the smirk in his voice.

I flung the covers off my legs and stumbled out of bed, the chain falling to the floor with a heavy clink. "I'll just sleep on the lounge chair by the fire."

It's not like I didn't like the idea of sleeping next to this psychopomp—or whatever he said he was. That was the problem.

I liked it too much. Everything about him drew me closer, like a spider pulling its prey into a web.

Even his scent was intoxicating and strangely familiar. Sweet and fruity, like ripe summer strawberries...

That's when it clicked. He smelt of sodium nitrate, a chemical found in shampoos, as well as embalming fluid. I hadn't had much experience with it–most of the corpses I'd dug up were too old for the scent to linger–but it was a fragrance that haunted my brain. Underneath the sweet scent were traces of pine, like a freshly built casket.

My heart ached at the aroma. It made me homesick.

I didn't *want* to want this man, but I did. That scared me almost as much as wanting the Lord of Bones. I stumbled away toward the hearth, but there was a jerk of the chain fastened to my collar. I hadn't noticed the chain had looped around my foot. With the tug, it caught around my ankle, and I went tumbling to the floor.

"There you go," the dark voice behind me drawled. "You look good on your knees."

I whipped around to see Belial sitting on the edge of the bed, the chain clenched in his fist. He gave it another tug. "I want you to sleep here, beside me."

"And *I* want you to fuck off," I snarled, trying to ignore the heat sweeping through my core at the thought of lying beside him.

He laughed, the sound dark and electric like thunder. "Liar. You want me to stay. Your scent betrays you." He leaned back on his bed, one hand braced behind him while the other held my chain, giving it a gentle tug. "Come closer, and I'll indulge your curiosity, little human."

The masked demon's visage blurred as angry tears pricked my eyes. He was fucking with me.

I hated how much I loved it.

"Are you my punishment for what I did to Catherine's body?"

"If anything, I'm your only chance at salvation, Rayven." Belial tilted his head, his eyes gleaming in the firelight. He was close enough now that I could see them staring out from the mask's eyeholes. They were a beautiful storm gray. "I could be of aid to you."

Hope soared in my chest. "You mean you'll help me?"

Instead of answering, he rose to his feet and approached me. I didn't dare move. I craned my head to look up at him as he loomed over me. He looked so terrifyingly handsome, doused in the amber light of the fire.

It wasn't until I was kneeling in front of him that I realized how tall he was.

He held his fist in front of him, the chain slack in his white-knuckled grip. Then, he started to circle me, wrapping the chain around my throat.

"You know..." He drawled on the second loop. "You were making the cutest little noises in your sleep, begging your lord to take you. You must be awfully pent-up. In need of relief."

He stopped when he came back round, standing right in front of me. My attention went straight to his bulge. How could it not? With how close he stood, it basically took up my entire field of vision. He arched down and pressed a slender index finger to my chin, his eyes capturing mine. "Let me sate your ache, and then I'll let you off your leash."

He turned his hand, running his knuckles down my jawline. The reverence in his touch had my heart beating faster than it ever had before. I wanted to say yes. Hell, before he'd dangled my freedom in front of me like a carrot on a stick, I'd wanted to say yes.

Now that he was offering to let me off this chain, how could I say no?

I worried my lower lip, my heart falling a little as he turned and sat back on the bed. His thumb rubbed over the chain links. "So, what's it going to be? Are we going to play? Or will we go to sleep and wait for the Lord to call for you?"

"How do I know I can trust you?"

He shrugged one shoulder. "You don't, but what other choice do you have? Holga won't defy the Lord, not for a second time. Nor will the other servants."

I frowned. "But you will? Why? What do you get out of it?"

"Easy." There was that smile in his voice again. "I get you."

My jaw fell open as I stared at him in disbelief. Who was this guy that he'd risk angering his god? For what? Living pussy?

But he was right, as much as I hated to admit it. Holga wouldn't help me. Belial was my best shot at getting out of here. "Alright. Fine. You have a deal."

"Smart girl," he praised, his voice rough and hungry. He pulled on the chain—this time with a gentle flick of his wrist. "Now, be a good girl and crawl to me."

# CHAPTER TWELVE

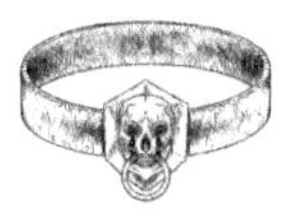

## RAYVEN

*He wanted me to crawl.*

Like a fucking dog. Like an animal. Like his plaything.

*And I couldn't be more turned on.*

I was into some pretty kinky things, but Mark's vanilla-ness had left me a bit starved in that area. So, before I could fully process my options—not that I had a lot to choose from—I crawled on my hands and knees toward the demon perched on the side of the bed.

Everything about this moment teased and plucked at my senses, heightening my arousal. The sweltering warmth in the room that had Belial's shirt sticking to his chest. The rattle of the chain dragged between my legs as I slowly knelt between his spread thighs. The way his lips parted through the mouth of his mask to praise me for being such a good girl for him.

He took the chain and unwound it from my neck before bending to take me by the waist and lift me onto his lap, like I weighed nothing at all.

His storm gray eyes turned my entire body to liquid. I could barely think.

"Why do you wear a mask?" I sputtered, not sure what else to say. The moment the words left my mouth, I regretted them. His eyes narrowed, and I whined when his fingertips bit into my hips.

"Is there an end to your constant barrage of questions, little human?"

"Yeah, when I start getting answers." I studied him carefully, drinking in all the parts his disguise didn't hide. His piercing eyes. His sharp jawline. His lips. There always seemed to be the ghost of a smirk tucked at the corner of them.

I raised my hand, bringing the tip of my index finger to his mouth.

He flinched—at least, I think he did. The movement was so slight, I wouldn't have noticed if it weren't for the jingle of jewelry draped from his antlers. To my surprise, he didn't move when the pad of my finger found the seam of his lips. I traced them, feeling the scars marring his flesh.

I resisted the compulsion to ask where he got them. What I couldn't resist was the urge—the need—to see more of him. My fingers moved to curl under the edge of the mask, but before I could lift it off, he captured my wrist.

"Ow! Fuck. You're hurting me!" I growled at him, trying to wrench my wrist from his bruising grasp. It was no use. I might as well have been wrestling King-Kong for how strong this guy was.

"Oh, little human," he clicked his tongue in disapproval, his tone mocking. "We were off to such a good start. Now you've lost your privilege to touch me." Both his hands clasped over mine in a suddenly sweet gesture, a stark contrast to the acid staining his voice.

He flipped me onto my back and pinned my wrists above my head with one hand. With the other, he reached for the manacles Holga had moved to the nightstand. I bucked beneath him, my tongue going slack as his cock twitched against my belly. He seemed to like it when I struggled.

In a million years, I'd never admit that I liked it too. Not that he needed my admission—by the cocky curve of his lips, he knew.

"Tell me to stop, and I won't," he muttered, his voice velvet-wrapped steel. "We'll need a different word for you."

"How about I just scream? Won't you stop then?" I whispered, feeling my body start to quiver with excitement.

"Oh, sweet little mortal. That will only make me harder."

"You're a monster," I breathed, more out of wonder than horror.

"Yeah, and monsters make you wet, don't they?" He laughed at my wide-eyed expression and sat back to admire my body spread out before him once the cuffs were secured around my wrists. "So we're going to come up with a new word for you to use if you want me to stop at any point."

"Like what?" My heart flitted wildly in my chest.

"Black widow."

I blinked. "Why black widow?"

His fingers drummed the chin of his mask in thought. "Female black widows are the most venomous. Seems fitting for you."

"I didn't think a demon would use a safeword."

"And I didn't think a young mortal woman would desecrate graves and steal from a primordial god of death. We're both full of surprises."

My breath hitched as his hand pressed against my navel then slipped to my waist. He looped the gown's tie around his finger, playing with it at a torturously slow pace, drinking in my every reaction.

His other hand was pressed over my heart, my pulse hammering against his palm. "I fucking love your frantic little heartbeat. It pounds so hard when I tease you."

We'd barely started. He'd hardly touched me, yet he already had me wrapped so tightly around his fingers. I wanted him so badly, I could cry.

I was just doing this to get off the leash, but I had a feeling I was going to enjoy it very much. It had me wondering, if I escaped this Hell, would my soul still be damned after all this? With how good Belial's fingers felt against me, I realized I wasn't sure I cared.

After a tense minute of driving me to the brink of insanity from sheer anticipation, the demon pulled the tie loose and opened my nightgown.

"You're beautiful, Rayven," he murmured as his eyes raked down my body, his hand skimming up between my breasts. His fingers tapped a frantic beat against my sternum, and it took me several moments to realize he was mimicking the rhythm of my heart.

I strained against my cuffs, wanting more of him. I wanted to taste his lips against mine, drink his breath as he sighed at the feel of my body around him. But he held me down firmly, forcing me to take his ministrations at his own pace.

His hands roved over the dips and curves of my body. I tensed, waiting for him to comment on my scars. He stayed quiet, tracing every line and contour, like he was intent on committing them to memory.

His hand moved to palm one of my breasts, flicking my pierced nipple. "I never saw these as anything more than body jewelry before, something pretty to adorn the female form, but on you?

His eyes lifted to lock with mine. "On you, they are fucking perfection."

An embarrassing sound tore from my throat when he pinched the tender peak between his fingers and tweaked it. There was a sharp pain, but it quickly turned to a dull ache that sank straight to my apex. "Oh God."

"God has no place here, nor prayers made to him. Here, there is no hope of his salvation. Only dust, darkness, and the screams of the damned." He leaned forward, so close his breath swept over me, heating my flesh. "Soon, your screams will join their forsaken chorus, and it will be my name in your mouth. Not God's."

"You seem pretty cocky," I teased, wondering if he'd speed up his pace if I pestered him. "You sure about that?"

His only response was the curve of his lips behind his mask and a gravelly, "hmph."

My heart lurched into my mouth when he twisted around and reached for the candle holder on the bedside table. I swallowed thickly, my attention honing in on the flickering flame and the molten wax dripping down the half-melted candle stick. "What are you going to do with that?"

"Teaching my bratty little human what it means to mouth off to a demon," Belial said with a dark chuckle. He held the candlestick holder over my navel, and slowly tipped it. "Now hold still, and don't be quiet. I want the entire castle to know what an insatiable slut our newest guest is."

Almost as soon as the last word left his lips, the first bead of wax dropped from the candle and landed over my belly button. There was a flash of searing pain, but it was over almost as soon as my brain had processed it.

Belial's throat bobbed with a swallow when I mewled at the next series of burning droplets. "That's right, mortal. Cry for me. Whimper. Beg for me to stop, or to give you more. I don't give a fuck, so long as you beg."

"P-please." I braced myself for the sting when the next beads of wax crested the patch of skin between my breasts. He snarled at the way I tensed in preparation for each burning drop. Reaching for me, he placed his hand over my eyes, which was so large, it swallowed half my face.

The next jolt of pain—braided tightly with pleasure—was more heightened by the anticipation of not knowing when the next drops would fall.  When the wax started to fall onto my nipples, hardening over the metal piercings, I screamed.

It was delicious torture.

After several more minutes—with a thick crust of wax coating my tits—he pulled his hand away and placed the candle back on the bedside table.

"We're done?" I asked, trying to keep the disappointment from my tone.

"Oh, we're just getting started." Goosebumps exploded over my skin at the grit in his voice. He grabbed and flipped me over, so I was on my hands and knees. He took my gown and pushed it over my hips, exposing my ass.

I craned my neck to look back at him, but his hand was in my hair, shoving my face down into the bed.

"No matter what happens, don't turn around. Keep your head down. Understand, human?"

"I–I understand," I stammered, so drunk with lust that I could barely speak.

"And what do you say if you want this to stop?"

I wouldn't want it to stop. Unless he did something truly heinous, I couldn't put an end to this, not when my chance at freedom was on the line. Plus, I was enjoying this way too much to quit now. "Black widow."

"That's a good fucking girl," he praised with a growl.

I heard him grabbing the candle again, and on the next breath, hot wax poured over the globe of my ass. My fingers curled into the blankets, and my body clenched at the searing warmth exploding through my body, turning my insides liquid.

I wanted it to stop, and at the same time, I didn't want it to end.

When the sound of rustling fabric met my ear, I knew he was taking out his cock. It took everything in me to keep myself from looking over my shoulder to see what created that huge bulge.

He'd punish me if I did, but I was learning pretty quickly that Belial's punishments weren't like the Lord of Bones'.

It was almost like he could see straight into my brain, because as soon as the thought popped into my mind, Belial snarled, "Don't even think about it. Be still and keep your eyes averted."

When I nodded into the pillow, another few beads of wax peppered my flesh. Soon, his masculine grunts filled the quiet. He was stroking himself with one hand while he covered my backside with hot wax with the other.

"Fuck me," I blurted out. I was so worked up, I needed relief. He'd promised to give it to me, but so far, all he'd done was work me into tight knots.

Shock and frustration rolled off him in waves. Then, silence as he debated. He was torn. I gave a little wiggle of my ass, hoping to tempt him.

He delivered a slap to the tender flesh, making me fall still. "*No.*"

"Why not?" I sobbed into the sheets. I felt pathetic, but I was so stupidly horny, I didn't care. "I thought you wanted me."

"Oh I do, little human. That's the problem. I want you too much. If I fuck you, and I feel the pound of that mortal heart kiss the tip of my dick, it's all over. I'll *never* let you go. You don't want that."

I didn't want that.

Right?

"Just—please. Make this ache go away. You told me you'd give me relief."

He growled again, this one low in his throat—almost a purr that calmed me. He continued to stroke himself, the noises tumbling from him turning sharp and harsh, deliciously masculine noises.

Curiosity was eating me alive. I wanted to see his cock. No, fuck that. I wanted to do more than look at it. I wanted to touch it, taste it—take it in whatever hole he'd give it to me.

Still, I stayed in place like he'd instructed, hoping he'd reward me for being obedient. I wasn't much of a rule follower, but something told me Belial's rewards were even better than his punishments.

As hot wax hit the base of my spine, beads of something cooler hit my back. He was coming, his cum joining the crust of wax over my reddened flesh as a string of curses fell from his lips.

I stayed there in the bed, holding my breath as I listened to him push himself back into his pants. Then, he placed the candle back on the table and he blew it out, the room going a little darker.

"You were such a good girl for me. Now…" His breathing was labored, his chest heaving. "Now it's your turn."

More rustling hit my ears. I couldn't resist the overwhelming urge to sneak a peek for a second longer. I turned my head, glancing over my shoulder.

He reached for the wine bottle Holga had brought in with my dinner, bringing the bottle to his lips and tipping it back, draining the last of the wine. A drop of red liquid slipped down the chin of his mask and dripped onto his chest.

My mouth tingled with the urge to lick it up.

When he caught my gaze, his storm gray eyes flashed behind his mask. "Turn back around, little human."

I did as I was told, pressing my cheek to the blankets. They didn't smell much like him. He must not sleep in his bed very often.

Then, I felt it.

The cold glass kissed my fever-hot skin. He rubbed the neck of the bottle through my folds, and he hummed in approval when he found me soaking.

*He was going to fuck me with the wine bottle.*

"You have the most beautiful cunt, little mortal. So pink and perfect. So much better than dead pussy. At least, that's what the other psychopomps tell me. As the Lord's ferryman, I have many duties, and I don't have time for either."

"You're fucked," I said on a moan as he sunk the first inch of the wine bottle into my pussy. It was cold at the base, but its tip was still warm from his mouth. It felt better than it had any right to.

He was gentle at first, careful to slip it in slowly, making sure my walls stretched to take it before feeding me more. He eased it out of me before pushing it back in, this time filling me all the way up.

"You take a surprising amount," he chuckled. "Shame. You'd fit me so nicely."

I bit back a yelp when he thrust it back inside me—this time harder than the first. "Fuck! Oh. Belial. Please. Please make me cum."

He began to pump the bottle into me with a pace that had me drooling into his blankets. My fingers twisted into them, holding on for dear life. It had been so long since I'd fucked Mark. It didn't take long to work me up. I was already so on edge, just a few more thrusts was all it would take.

I didn't expect the pleasure to crash over me so brutally—like a tidal wave intent on drowning me. I gasped for breath, my body shaking violently as my nerves struggled to process this feeling.

"You did well." Belial fell back onto the pillows, the arm holding the wine bottle propped on one knee. He tipped the bottle back and this time, a milky substance—the cum that had dribbled into the bottle—slipped through the glass, past the mouth hole of his mask, and down his throat.

A sated sigh fell from his lips—like he'd drunk a refreshing glass of lemonade and not my cum.

He snapped his fingers, and just like that, the chain fell off my collar. I'd half hoped the collar would come off too, but I guess that wasn't part of the deal. The restraints binding my wrists undid themselves, and I pulled my hands free.

"You better get out of here," he said with a sigh. "Before I decide I like the taste of you too much to let you go."

# CHAPTER THIRTEEN

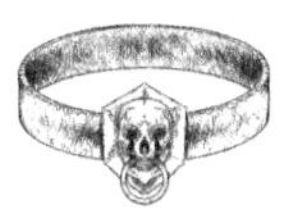

## RAYVEN

I TORE OUT OF Belial's room, gasping for breath. My back hit the wall, and I slid down, burying my face into my knees. My flesh was hot and sticky and still crusted in wax.

I felt utterly spent—used.

Disturbed.

Oh so fucking *wet*.

What I should have felt was shame for what I had to do for that demon to release me.

Instead, I felt...alive, surrounded by all this death. Then again, I'd always felt more at home surrounded by the dead.

There was a little voice in the back of my head telling me that I belonged here, probably because I deserved to rot in purgatory, given my career choice. Maybe an eternity in this place wouldn't be total Hell with someone like Belial doling out my punishments.

No, *bad vagina,* I scolded the throbbing flesh. Not that I blamed it. I knew all my previous lays had been disappointing, but after what just happened with that demon, I had more perspective on just how bad they'd been.

Still, I couldn't stay in the land of the dead just because it had better dick.

I stood up and shoved my hand under my dress, picking off the wax.

My chances of escape were slim, but I still had to try. I was determined for it to go better than last time. A shiver shot through me at the memory of the hands, grabbing me from all directions—*touching* me.

Then, the fresher memory of Belial's hands smoothing over me, firm and dominant, took over.

I took one last look at his door, my heart twisting into knots, before launching into a sprint.

My bare feet pounded against the tile floor as I raced down the hall, the white nightgown flapping wildly behind me. The collar around my neck felt heavier as I ran, but I ignored it, shoving away every ounce of discomfort and focusing solely on getting out of this damned castle.

Before I knew it, I was following a familiar path. *Left at the suit of armor, right at Catherine's painting, down the stairs...* It was foolish to retrace the steps I'd taken last time, but I had a feeling it didn't matter which route I took. I'd end up in the same loop of hallways, the same walls mocking me and my inability to figure out the maze.

What if the only way out was through magic?

When Catherine's painting came into view a second time, my shoulders fell slightly and I slowed to a stop, staring up at her solemn expression enviously.

Her likeness and memory were locked up tighter than a pharaoh's treasure within this place, but her body was free. Had she escaped the Lord of Bones? Would he be so broody if she hadn't?

"Think, Rayven," I whispered, my voice barely audible to my own ears.

I'd broken out of the labyrinthine halls before with the help of the letter opener, even though it had led me somewhere far worse than the corridor. I didn't have the knife to beg for answers—the Lord of Bones had taken it from me—but there was someone else I could ask.

My eyes darted to the chair and side table across from Catherine's painting, the toad-shaped teapot sitting stone still on the same pile of books.

"Teapot!" I hissed, hurrying to kneel next to the table. I stared at its unblinking, porcelain eyes like it could somehow see me. "Baker! Do you know the way out of here?"

"Oh, it's you again," the toad said, its lid clinking as it came to life. "Didn't I tell you before? There was no way out then and no way out now. Only if the Lord allows it, and he doesn't make a habit of letting his pretty trophies go."

"But what about Catherine?" My eyes flicked back to the painting. "She escaped, didn't she? Tell me how?"

"How? Out the window once. Then, the bars came up. Then again on a suit of armor's sword."

My blood turned cold in my veins. "You're talking about death. She *killed* herself."

"Each time, he brought her back. Until he didn't. She lost her mind wandering in circles, dearie. You'll do the same."

My jaw hardened at the frog's words. "I'm not giving up. There has to be some way out."

The teapot laughed. "At least mind your step. The old mistress once got crushed to death between the shifting halls."

"Crushed to death?" I glanced at the hallway next to us, knowing the stone would shift and swallow the corridor beyond it soon. The walls seemed to shift most when I wasn't watching.

"And watch out for the corrupted souls," the candlestick beside the teapot added.

"Corrupted souls?"

"The dark magic in the air starts to corrupt souls after a time. It's why most of us seek refuge around the castle. Can't grow bones out of my eyeballs if I'm a ceramic pot."

"Maybe you should cut your losses and ditch that pretty little body of yours," the candlestick said. "Find something to hide in."

"There's nothing left for her to take, except maybe a chamber pot in one of the spare rooms. The Lord might not be so keen to have you then."

"There, problem solved!" a figurine of a fat gargoyle sitting on the buffet below Catherine's portrait said.

The objects laughed together, their raspy chuckles echoing in the silent hall.

I rolled my eyes. These souls weren't going to be any help. Groaning, I got to my feet and approached Catherine's painting, my thoughts spinning out of control.

If I wanted to find the exit, did that mean I'd have to take one of the shifting hallways to get there?

My stomach churned.

If I was right, I'd be that much closer to escaping, but if I was wrong... I didn't want to think about the alternative.

I stared down the hall, trying to guess how long it was. Could I make it in time before it shifted? The hall seemed to go on forever, but the stone walls shifted slowly.

I could make it. I hoped. It wasn't like I had more than one shot. Worst case scenario, I'd die. Game over.

Then, the Lord of Bones would come to revive me, like he had for Catherine.

A chill shot down my spine. I didn't want to see him again. I hated him. After that dream, I wouldn't be able to make eye contact with him.

I drew a shaky breath. Dying was out of the question.

After what seemed like forever, seconds before I was ready to give up and take the stairs again, the rumble of stone against stone grumbled to life, breaking the silence. The left wall began to close in, making the long hallway narrower by the second, and I broke into a sprint without a second thought.

I pumped my legs as fast as they'd go, darting down the narrowing hallway. The walls got closer and closer together while the hallway felt like it was stretching on even longer.

My stomach bottomed out. Had I miscalculated the distance? Fuck. Fuck. *Fuck!*

Blood pounded in my ears as the hallway grew narrower. The stone walls were now inches from me on either side. Jesus Christ, what kind of Indiana Jones nightmare bullshit was this?

The stone wall brushed my arm, pressing against me. I had to turn my body and shuffle sideways. When there was only a few feet left, I leapt, diving into the room at the end of the passage.

I hit the stone hard enough to knock the wind out of me, nearly smacking my chin on the floor. A curse dropped from my lips at the insanity of what just happened.

I'd come so close to getting pancaked, but I'd made it.

When I looked up at the space around me, my jaw dropped.

I was in what appeared to be a well lived-in study, filled with all sorts of books and furniture made of bone. It was a little messy, but the space didn't have the same heavy atmosphere as the endless halls outside.

As I pulled myself to my feet and examined the space, I realized it was because none of these objects appeared to be possessed by dead people.

An ornate mirror sat at one end of the room. It was huge, with a pane of glass large enough to reflect the entire room.

I moved toward a desk, which was pushed up against the far wall, and sat in the huge chair that wasn't unlike the throne of bones in my dream. My eyes moved to the window over the desk.

The view had tears pricking the corners of my eyes.

The window I'd climbed out of had overlooked an ocean, so I must have been on the other side of the castle, because there was no water in sight. Instead, the largest hedge maze I'd ever seen stretched as far as the eye could see.

It was like Alice in Wonderland, only instead of a maze of pretty rose bushes, this one was brown and dead and filled with twisting bramble. Even if I found a way outside, it would take me a million years to find my way through it...

"Enjoying the view of my labyrinth, little thief?"

Hatred snaked through my veins at the sound of that deep as Hell voice—hatred mixed with something else, something I didn't dare try and dissect.

I hadn't heard him come in, not the sound of footsteps or the rustle of his cloak. It's like he'd been here all along.

I pushed out of the chair, but a heavy hand gripped my shoulder and shoved me back into my seat.

I looked up to see the Lord of Bones standing behind the chair, looming over me with that ominous gleam in his eye sockets. He kept one hand on my shoulder while he toyed with the amulet in my collar with his other. "You're an insistent little thing. What am I to do with you?"

"Let me go."

He gave a dark, guttural chuckle.

"So eager to escape me when you've yet to know the sweet torment of my embrace. Or maybe…"

He gripped the chair by the arms and spun me around to face him, the legs of the chair scraping against the stone. He kept his hold on the armrests, caging me in. "Maybe you do know."

"What are you talking about?" I snarled, trying to keep the fear out of my voice.

"Have any sweet dreams lately?"

"You asshole," I seethed through clenched teeth. "There *was* something in the food."

"Don't sound so vexed. You thoroughly enjoyed it."

"I–I didn't."

My heart lurched into my mouth when his jowls parted, and a black tongue wriggled out. It was just like the one in my dream, only it was split down the middle.

*Jesus Christ.* The sins a tongue like that could commit.

I froze, my breath coming out in short little pants as the Lord of Bones draped himself over the chair and painted a lick over my lips, tracing the seam of my mouth with the point of the monstrous appendage.

"Your sweet little lies are so delicious. Careful, I might become hooked on the flavor."

"Let me go," I reiterated, my eyes landing on the door just visible over his shoulder. "I don't belong here."

"Do you really believe that?" His dark voice swirled around me, sending goosebumps crawling over my skin. "I wonder…did you rob graves for riches? Or was it just an excuse to be closer to death?"

His huge hand cupped my cheek, his claws scouring my flesh as they sunk into my hair. "I can give you a new home."

My heart slammed mercilessly against my ribs as I gaped up at my captor. His horns stretched high into the air as he loomed over me like an angel of death, offering me eternal damnation in the guise of salvation.

"Home? You mean my new prison?"

"It will be a gilded cage, the prettiest one ever gifted to a mortal."

"What am I supposed to do? Sit around and be your palace pet?

"Oh..." He drawled, his gravelly rumble sinking straight to my core. "You will be so much more than my pet."

His clawed fingers tightened around my arm, his hand so big, it swallowed me from my wrist to my elbow. He wrenched me out of the chair and pulled my body flush against his chest.

This monster towered over me, all eight feet of him casting a shadow as palpable as his collar around my throat.

"You will be my slave. You will suffer at my hand, and I will draw pleasure from your beautiful little screams. I will brand my name upon your bones, and carve it into your flesh. You will endure me and my brutality for all eternity. As my pet. My mate. My queen."

Mate? *Queen?*

The realization of what was happening came slamming down over me like one of those falling pianos in old timey cartoons. This was my punishment for desecrating Catherine's corpse.

I was her replacement.

He would torture me. He'd drive me to madness, just as he'd probably done to her. Unlike Catherine, though, there was a part of me that would enjoy the way he'd hurt me.

And he knew it.

I couldn't let that part of me determine my fate. I couldn't be the Lord of Death's plaything. Because if I accepted, there'd be no escaping him.

Not even death would end our union.

I thrashed against him, but he only held me tighter. "You can't do this. You have to at least give me a chance to escape."

The light in his eye sockets glowed with malice. "I don't have to give you anything."

"Then I'll hate you forever, just like Catherine. Is that what you want? Give me a chance to get back home, and if I fail, then I'll accept my fate. I'll be your mate and queen."

He seemed to consider my words as he canted his skull and peered out the window over my head—deep in thought.

"Very well."

My breath caught, making it impossible to force air into my lungs. I hadn't expected him to agree. "Really?" I choked out.

He slowly reached for my face, dragging a single finger along my jawline as he stared me down.

"You want your freedom so badly? I want to see you fight for it, bleed for it, die for it," he said, tilting my chin up higher. "You must escape my grounds before time runs thin…"

His hand dropped from my chin to grip my ass, grinding me against the impossibly huge bulge pressed against my stomach. It was a threat—no, a promise.

"Or become mine forever, until eternity's end."

*Eternity's end.*

As much as that twisted part of me perked up at this monster's demented proposal, an eternity was too long. He was too brutal. Too big. He'd split me open, make me bleed. Then he'd piece me back together just so he could do it all over again.

My pussy throbbed at the thought.

*No.* I couldn't let this monster crawl under my skin like he was.

He'd fucking kidnapped me, collared me.

He'd threatened me, manhandled me, invaded my mind.

And I couldn't forget his worst crime.

He'd murdered Mark. Sure, I never loved him, but he didn't deserve to die in the way he had.

"How much time do I have?"

"Three days."

A second after my hope shot through the roof, it came plummeting down again. I turned my gaze back out the window to the sprawling labyrinth below. "That's not enough time."

"That's all you get."

I flung my glare up at the leering skull, my eyes stark with rage. He held my arm so tightly, it felt like it might snap at any second, but I refused to let the pain show.

"At least give me some decent clothes." I was still wearing nothing but the tissue-thin nightgown. "You can't expect me to wander around your creepy garden without underwear or even shoes."

I winced as he jerked my arm, pulling me up so my toes barely touched the ground. The snout of his skull was a kiss away from my lips, his hot breath washing over my flesh. "You're lucky I don't tear this gown off you and make you traipse through the mud and bramble naked."

Angry tears made my vision swim. "I fucking hate you."

"Yet your mortal cunt still weeps for me." He pointed to the floor, and I followed his gesture to see a small puddle between my legs.

It wasn't piss—I probably would have been less mortified if it was. Wetting myself out of fear in this scenario would have made sense. No one would blame me. But it wasn't urine. It was my arousal. I'd always been extra wet, to the point where I usually made a habit of carrying an extra pair of panties with me wherever I went. Mark had poked fun at me because of it, but this was a lot, even for me—too much to pass off as natural lubrication.

"That means nothing," I seethed. "My body, it..." My voice trailed off.

It betrayed me.

"So how about it, little thief? Do we have a deal? You have three days to escape. If you fail, you become mine. Forever."

A tumultuous storm of emotions tore through me. What choice did I have? Making a deal with the devil was going to come back to bite me on my wax-coated ass, but bargaining with the King of Limbo for a slim chance at freedom was infinitely less stupid than agreeing to be his sex slave.

"We have a deal. So, what? Do we shake on it? Or do I sign some flaming contract?"

He slowly shook his head, his fingers unfurling from my arm. "No. Not for you. You will get on your knees."

My thighs clenched, sticky with sweat and arousal. "What? I'm not doing that."

The Lord of Bones turned to leave. "Have it your way. I will summon Holga to chain you back up. You can warm my ferryman's bed until I decide to claim you as mine."

I flinched at his words. Why did I feel so betrayed? This really was about tormenting me. If he truly cared about me, he wouldn't be so casual about throwing me to another demon.

The pain sweeping through me didn't make any damn sense at all. Why was I surprised? Why did I care?

I didn't want his love or his obsession. I needed to get the fuck out of here.

My hand snapped out, snatching a fistful of his cloak. "Wait..."

He paused and slowly lumbered around to face me once again, waiting expectantly.

Slowly, I lowered myself to my knees. Extending a finger, he pointed at the puddle of moisture I'd left behind on the floor of his study. "Lick it."

My heart hammered in my throat as I stared down at the puddle. "But…"

"Don't leave me waiting." He crouched to one knee and reached for my hair, gathering the long strands and wrapping them around his hand like a leash. I'd expected his grip to be rough, like before. Instead, he gently nudged my face toward the puddle in encouragement.

"Be a good girl for me. You can do it."

This gentler side of him dazed me. I didn't trust it for a fucking second, but the praise fueled me.

Crouching down, I put my face to the floor. His eyes burnt into the back of my head as he watched my tongue slide over the stone, lapping up the liquid.

He laughed darkly, the sound making my head swirl. "How does it taste? Your desire for me?"

It didn't taste good, but my pussy didn't care. Licking up my own juices from the floor had the heat stirring in my core, and that terrified me. There was no denying my intense attraction to this monster—this ancient, evil demon of death and bone.

"Look up, little thief."

My gaze lifted to see the Lord of Bones, the hollows of his eyes hot and full of fire. My heart clenched as my attention dropped to the object he now held in his hand.

It was a crown made of bone—specifically, a spinal column.

"Fail to escape my palace grounds in three days, and this will be the first of many gifts. Recognize him?"

I stared at the crown in confusion, trying to make sense of his words. What did he mean by 'recognize him'? Then, it clicked.

Horror turned my stomach, bile burning in the back of my throat.

"That's not..."

"Your dead mate? Oh yes, little thief. I make use of all the bones that are no longer needed by the souls they once hosted. Sitting atop my queen's head will be the greatest accomplishment a worthless mortal like him could have ever hoped to achieve."

"Y-you're a-a f-fucking monster..." I stammered, barely able to get the words out as I crumpled to the ground.

Belial chuckled. "Yes, and when the three days are up, I'll be *your* monster."

His words were the last thing I registered as I fainted, darkness rushing in to claim me.

# CHAPTER FOURTEEN

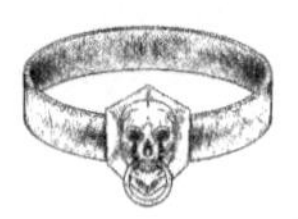

## RAYVEN

THE TICKLING OF SOMETHING soft against my skin was the first thing I registered as I regained consciousness. I knew before I opened my eyes that I wasn't in the castle anymore. The air filtering into my lungs wasn't laced with the castle's heavy aroma of woe and dust.

It smelled like rain and mud.

I pried my eyes open and found myself staring up at the sky, blanketed in a layer of heavy, sagging rain clouds. The softness against my skin turned out to be a dense bed of heather—at least I think it was heather, but these flowers were gray instead of pink. My head swam a little as I dragged myself up into a sitting position and looked around nervously, taking in my surroundings.

*How the hell had I gotten here?*

Had the Lord of Bones carried me here?  Why would he have done that when I was now steps closer to escape? I wasn't naive enough to think it was for me to have a head start. I didn't think he had a kind bone in his body, not after what he did to Mark's bones.

Had Belial showed up to help me? When he'd let me off my leash, he hadn't seemed concerned about pissing off his Lord. Was he so cocky that he didn't care, or was he that high up the food chain that he wasn't worried? Maybe he could be an ally. But if he helped me again, he'd probably want something else from me...

I didn't have time to sit around and fantasize.

As much as I wanted to sit around and daydream about it, I could barely think through my splitting headache. Had I hit my head on the floor when I passed out? I closed my eyes and flinched, immediately prying them back open. The image of the Lord of Bones looming over me with the crown made of Mark's remains was seared onto the back of my eyelids.

I forced the memory to the back of my mind and dragged myself to my feet, retying the sash around my waist as my eyes drifted over my surroundings.

I had to be in the courtyard.

The castle wall was a few meters from where I'd been laid to rest, towering menacingly overhead. Vines crawled up the stone to ensure there was no space between the castle and the thick maze of twisted plants that surrounded the courtyard on all sides. The brambles looked thick and impossible to penetrate, leaving no room to slip between them.

In the middle of the courtyard was a black stone fountain spewing red liquid that resembled fresh blood too much for my liking.

Judging by their color, the plants were dead, but something pale–possibly fruit or flower blossoms–dotted the thorny brambles. There were three gaps in the wall where the branches arched, creating entrances to the labyrinth. A shiver worked through me as my attention settled on them and realization set it.

The only way out was through the maze.

The thought of making my way through a thorny bramble labyrinth wearing nothing but a sheer nightgown was horrifying, and I wished I at least had my boots on, something to protect my feet. I would have settled for anything–bunny slippers, or those little booties you got at rich people's open houses, but no. The Lord of Bones had to be a fucking sadist.

He was probably watching me now from his study window, jerking off.

I was determined to give him a real show and take whatever this labyrinth had to throw at me with my head held high. I had three days to get through it.

Or I'd be his forever.

Stomach flipping with nerves, I turned and headed toward the towering forest of brambles. I had no idea what nasty things

I would find inside. It was hard to fathom anything worse than the Lord of Bones.

I stopped short when I was close enough to see the pale objects decorating the dark, twisted branches. My stomach gave a sickening lurch. They weren't blossoms or fruit at all.

They were body parts, hundreds of severed body parts strewn amongst the brambles. Hands, toes, torsos, heads.

The worst part: they were moving.

Bile burned up the back of my throat, and my heart slammed painfully against my ribs. It was like the oubliette all over again. Thankfully, there was enough space between the high hedges that I could make it through without any of them touching me, but deeper in the maze? Would it be different there? Thicker? *Would I have to fight my way through walls of severed limbs inside?*

I squirmed with nerves.

I took a few steps closer, and that's when I heard them. Whispers. A low roll of murmurs drifting through the hedges, the voices an indecipherable song. The blood drained from my cheeks, fear pushing its way up through my confidence and gripping me with its icy claws.

*Fuck.* This wasn't good.

Just seeing these limbs—especially the grasping hands—was triggering.

I could *not* have a panic attack here. I refused to let the Lord of Bones see me crumble before I even started.

I swallowed down the nausea threatening to undo the rest of my determination, and turned to march into the thick of the brambles. I kept my head high, my arms tucked tightly around me to maintain as much space as possible between me and the wiggling body parts in the walls of the maze. The whispers grew louder, dancing over my skin and leaving goosebumps on every inch.

I hated being here, but I hated the thought of losing to the Lord of Bones even more.

Step by step, I slowly made my way deeper into the maze, eyes darting around, nervous that the wiggling hands would grab me unexpectedly. Thankfully, they didn't seem as greedy as those in the oubliette.

When I made it to the first fork, I paused, hesitant to make a decision, but my thoughts were interrupted by a rustling sound behind me. Stomach pitching toward the ground, I spun around with my fists held up to prepare myself for an attack, but there was no one there. I was still alone.

Movement at the end of the path caught my eye, and I watched in horror as the brambles came to life, the walls shifting and moving toward one another, until the place I'd entered the maze was a dead end.

*Holy shit.* My brain could hardly process what was happening.

Just like the castle, the maze was alive with dark magic, and it was sealing me inside as I watched helplessly, unable to do anything to stop it. Going back the way I came wasn't an option.

I ran down the path on my right, afraid the walls would continue to knit together until they swallowed me whole, the rough terrain stabbing into my bare feet as they slapped against the sodden ground. It had stopped raining, but the soil was muddy and filled with rocks and broken pieces of thorny bramble.

Despite all that, I didn't slow down. I fucking refused.

A left, a right, another left. I was lost before I had a chance to come up with a plan, hoping that luck would lead me somewhere.

It didn't.

Every passage was the same. The same tall walls, the same severed bodies littered throughout them, the same haunting whispers that feathered over my skin like an unwanted caress.

I slowed to a stop, my lungs screaming for me to catch my breath. I gasped for air, trying to take steady breaths, and tilted my head back to look at the sky. Dark clouds still swirled there. Was it perpetually cloudy here or would sunshine follow the rain?

*Was there even a sun here?*

"You'll fall into the sky staring up like that," someone said behind me, making me jump. I whirled around to search for the owner of the voice, only to find there was no one there.

I was still alone, but I'd clearly heard someone.

"Hello?" My voice sliced through the whispers, and I kept my eyes peeled for movement.

"There's no need to yell." The voice came from my right, and my head whipped to the side. There, stuck amongst the dark brambles and twisted vines, was a severed head. Sunken cheeks, patchy hair, and sallow skin, it looked to be asleep...until one of its eyes popped open and glared right at me.

It was milky white, but darted around as though it could still see.

"I'm sorry?" I said, taken aback. I wasn't sure what else I was supposed to say to a severed head.

"You're going the wrong way." The head's other eye popped open to reveal an empty socket. The maggots must have eaten the other eye.

I sucked in a sharp breath. "Do you know the way out of here?" I asked, hoping I'd finally gotten lucky.

"Of course."

My heart leapt into my throat. "*Really?* Can you tell me?"

"Tell you what?" His brows knitted together in a scowl.

"How to get out of here."

The head scoffed. "Who said I knew how to get out?"

"You did," I snapped, irritation flaring through me.

"Did what?"

"Said you knew how to get out of the maze," I ground out, my irritation morphing into quiet rage. If I wasn't terrified to get closer to the shrub, I would have punched the head. "Do you know how to get out of here or not?"

The head cackled, grinning wide and revealing several missing teeth. "Nope."

I stomped my foot on the ground, regretting it when a sharp twig stabbed into my little toe. The severed head laughed at my howl of pain. "Don't lose your head, maiden!"

My jaw clenched, teeth grinding. What a waste of time. This guy—what was left of him—had lost his mind along with the rest of his body.

"Thanks for nothing," I muttered as I turned to head down the path. I didn't make it far before the head started yelling behind me.

"Not that way! You're going the wrong way!" he yelled, but I ignored him. He obviously didn't know what he was talking about, and listening to him would probably get me more lost. I trudged on, anger heating my cheeks. I'd show him, just like the Lord of Bones. I didn't need either of their help to get out of here.

As I marched on toward the end of the path, the ground became even softer than before. For a moment, I was relieved—there weren't any sharp rocks or thorns here to eat at my feet—but as the ground began to squish between my toes, I stopped in my tracks. Only, I didn't stop moving.

I was sinking.

My feet slowly disappeared beneath the ground's surface. I tried to pull my feet free, but they didn't budge. The more I moved, the deeper I sank. The ground was swallowing me, dragging me under, and the more I struggled, the faster I went under.

*I'd wandered into a patch of quicksand.*

I screamed, the shrill noise tearing up my throat, and the whispers in the air turned to grumbles.

"Keep it down," a voice snapped.

"Yeah. Try to die quietly, please."

Ignoring the mocking voices, I reached for the brambles, grabbing onto the spiky vines despite the pain and clinging to them for dear life. I pulled, I tugged. No matter what I did, I continued to sink. My legs disappeared, then my hips. I clawed at the ground, my nails frantically dragging track marks through the sand in a vain attempt to find solid purchase.

I was going to suffocate beneath the surface in mere minutes.

I screamed again, even though I knew there was no one coming for me. Even if they heard me, I doubted that they'd make it to me in time.

The ground devoured half my torso, squeezing me and making it hard to breathe. The more of me it swallowed, the tighter it constricted every bone in my body until it felt like they'd shatter under the pressure. As my arms slipped below the surface, I lost my last shred of hope.

I couldn't fight.

There was nothing left for me to do.

I'd die, and the Lord of Bones would bring me to life in an endless cycle of torture.

My chest seized, but I wasn't sure if it was out of fear or the crushing sand.

Would it hurt to die? To take my last breath?

Would it be like falling asleep in my last moments?

Somehow I had the feeling that dying would be easier than coming back to life, where I'd have to come face to face with the Lord again.

I choked on a breath, still trying to force air into my lungs. How many breaths did I have left before my last?

"I figured you'd die quickly, but I didn't think it would be this quick, little human," a familiar voice said, grabbing my attention. I frantically jerked my head up to see a tall, masculine figure melt out of the fog.

Hope thrummed in my veins when I registered the antlers dripping in jewelry and the black mask.

*Belial.*

"Wait, be careful! It's quicksand!" I tried to warn him, but his boots were already walking across the soggy ground. I waited for the sand to swallow the soles of his black boots, but they didn't.

He didn't sink at all. He walked across the surface with sure strides, and came to stand right in front of my face. As my breasts slipped underground, his head tilted to look down at me, the silver charms dangling from his horns clinking together with the movement.

"How are you doing that?" I gasped in disbelief, my voice coming out ragged from all the screaming. "What are you? Monster Jesus?"

He chuckled once, squatting in front me, and reached his gloved hand down to tilt my chin up. His smokey gray eyes met mine, and for a moment, I forgot I was seconds away from death, lost in the pull of his gaze. "Here you are, caught in the maw of death, and you still can't help but run that bratty little mouth of yours."

Then, my ribs constricted harder, and I choked on my breath. "Help me. Please."

"Aww, you can beg better than that, little human." He chuckled darkly. Through the mouth slit in his mask, I could see him biting his lower lip. The bastard was enjoying this. "Again. This time with feeling."

I clenched my jaw, and my throat throbbed with anger. "Now isn't the time for your sadistic little games. I'm going to die if you don't do something!" I begged, letting the fear slip into my voice as my shoulders sank into the ground. "Save me. *Please.*"

"You're *so* cute when you're desperate." His gloved index finger traced my mouth. "Your lips are so fuckable when they purse around your pathetic little cries."

I gasped, and this time, the lack of air in my lungs had nothing to do with the quicksand. Belial was no Lord of Bones, but he was still a sadistic bastard. What did I expect from such a high-ranking member of his court?

What I hated most, though, was how his depraved words ignited a fire inside me—a dangerous inferno of fury and lust.

"All right," the demon finally said after a tense beat. "I'll save you, but you have to do something for me first."

I blanched. Was he fucking serious?

"Um, I don't know if you noticed, but I'm a little tied up at the moment. Whatever you want, we're probably gonna have to raincheck it until after I'm not slowly sinking to my death. Kay? Thanks."

He ran his fingers over the track marks I'd left in the sand, and then he returned his gaze to mine. My heart galloped in my chest at the way his eyes darkened through his mask's eye holes.

"Kiss my boot, Rayven," he said, rising to his full height and planting his foot right in front of me. "Show me that pretty little mouth is worth saving."

"Fuck you." I bared my teeth at him, wishing I were free so I could punch him in his huge bulge.

"That's on the table for about another minute. Then you'll suffocate, and I'm not in the habit of making love to corpses." He admired the rings on his fingers like a cocky asshole, refusing to look in my direction. "Though I'm not sure I'm patient enough to wait for the Lord to revive you either."

*Fuck.* He knew he had me. I didn't have time to argue, and it's not like there was a chance of another handsome stranger happening across me in the next minute.

Either I kissed the boot of this demon, or I'd die and face his Lord later. Who knew how long it would take the Lord of Bones to revive me? He'd probably wait until after my three days were up.

Kissing the boots of this sexy bastard was the much better option.

"Fine," I gasped as the ground brushed my chin. I glared up at him, eyes full of the fire raging inside me, before leaning forward and pressing my lips to the toe of his black leather boot.

I hated how wet it made me, even with the crushing sand pressing in from every angle.

I expected Belial to grab me the second my lips left his shoe, to start digging against the quickly sinking ground to dig me out.

To my horror, he only stared down at me with a dark smile that had my stomach twisting with unease.

"Belial!" I screamed as my ears dipped into the dirt and the ground swallowed my mouth. I could only watch in terror as he stood there, doing nothing, and allowed the ground to swallow me whole.

# CHAPTER FIFTEEN

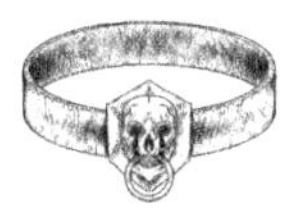

## Rayven

*This was how I died.*

I knew it in my bones.

My lungs began to ache, begging to release the air caught in my chest, and I became hyper aware of the blood pounding in my veins. Everything slowed to a painful crawl. My last moments with Belial played in my mind on loop, the gleam in his eyes as he'd watched me disappear beneath his boots seared into my brain.

What. A. Bastard.

I resisted the urge to open my mouth and scream. This was uncomfortable enough without soil spilling inside my mouth. Plus, what good would screaming do?

No one was coming to help me.

All I could hope for was a quick death and for the Lord of Bones to revive me before my three days were up.

Doubtful. Knowing that sick fuck, he'd probably leave me to rot in the mud for a while before unearthing me for round two of torturing his new pet.

My chest squeezed tighter, and my mind grew fuzzy from the lack of oxygen. I was only seconds away from death when the ground around me began to shift and dirt fell away. The crushing pressure around me dissipated, and I could finally breathe again.

I choked the fresh air down like I hadn't known it for an eon.

Strong hands gripped me, pulling me up out of the ground. When I forced my eyes open, Belial was hauling me into his arms. The muscular expanse of his chest was warm, comforting. I had no idea why I felt safe in this fucker's arms. He'd made me believe I was going to die.

He carried me away from the quicksand and lowered us to the ground in a sitting position—with me still cradled in his arms. As relieved as I was to still be alive, I wanted to shove away from him and run, to put as much distance as I could between us.

But my body was spent from the struggle of trying to escape. I needed to gather my strength.

"What the hell was that?" I said, unable to get enough air into my lungs between my shallow, panicked breaths. "I could have died."

"But did you? No, so I think thanks are in order," he muttered, his eyes glittering with mirth. This asshole thought this was *funny.*

"Eat a dick, you horned prick." I slapped my hands against his chest, trying to shove away, but his strong arms held me in place. "You're out of your fucking mind if you think I'm going to thank you for letting me get buried alive."

He laughed, throwing his head back as the sound echoed over the steady roll of whispers, and looked back down at me again. His stormy gray eyes gleamed with mischief, and he shifted so that the hard bulge in his pants pressed against my ass.

He'd obviously enjoyed watching me almost die...*really* enjoyed it.

If I wasn't so pissed, I might have been inclined to closely explore exactly how my near-death experience affected him. As it stood, I wanted him to get the hell away from me.

I shoved against his chest again, but the circle of his arms held fast.

"Thank you for saving me, even if your timing was shit," I said spitefully. "Now let me go."

His head tilted to the side, the chains on his horns clinking with the movement, and his gaze darkened. When he spoke, his voice was a coarse growl. "Weren't you just screaming my name?"

I stilled as tantalizing jolts of electricity zipped through me, rocketing to my core.

Fucking Hell. I should have found his stupid one-liners annoying, but his words were dark and twisted, wrapped up in his silk and honey voice.

I wanted him to say it again.

One hand pressed against the small of my back, the other slipping up to grab my throat. His gloved fingers closed in on the sides of my neck, creating a collar with his hand over my other made of iron. He brought his face close enough to mine that I could see the pale skin rimming his eyes and hear his breath behind the mask. My heart skipped a painful beat.

My chest seized as my knees turned to jelly, the desire to reach up and tear his mask off overwhelming. I wanted to see his face, feel his lips. I wanted a peek at the monster beneath the disguise—a glimpse of the man who'd both put my life in danger and saved me all in the same beat.

"Belial," I stammered, not sure what I planned to say after.

His name in my mouth felt like a lifeline.

Even if I wanted him to throw me down and fuck me into the ground, it didn't change the fact that the clock was ticking. There was an hourglass in the back of my mind, every grain of sand counting down the seconds until my time was up.

Until my fate was sealed. Until I belonged to the Lord of Bones forever.

I didn't have time to waste, but I also had burning questions begging to be answered. Like how the hell had Belial found me in the middle of the maze when I'd been stumbling around for what felt like hours?

Had he been following me this whole time? Or had he found me out of sheer luck?

"Do you know the way through the maze?" I asked, staring up breathlessly into his eyes. I was thankful for his hold on me. Otherwise, I might have fallen over at the way he looked at me.

Damn him.

"There are many ways through it," he mused after a moment of silence, as if he was debating answering me at all.

I huffed out a sigh. "Do you know any of them? Can you take me out of this place? You are the ferryman, right? You must have a boat or something. You kinda owe me after that stunt, don't you think?"

He stiffened against me, muscles tense, as though I'd asked something offensive, and shook his head. "No. I *don't* think. You asked me to save you from the quicksand, and I did. I don't owe you anything."

Slowly, he let go of my throat. "Even if I wanted to show you the way out, I can't. My job is to bring souls to this realm, not take them out."

To my surprise—and dismay—he pushed me out of his lap and rose to his feet.

I followed suit, but he was already stepping away, putting space between us.

"Can't you help me some other way?" I pressed, unsettled by how wrong the space between us felt. "Take me most of the way there? Halfway?"

Considering I'd been buried alive minutes ago, the white dress wasn't all that dirty, just wet. Very wet. It clung to my skin, leaving little to the imagination. I didn't bother trying to cover myself. Belial's eyes were skimming down my body, his eyes wide with something feral—masculine hunger.

Maybe I could convince him to help me.

"Help me, and I'll help you in return."

He laughed. "Help *me?* If I'm caught helping you, I'll be demoted to serve one of the Lords of the lower Hells. How will you help me then?"

I propped a hand on my hip. "Would that be so bad? They can't be worse than the Lord of Bones."

I didn't understand the look behind Belial's eyes. "You know nothing. They're worse, more than your little human brain could ever comprehend."

"Can you at least point me in the right direction?" I sighed, feeling like I was talking to the decapitated head all over again. If Belial wasn't going to budge on helping me, this conversation was pointless. I was wasting precious time. "What if I fall in quicksand again? Or get eaten by a bush?"

"I guess you should pay more attention then," he mused, once again examining the glittering rings on his fingers.

It annoyed me that he seemed to be more interested in his jewelry than my body, which was pretty much on full display.

It was almost like he could read my mind, because his gaze jerked up to land on my breasts, his lips bowing with a smirk. "Besides, the bushes wouldn't eat you. The trees would. And what a meal they'd make out of you. It's been some time since they've feasted on a beautiful woman."

This man was absolutely infuriating. *And annoyingly sexy.* My brain and libido were at war, and I couldn't decide if I wanted to suck his cock or punch him in it.

"I will do whatever you want if you help me," I say, glaring at him. "I need help if I'm going to make it out of here. Please."

Belial chuckled. "Whatever I want, huh?"

The bastard didn't deserve whatever he wanted, but at the moment, he was my only solid hope of escape. Plus, I couldn't lie—after last night in his bed, my pussy was already dripping for him.

"Maybe. It depends on what you want. We can, um, do the wine bottle thing again?" I tried to keep the excitement out of my voice, without much success.

"That was fun," he mused on a wicked laugh. "But we already did that."

He considered me for a moment, tapping his fingers on his chin in the most condescending way possible. My mind careened out of control at the silence, the whispers of the souls around us making my skin crawl again, waiting for his response.

Needless to say, it wasn't what I expected. "I want certain parts of your body."

"Excuse me?" My brows shot up toward my hairline. "Can I at least keep them attached?"

Belial sighed heavily and rolled his eyes. "You're no fun. Yes, you can keep them attached. I'll give you a way to summon me—only when you need me—but I have a condition." His eyes darkened as he took a step toward me.

My breath caught in my chest. "What kind of condition?"

"I'm going to use you however I want, so long as I keep you in one piece."

I swallowed hard, thoughts of the night we spent together in his bedroom filling my mind. I felt a little like an ant under a magnifying glass with this guy. He was a mischievous demon, and I was the helpless little creature he could amuse himself with.

He should have terrified me, but the only thing that scared me was the fact that he didn't.

I wanted to feel his hands, his tongue, his cock… and if giving myself to him got me through this forsaken maze quicker, and kept me alive, I'd accept his help.

I probably should have hesitated more, taken time to truly consider his offer. I didn't trust this guy as far as I could throw him.

There was something off about him. Whatever that quality was, it was the same thing drawing me closer. Besides, making a deal with a demon wasn't so bad when it was all to escape the devil himself, right?

"Deal."

His gray eyes flashed, and through the slit in his mask, I caught him licking his lips.

Yes. I had him, hook, line, and sinker.

He reached for his ear and took out his dagger earring, dangling it in front of me by the hook.

"Your blood on this blade will summon me to your side," he explained, dropping the tiny dagger into the palm of my hand and curling my fingers over it. "When you call me, I will come to you."

My heart fluttered at the idea of him running to my aid, imagining the next time I saw him and all the things he planned to do to me.

Without another word, he turned to walk away, back toward the way we came, leaving me in the middle of the path.

"Wait!" The word flew out of my mouth before I could stop it. "Can't you at least point me in the right direction, since you're here? Please."

He froze, waiting a full second before turning around to face me again. Behind me, I heard the plants begin to shift, twisting and crunching against one another, and when I checked back over my shoulder, there was a brand-new path that hadn't been there moments ago, and my heart leapt into my throat.

"Don't die, Rayven," he said.

Then, in a swirl of sparkling blue magic, he disappeared, leaving me alone once more.

I stared at the spot he'd been seconds ago, this time a little less lonely, and a little less afraid.

# CHAPTER SIXTEEN

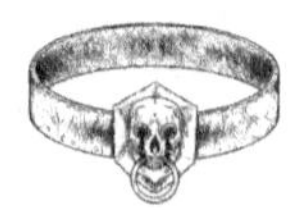

## BELIAL

I WASN'T JUST PLAYING with fire—I was stoking an inferno that threatened to destroy everything if I wasn't careful. Though, truthfully, I didn't mind getting burned. Not when it meant I'd be using every one of my little thief's orifices to bury my cock in.

It was only supposed to be a game, but it had quickly turned into so much more. *She* was turning into so much more.

I'd meant to toy with my little human, to get her hopes up only to crush them later. To earn her trust, only to break it. I'd wanted to be her ruin, her destruction.

But now...

Now, I was pacing in my study, twirling the tiny dagger earring between my fingers, waiting for her to summon me with its twin. Waiting to race back to her in the maze and help her in exchange for free use of her body.

Waiting for her to need me.

For hours, I'd watched her in the maze as she tried, and failed, to get anywhere. It shouldn't have been as entertaining as it was, but...I could watch her forever.

I expected her to call for me almost as soon as I'd given her the earring. She was hopelessly lost, endlessly frustrated, yet the call never came. Was she trying to prove a point? Trying to show me just how strong she was? Or was she that reluctant to let me use and worship her body?

Stubborn human.

Every one of her attempts were futile. She'd never figure out the labyrinth's cryptic paths. No one ever had—not that many had tried. I alone knew its secrets, for I was the one who'd planted it centuries ago. I was the one who'd enchanted it, tended to it, fed it corpses to keep it content.

My little thief would try desperately to escape the dark, endless pathways, and it wouldn't be enough. Not by a long shot.

Then, when her time ran out, she would belong to me... not that she didn't already. At least this way, she'd come to accept that fact once she failed.

In the meantime, I'd let her come crawling to me for my help, thinking she had an ally in the masked ferryman.

I couldn't wait to see her break when she discovered the truth.

I could do it now, give in to the desperate fire in my veins and pluck her from the labyrinth. I could break our deal and claim her as my queen, abandoning this plan of psychological torture.

But she was so beautiful when she suffered, so stunning when she cursed, when she cried. When her emotional fortress came down and she sank into complete and utter despair, knowing I was the sole cause of it all, that made it all the sweeter.

Besides, I might have been a heartless, callous monster like so many had claimed, but I was a beast of my word. I could summon enough patience to wait until her time ran out.

Three days was nothing compared to how long my little thief would belong to me. A blink of time compared to all of eternity.

In the meantime, I'd wait for her to beg for my help. I'd give it. In return, I'd use her, play with her, taste her. She'd be willing. For the first time, I'd fuck a living woman, one who wouldn't cower or sob at the sight of me.

My fingers tightened around the earring, the blade slicing through my flesh. With a curse, I pushed the digit into my mouth to suck my blood clean.

"You must be in quite the dry spell to be sucking your own body parts, brother," a voice hissed behind me. I turned to find a man with angular cheeks, green scaly skin, and serpentine eyes glaring at me from the mirror in the corner.

Fuck. I usually kept a sheet over the damn thing to keep my brothers from contacting me, but I'd forgotten to put it back after my conversation with Asmodeus.

Of course one of them would contact me when I wanted to be alone with my thoughts. Irritation burned through me when I saw who it was.

"What do you want, Leviathan?"

He laughed, a sinister noise that coiled through the room like a viper, leaving me feeling unsettled. "Why do I have to want anything to talk to you?"

The slits of my eyes glowed with malice. "You're the Lord of Envy. You want everything."

"Fair enough," he hissed, shifting in the mirror. Beyond him, I could see a sliver of a dark, wet cavern, stalactites stretching down from the ceiling. The faint, steady trickle of dripping water could be heard between his words. "A little ghoul told me you were hosting a party on All Hallows' Eve and that I'm invited. I was a little crushed that I didn't receive a direct invitation."

*Hells.* I had to admit, I'd been so caught up in my little thief's delicious suffering, I'd nearly forgotten about my bargain with Asmodeus. In exchange for Holga's return, I was to hold a party. *A masquerade.*

Apparently, word was quickly spreading through the layers of Hell.

"Ah," I said, clearing my throat. I hated all of my brothers, it was true, but there were a couple I could stomach more easily than others. Leviathan, despite his selfish, cunning ways, was one who didn't make me cringe. Usually. At least he didn't berate me for appearing in my "weaker" form. If this were Asmodeus or Belphegor, I'd never hear the end of it. "Yes, something like that. My deepest condolences brother. I've been a bit... *occupied.*"

I didn't miss the way his yellow eyes shone at my words, nor the devilish smile that contorted his features. "If not your duties, I wonder what could possibly be taking up so much of your time." Dread settled in my gut before I could even form a reply, and Leviathan didn't wait for an answer. "Could it be that you've found a new little pet?"

I froze, thankful for the mask I wore. Asmodeus had obviously been busy running his mouth to our siblings about me resummoning Holga.

"What I have is none of your business," I snapped, trying and failing to keep the sharpness out of my tone.

Leviathan's grin only widened. "You never learn your lesson do you?"

He wasn't asking anything I hadn't already asked myself. They'd all warned me before with Catherine. They'd think I was making the same mistakes. I didn't need to be chastised. This time was different.

I'd found a queen who wanted me, even if I had to twist and torture her to get her to admit it.

"I hope you'll bring your little pet to the masquerade," he went on, ignoring my silence. "It's been a millennium since I've seen a living soul. I'm not sure I'll be able to refrain from sinking my teeth into her."

Something snapped in me at his words, and I saw red, taking several steps toward the mirror. Blinding rage swallowed me at the thought of any of my brothers—any of them—laying a finger on her. They couldn't die, but I could make them suffer. She was mine, and mine alone. Anyone who dared to look at her the wrong way would pay for their insolence.

"You won't touch her." My voice was pure venom that had Leviathan flinching away from the mirror.

"Temper, temper. You're stubborn *and* greedy, Belial," he mused, and I wished I could reach through the mirror and punch him in the fangs.

"What do you want, Leviathan?" I ground out, eager to end this conversation. "I have much to do and you're wasting my time."

"Is your pet's name *much*?" He chuckled once, clearly humored by his own joke. "I'll leave you to it then. Get that dusty skeleton of a castle ready. We'll be seeing you soon."

His image shimmered, then disappeared completely, leaving me staring at my own reflection.

If Leviathan knew about my little thief, it was safe to assume the rest of my brothers did as well, which left me uneasy. I didn't trust half of them with dead souls, much less living ones, and least of all with my delicate little human.

I feared what might happen if all of them were in a room with her, but I wasn't afraid for her. I was afraid for *them*. Afraid I would tear them apart limb from limb and disturb the ancient balance between the layers of Hell if they touched her. I'd do it all with a smile on my face.

Grabbing the dark sheet on the table, I tossed it over the mirror with a curse before I marched toward the door. As much as I hated to admit it, Leviathan was right. I needed to get the castle in order if the other eight princes of hell would be roaming the halls in three days' time. There was so much to do, so many things to prepare.

I needed to start with moving some of these souls waiting for Judgement off the grounds. They all knew I was decades behind by the lack of souls trickling down to the lower layers, but seeing just how many were sitting around would enrage them.

As concerning as that was, the masquerade was the furthest thing from my mind. There was something more important that would take place on All Hallows' Eve. Time would run out for my little thief at the stroke of midnight, making her totally, irrevocably mine.

The thought spurred me on, my steps quicker as I headed for the Library of Souls. It would take a lot of souls to whip the place into shape in time, but it could be done. It would be the most magnificent party the nine realms of Hell had ever seen.

It would also be the first time in all the realms of Hell there'd been a queen.

I glanced out the window, noting the blood red sky. In my realm, the sky turned red as brutal death at nightfall.

Day one was up.

She still hadn't called for Belial.

It didn't matter. I'd see her soon enough as the Lord of Bones. Rayven needed to know I was watching, waiting.

Counting the days down until she became mine.

# CHAPTER SEVENTEEN

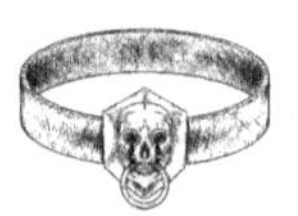

## RAYVEN

THE SKY TURNED BLOOD red as it grew darker. Was this supposed to be dusk?

It would be night soon, leaving me only two days to escape. Frustration twisted my insides. I'd accomplished so little.

It started to rain again, saturating the ground and making muddy puddles. I was water-logged and freezing, and it only got colder as the sky grew darker, bloodier.

Pain lanced up through my legs as I slowly made my way through the winding paths of the labyrinth, hoping to find a way out.

"You look awful," one of the heads in the brambles noted as I hobbled past. He was missing his nose and half an ear.

"At least my body is still attached," I grumbled, trudging past him.

Another corpse gasped up ahead. "How rude."

"So rude," the one behind me called. "See if I help you find the garden."

I froze in my tracks, whirling around to face the head that had insulted me. "The what?"

"The Master's garden," he said, and I took several cautious steps toward him. He stared at me with milky white eyes and a lopsided grin. "That's where you're headed, isn't it?"

"I'm looking for the exit, but the garden could be useful," I mused. "Does he plant food there? Fruit? Or only flowers?"

"You'll find a fine plum tree there."

My stomach fluttered at the thought of the juicy plum I'd eaten and everything that had transpired afterward. Dirty thoughts exploded to life in my mind, images of a throne and chains. Wine and wax. My cheeks flushed as I recalled it all. I was starving for food, and other things...

"That's perfect," I said, my spirits lifting. "Can you tell me how to get there?"

The head's forehead crinkled. "Get where?"

"The garden," I bit out. "Can you tell me how to get to your Master's garden?"

He pursed his lips. "I don't know of a garden."

"But you said..." The disappointment in my voice was obvious, and I hated how much I'd gotten my hopes up, if only for a brief second.

"I said nothing. The maze is making you crazy."

"Loony as a tune," another head said, making the last vestiges of my patience snap like dry spaghetti.

Stupid, useless fucking corpses. Before I could stop myself, I reached for the decapitated head, grabbing hold of its crusty hair, and wrenched it from the bush. It screamed, a raspy, choked noise.

"I'll show you loony." I dropped the head and punted it as hard as I could, sending it flying down the path and rolling into a puddle. It gurgled, twitching in the water.

With a huff, I glared at another head a few feet away. "Want to join him?"

"No, thank you, maiden. I'll just, eh, be quiet. Mind my own business."

"That's what I thought."

Annoyed, I kept moving, making a right at the fork ahead. Maybe plucking all the severed body parts from the bushes wasn't such a bad idea. It would help me mark the paths I'd been down—like the breadcrumbs from Hansel and Gretel but fucked up. I considered it for a moment but then dismissed it. If the paths kept changing, it wouldn't make a difference.

The rain eventually stopped, and the sky got darker.

The maze was just as confusing as ever, but something about the path Belial created was different. Trees and small bushes broke up the monotony of the knotted brambles, and the identical pathways opened into clearings the size of rooms.

I was still trapped, but it felt less ominous. It felt like I was making some kind of progress.

A river, deep and wide, wove its way through the maze. The crimson water was filled with decomposing corpses flowing lazily between the plants, disappearing beneath the walls of the labyrinth and blocking paths. Every time I ran into the river, I had to turn back. I was too afraid to cross it, or even go near it. It was a place for the dead, and I couldn't shake the feeling that if I got too close, I'd join them.

As the last light of day faded overhead, fear crawled through my blood. Where would I spend the night? There was no shelter, no place to sleep, nothing but the never-ending walls of hedges and the not-so-comforting whispers that followed me everywhere I went.

The only thing that gave me the slightest reassurance about being stuck out here all night was the lack of predators. Aside from the countless corpses surrounding me, I seemed to be alone. The disembodied heads might have been royal pains in my ass, but they weren't threatening. There were no beasts lurking around the corners—except for maybe Belial and the monster he kept in his pants.

I was utterly alone, forced to endure the night out in the wilderness, hopelessly lost in the maze. I could have given up, asked Belial to lead me back to the castle so I could sleep in a bed.

Fuck. A bed. My aching muscles rejoiced at the thought, but I quickly shoved the notion away. Nope. Not an option. After all I'd been through, I couldn't turn back now.

I reached up to thumb the dagger earring I'd pushed through my right earlobe. Even if it wasn't to whisk me away to the castle, I could still summon him, but what would I ask for? A massage? A bubble bath? My phone back so I could fall asleep to my latest monster romance book on audio? No, those were all stupid human things. He'd make fun of me, and I didn't have the energy to deal with that right now.

I fucking hated that I cared about what he thought.

I shouldn't have cared at all.

All thoughts of Belial drained away when I rounded a corner and stepped into an enclosed courtyard filled with several trees. *Fruit* trees! I rubbed my eyes, half expecting them to be a figment of my imagination. Surely, I wasn't hallucinating.

I stumbled toward them, delighted that the lowest fruits were just within reach; I didn't have the energy for tree-climbing. My mouth watered, excitement bubbling under my skin, until I plucked one and registered the deep purple skin.

It was a plum.

I turned it over in my hand, my mind drifting back to my dinner in the castle. I'd suspected there was something wrong with the food when Holga had given it to me, insisting I eat every bite. Then I'd had that dream, the one where I was chained to the Lord of Bones' throne and he'd made me pleasure myself in front of a room full of souls.

He'd all but admitted he caused the dream. It had been some kind of dark magic, and I was sure the food had been the source. There had been a few other items, but the plum had a weight to it that the bread and the wine hadn't. *And Holga had stayed to make sure I finished the fruit...*

Had the plum been picked from this same tree? Would I have strange dreams again? My eyes slid to the few other trees in the garden, but they were all the same. Plums. Weird, magical, sex plums.

My stomach growled in anger. I had to eat.

I sat down on a stone bench beneath the plum tree, my muscles unclenching in relief. This garden was relatively protected from the rest of the maze, so it would be a nice spot for me to rest for the night. The bench wouldn't be comfortable, but it beat sleeping in the mud.

Plus, there were countless plums for me to gorge on, so I wouldn't go hungry.

What if I dreamed of him again?

It wouldn't be the worst thing. The nightmare the plum gave me hadn't been bad. I was pretty fucking sure he intended it to be a nightmare, but instead, it was the best dream I'd ever had. It had been dark and luscious, calling to a part of me I hadn't even known existed.

*Bend over and show me all that I own.*

His words played in my head over and over, making my thighs clench and my palms sweat. I should have felt exposed, obscene, wrong. Embarrassed, degraded. While I'd felt all those things, it had felt *right*, like a part of myself had come racing to the surface for the first time. That part of me had felt safe under the heated glare of the Lord of Bones.

It had just been a dream. A lie. A spell, fabricated to crawl under my skin and leach into my mind, leaving me to question everything.

It didn't change the fact that I loved every second of the fantasy. If I took a bite of the plum, and it ended up magical like the other one, I wouldn't be disappointed.

Before I lost my nerve, I put the plum to my mouth and sank my teeth into its flesh. The flavor exploded in my mouth, so sweet and delicious that I moaned. It was probably just the hunger talking, but I was pretty sure it was the best thing I'd ever eaten.

I took another bite, and then another, until it was finished. Then, I plucked a second fruit, and a third. I feasted on them like a starving animal, juice and bits of pulp streaking my chest. I didn't care. No one was here to see, and even if they were, the plums were too intoxicating to pay attention to anything else.

"I see you've helped yourself to my fruit trees," a guttural voice snarled from the darkness. "Then again, I should have expected as much from a little thief."

That familiar voice sunk into my bones and turned my marrow to stone. I couldn't move for several intense beats as my mind reeled, grappling with the fact that the Lord of Bones was here, and he'd caught me stealing. *Again.*

I gathered my nerves as the Lord of Bones emerged from the shadows, the dense blanket of fog that had settled on the ground coiling up around his ankles. He looked so ominous shrouded in the night, with the tips of his horns scraping the blood-red sky.

He took a step forward, eating up the precious distance between us. I remained seated on the stone bench and took another bite of my third plum, smiling as the juices coated my fingers and dripped down my dress, slipping beneath the neckline. I was using every ability I had to sell the lie that I wasn't flustered by his sudden presence, that I wasn't absolutely terrified.

"I wasn't expecting a dinner guest. Want some?" I held the plum out to him. "Careful, though. They're known to give you filthy dreams."

He took another step toward me, then another, until the tips of his giant boots nearly touched my bare toes.

Instead of taking the plum, he captured my wrist and wrenched me off the bench. I thrashed, trying to get away, but his arm banded around my waist and drew me close to his hard body.

"If you're so sure these plums are enchanted like the one served with your dinner, why are you stuffing yourself silly?" he growled, the blue lights in his eye sockets glinting through the dark.

"B-because I'm starving."

"For what, little thief? Food, or me?"

I swallowed thickly and narrowed my eyes, refusing to answer.

His jowls parted, and that thick black tongue slithered out, oozing saliva. Its hot tip slid over my jaw, slipped down my throat, and flicked at the skull amulet on my collar. "I will always know where you are because of this. At the end of each day, I will come to you and bid you goodnight. Together, we will count down the days left until you are mine."

His tongue roved lower, slipping beneath the neckline of my dress to taste the plum juice that streaked down my front.

I was so caught up in the sensation of his tongue against my breast that I hadn't seen him take his claw to my wrist until it was slicing into my flesh.

*He was cutting me.*

I clenched my teeth together, biting back the scream bubbling up from my throat. I wouldn't give him the satisfaction.

He dragged the razor-sharp claw down my skin, leaving a two-inch mark. Then, he brought his tongue to my bleeding wrist to lick up the blood. "This marks one day passed. You have two more, little thief. Or, you can give up now and become my queen without all this added suffering?"

"Fuck you. I'm not giving up," I snarled.

The monster chuckled. "Good girl. I'd be disappointed if you did."

With that, he released his hold on me and turned around. The swish of his cape stirred the fog up behind him and in a blink, he was gone. My hand raised to my throat, toying with the amulet—the *tracking* device.

No matter how deep I went into the labyrinth, how far away I got from the castle, the Lord of Bones wouldn't be far away.

He'd always be able to find me. Always watching.

Waiting for my time to run out.

# CHAPTER EIGHTEEN

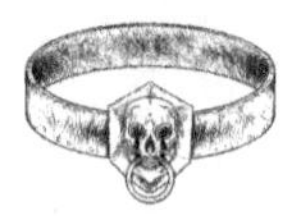

## RAYVEN

I woke up with a scream. Something was touching me.

My eyelids flung open to see a vine slowly winding around my ankle.

I shot up into a sitting position and tried to pull the vine loose, but it wouldn't budge. It only wound tighter, cutting off my circulation.

Fuck.

My gaze followed the vine, trying to find the plant it came from, and my heart clenched when I saw it disappeared beneath the hedge wall. Whatever this plant was, it wasn't from the garden of plum trees.

It must have sensed me, searched for me. Whatever it was doing, it couldn't be good.

No matter how much I pulled at the vine, it wouldn't loosen. If only I had something to cut through it...

Belial's dagger earring!

My hand shot to my ear and pulled the silver piece of jewelry free. It was only a few inches long, but the blade was sharp enough to slice through the vine.

I swung, stabbing toward the vine around my ankle. The instant it met the metal, the vine recoiled and jumped back into the bushes, taking me along with it.

A scream was knocked back into my lungs as it jerked me off the bench, and my back slammed into the ground. Then, I was being pulled across the garden at a speed that had my head spinning.

I exploded through the hedge, and then another, thorns slicing my skin and branches jabbing at every part of me.

The vine dragged me through the mud, my head whirling as I was viciously jerked down turns and through several more hedges. The disembodied heads laughed as they watched me zing past.

"Ha! Looks like the blood oak caught her!" one head snickered, its voice gone as soon as it had come.

Blood oak? Belial's words from when he'd pulled me from the quicksand came rushing back. He'd mentioned something about carnivorous trees. Was that what the head was referring to?

Of all the ways to die in this stupid maze, being eaten by a fucking plant wasn't going to be the way I went down.

With the dagger earring clutched in my fist, I tried to haul myself up to reach the vine dragging me, my muscles screaming, but it was no use. At the speed I was moving, I couldn't pull my back off the ground.

Mark had once tried to get me to join a Pilates class. I'd laughed in his face when he suggested exercise, especially in public. At a strip mall of all places. Not exactly my scene.

Now, I regretted turning him down. If only I'd known weekly core exercise would have saved me from a flesh-eating tree on my unexpected vacation to fucking Limbo.

I smelled it before I saw it, and I had to resist the urge to vomit. I was no stranger to death, but the corpses I was used to were dusty and had long since decomposed. This smell was pungent, the kind that seeped into every pore, leaving a film on your skin and hair.

The scent of decay in the air was so intense, so thick, my eyes watered and my stomach churned.

I was pulled through another thicket and emerged on the other side to find myself in a walled-off garden. That's when I saw it.

The blood oak was a colossal tree with the thickest trunk I'd ever seen. It had twisting, gnarled branches that looked like something straight out of *Sleepy Hollow*. There were no leaves, no traces of greenery, just dead branches and snake-like vines, identical to the one that had dragged me here.

The bark was stained with dark sap. No...*blood*. It streaked down the trunk, and bled into the ground around it, turning the dirt an ominous crimson color.

The vine around my ankle was still retreating, coiling around the tree, reeling me in. I stared up at the branches, noting pale chunks of something caught amongst them, which blended with the overcast sky at first.

When I got closer, I was able to register what they really were: body parts. They were being chewed by the thick knots in the branches. Each bulbous knot and burl on the tree had *teeth*, sharp and yellow, munching on the rotting pieces of flesh, dripping more blood down its bark and staining everything red.

I was so horrified, so scared that I would be just another corpse strewn amongst the blood oak's branches, that I couldn't scream. For a painfully long moment, I could only watch as the tree continued to drag me toward it, and the blood-soaked space between it and me disappeared.

Then, something kicked on in my brain.

A surge of adrenaline and determination summoned every ounce of strength I had left to pull myself up and grab onto the vine around my ankle. Gripping it with one hand to anchor myself, I started sawing through it with the dagger earring.

The tree howled in pain, dozens of disembodied souls blending together to create the most disturbing sound. I worked frantically as the vine lifted me up in the air, desperate to free myself from the blood oak's clutches so I could hit the ground running.

Sweat streaked down my body, and my breath turned to tiny little huffs as I focused on the vine, honing in on the fraying fibers so I could try to ignore the tree's movement in my periphery.

I shouldn't have looked.

The blood oak's trunk had a slit running down its center that opened into a gaping maw lined with countless rows of needle-sharp teeth. Inside its mouth were pieces of chewed up limbs all tangled together.

"Oh, *fuck*." I fought the urge to retch as a fresh waft of decaying flesh slapped me in the face.

"Keep it down, would ya? We're trying to rot in peace," one of the heads stuck in the hedge nearby griped.

"Just hurry up and let it eat you," another head snickered. "It's not so bad. Not once you're dead, anyway. Before you're dead, it's pretty bad, actually."

All the other heads nodded as much as the brambles holding them up would allow, and murmured in agreement.

Pure, unsaturated panic had me sawing through the vine as fast as humanly possible as it hoisted me higher into the air. I sliced through the last of the vine's fibers with a snap, the blade cutting into my ankle from the pressure.

I cried out in victory, but the celebration turned to sheer petrification as I started falling, plummeting through the air.

The ground was an alarming distance away. I'd probably break my back or my neck with the angle I was at. Then I'd die, and the blood oak would eat me anyway. How was that for bitter fucking irony?

I closed my eyes, waiting for impact.

Instead, strong arms caught me and pulled me close to a hard, warm chest.

I knew who it was before opening my eyes. His scent of pine and strawberries chased away the rot and decay of the carnivorous tree.

"You called me?" He sounded mildly amused.

I looked up to see Belial's storm gray eyes peering at me through the holes of that dark, faceless mask.

"On accident. I had things covered," I snapped, unable to keep the relief out of my voice.

Several vines whipped in our direction, but Belial held up his hand, a wall of blue magic shielding us against the blood oak's attack; all the while, the demon's eyes never left mine.

"Covered?" His voice lifted, and I could picture his brows arching. "Let me get this straight. You were about to get devoured by a carnivorous tree, and instead of using the three-inch decorative blade I gave you to summon me, you decided it was better used as a weapon."

"Pretty much."

"Your survival skills are shit."

"I was trying to avoid you, so they're pretty good, if you ask me," I said through a smirk.

Christ. I'd just come awfully close to dying in the most horrific way possible, and here I was, smiling.

*I felt so safe in his arms.* Like he hadn't been that far off all this time.

I allowed him to carry me away from the blood oak, the only thing filling the silence the rapid pound of his heart against my cheek.

So he did have a heart, a functioning one at that. I guess that made sense. It's not like he was a dead soul. He was a demon. Maybe not like the Lord of Bones—definitely not like the Lord–but he wasn't human.

I peered up at him, the questions piling up in my mind easily making up for the silence between us. My eyes followed the edge of the mask to where it sat on his chiseled jawline. What horrors was he hiding beneath? Would he ever show me?

Where was he taking me?

Then, there was the biggest question of them all: what was he going to ask of me in payment for saving my life... again?

# CHAPTER NINETEEN

## RAYVEN

BELIAL CARRIED ME TO a clearing where the hedges weren't so close together. When I looked up, my gaze flicked between all the stone markers and the few decorative plants with actual flowers on them instead of body parts.

We were in a graveyard. The moss-covered stones looked ancient, with engravings that had faded over time.

It had obviously been forever since anyone had been buried here. "What is this place?"

Belial snorted. "You'd think the grave robber would know a cemetery when she sees one."

"I know it's a cemetery, but...why is it here? What's the point when bodies are just strewn all over the place?"

He tsked. "The body parts you've seen belong to lost souls who never went through Judgement. If they wait too long, they go crazy and wander off, usually eaten by other corrupt souls. The blood oak tree was once a Roman blacksmith, if you can believe it. The smart souls seek refuge outside of their bodies."

"The haunted furniture around the castle are souls waiting to be judged?"

He nodded, the silver chains jingling against his horns.

I strained my neck, looking around at the graves as Belial carried me between them. "So who are all these people if not human souls?"

"Demons—natives of this realm without souls to keep in the archives. The ones who served him—past reapers and ferrymen mostly—lie here, in eternal peace. At least, as much peace as a demon can hope for."

He lowered me down onto a stone ledge. When he perched himself on a gravestone opposite me, I craned my head up to find I was sitting on the base of a statue. It was enormous, with a long skull face and twisted horns that reached up toward the sky. "You had to bring me to a statue of *him?*" I grumbled.

"I can take you back where I found you," Belial replied in a tone mixed with irritation and amusement, "if you think the blood oak will be better company."

"Don't tempt me." I reached down, rubbing my sore feet with a scoff, but my eyes kept traveling back to the stone sculpture looming over me. "Why do you serve him, anyway? He's a dick."

"Careful what you say about the king of this realm. He has ears everywhere."

My eyes snapped in his direction, hot and full of rage. Adrenaline still coursed through my system, making me shake from the aftershock of almost being eaten. "So what if he hears? That monster threw me into a labyrinth with annoying body parts and carnivorous plants. I bet he saw me almost get eaten—he's probably up in his castle somewhere, jerking off to the show."

Belial's eyes gleamed, as if I'd said something funny. "Maybe, but you lived, didn't you? You could have called on me to save you, but you didn't. Maybe he's testing you?"

"Testing me for what?"

"To be queen."

"Right," I spat, kicking at the dead grass beneath my feet and wincing when I stubbed my battered toe on a rock. "Forcing me to be his queen is just another way for him to torture me. He'll probably torture you too once he finds out you're helping me."

The demon ran a hand between his horns, slicking back his inky hair. "Probably."

"Aren't you worried about what he'll do to you?"

"My punishments will be my business, not yours." His smooth, velvety voice had a sharp edge to it that warned me not to press the issue. "Anyway, they won't be worse than yours if you don't get out of here before your time is up. Either way, you seem to enjoy pain to an extent..."

Judging by the lines at the corners of his eyes, he was smirking beneath his mask. "So maybe you should just give up."

His eyes dropped to the skull amulet dangling from the iron cuff clamped around my neck. "The only queen to ever wear the crown of a monarch and the collar of a slave. Actually, that has a nice ring to it. Rayven, the slave queen."

I glared at him, trying to ignore the knot of nerves tightening inside my gut. "I'd rather dig up one of these graves and pitch myself inside, thanks. But if we're done here, I better get going. Time is running out."

Every part of me was sore, my muscles throbbing as I scooted myself off the ledge. As soon as I was upright, my knees buckled, sending me crashing back to the ground. The bottoms of my feet were shredded from my traipse through the maze, my nightgown torn to shreds, soaked through with mud and water.

I might as well have been wearing wet toilet paper for all the coverage it gave me.

I flung a glare at the Lord of Bones' stone likeness.

"Fuck you," I hissed, fighting the urge to cry.

It was like I'd been thrown into a post-apocalyptic movie with no provisions and expected to survive...only I'd done this to myself. I wanted this chance to escape.

I just wasn't ready for how fucking impossible this whole thing would be. I hated how weak it made me feel, how utterly helpless I was. This wasn't how I expected things to go, not by a long shot.

If only I had shoes and some actual clothes, instead of this tattered nightgown.

If I asked Belial for boots and some pants, what would he have me do for payment?

Just the thought had a heartbeat forming between my thighs.

The not knowing and not being able to say no was what terrified me, but it also thrilled me. I didn't think he would hurt me—at least, I hoped he wouldn't—but giving him freedom over my body was nerve-wracking.

Last time, I'd had a safeword.

This time, I probably wouldn't be so lucky. He'd expect me to follow through with whatever twisted little sex game he had in mind, or he wouldn't fulfill my request.

I turned a pointed look to where he was still lounging on the headstone, looking sexy as fuck with his elbows propped over his knees. "So, are you going to demand something in exchange for catching me? Even if I didn't ask for your help?"

He shrugged one shoulder. "Consider it a freebie, as long as you ask for something else. Otherwise you're wasting my time."

"Why are you so interested in me? Don't you have some woman to occupy all this free time you seem to have? Some castle servants to tie up and shove wine bottles into?"

"They aren't the same." He chuckled. "Their flesh doesn't turn pink, their pussies don't throb and heat. They don't bleed like you. They don't scream like you..." He leaned forward, and my heart stuttered at the flash of pointed teeth I caught through the mouth of his mask. "And they certainly don't cream like you do."

I had to swallow down a gasp at his words as they caused heat to bloom in my chest before sinking between my thighs. *Holy hell.*

"So, spit it out," he demanded, his voice nearly a growl as he stood up from the gravestone, towering over me. "What do you want from me?"

If only we were under different, sexier circumstances; then I would have asked him to take his clothes off.

Maybe he would anyway, depending on what he wanted for payment.

"Shoes," I said, gesturing to my feet. They looked worse than yesterday, and I was beginning to worry about infection. "Specifically my boots."

He tilted his head to the side, the jewels on his horns jangling. "Your boots?"

I nodded. "The ones taken from me. I want them back."

"Your clothes—including your shoes—were torn off by the corrupted souls in the dungeon's oubliette."

A sharp, uncomfortable pang jabbed under my ribs and burrowed into my gut. "You know about that?"

Belial's eyes darkened. "The whole castle knows about that, Rayven."

"Oh..."

"Those boots are in the deepest, darkest part of this realm. You expect me to just fetch them?" he asked, considering me.

I panicked. There were a million other useful things I could ask for, like a giant pair of hedge clippers to bulldoze my way through this maze. However, judging by how the shrubs grew whenever and wherever they pleased, I doubted it would do much good.

Shoes were what I needed. Besides, I'd lost everything else that belonged to me. The least I could have were my goddamned boots. I didn't know how much farther I could walk without them—that is, if I could walk at all.

"Yes."

The second of silence that followed was palpable, and my heart clenched hard.

"Fine." I expected him to disappear in an explosion of blue magic, to head for the oubliette to find them, but he didn't move. Instead, he produced the boots with a flourish of his wrist, and dropped them on the ground before me. "There you are."

I stared at them, unsure if I should laugh or cry at how simply he'd pulled them out of the air. Any form of thanks died in my throat as I reached for them in disbelief. They were well-worn, well-loved, and all mine.

"How did you do that?" My voice trailed off. "What else can you just pull out of thin air?"

"A lot of things."

"You also cast that shield back at the blood oak," I said, pursing my lips. "Seems like powerful magic for a guy who drives a boat. Where is your ferry, anyway? How do you get it through the river?"

"Always with the questions." He massaged one of his temples with two fingers. "I got your boots with magic. I cast that shield with magic. I steer my ferry through the narrow canals with *magic*."

With a scowl, I scrambled to untie the boots, pulling them on and lacing them up tight. I slowly stood, testing them out. My feet still ached, but I was too relieved to care. My determination renewed, I looked up to find Belial's eyes glowing with intrigue.

"You could have asked for a new pair." He folded his arms over his chest and nodded toward the worn shoes. "Why ask for your grubby old boots back?"

"*Excuse* you, but these are Doc Martens, pal. I spent a lot of money on these."

"Money you took from the dead?" Acid stained his voice.

"Maybe."

His jaw set, and for a second, he looked angry. Then, he shook his head, as if to dismiss whatever he was about to say. "What else do you need from me?"

I hesitated, chewing the inside of my cheek as I considered asking for more. Water would be nice, or another point in the right direction, but there was the big fat question of payment. The more I asked for, the more I'd rack up the bill, and who knew if I'd be able to afford it.

I didn't even know what he expected in exchange for the boots.

"Nothing," I said, swallowing hard.

He cocked his head to the side. "Nothing at all?"

"No."

His eyes narrowed, turning dark and stormy, and he was silent for a long moment. His gaze on mine made my skin prickle, a heat stirring in my middle, but I shoved the thoughts aside. The fact that he turned me on so much by just standing there was alarming.

"In that case," he said finally, uncrossing his arms, "I have a gift for you."

"A-a gift?" I was skeptical, but the excitement in my voice was clear, my mind spinning with possibilities.

I probably should have been more suspicious, but at this point I wasn't going to turn down anything that could potentially help me find my way out of this hellhole.

With another flourish of his wrist, Belial produced a piece of bread. It might as well have been a Thanksgiving feast for how happy I was to see it.

"Food," he said. "To keep your strength up."

I wanted to tell him how little strength I'd get from a scrap of bread, but I was so hungry I didn't care. Bread was better than no bread.

I reached for it, and paused, cocking a singular brow at him. "This isn't going to cost me, is it?"

His mouth curled into a smile beneath his mask. "A gift is a gift. You don't owe me for this."

I was hardly dignified in the way I snatched it from him and shoved it into my mouth, tearing a bite out of it. I was pretty sure it was the hunger talking, but it was the most delicious thing I'd ever tasted.

"Wine to wash it down," he said, conjuring a wine bottle filled with red liquid.

My lungs slapped together at the sight of it. It wasn't water, but it was better than nothing. "Uh, thanks..."

I swallowed down about a quarter of the bottle, my cheeks flaming red from the alcohol's warmth.

"Thank you." I was thankful, grateful, and in his debt more than ever.

When I handed the bottle back to him, he brought the glass to his mask's mouth and ran his tongue over the rim, tasting where my lips had been.

The noise he made was caught somewhere between a moan and a growl. He threw the bottle aside and it disappeared into a cloud of glimmering blue magic before it could smash into a headstone.

"Don't thank me." His eyes darkened as he stalked toward me, like a predator about to pounce. "You're about to show me just how grateful you are."

# CHAPTER TWENTY

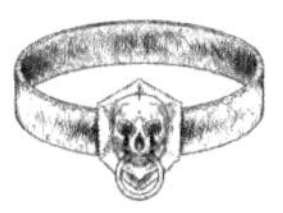

## RAYVEN

THERE WAS SOMETHING IN Belial's stride that put me on edge and made my pulse race.

"You should have told me what you wanted before you gave me the boots," I said.

"That's not how this game works, little human. I make the rules." His tone was dark and full of hunger, but I could still hear the smile in his voice.

"What do you want me to do?"

He came to stand in front of me, his eyes roving down my body and gleaming with satisfaction at the way my skin flushed. "I want you to worship me... while the Lord of Bones watches."

A chill skipped down my spine, and my eyes swung wildly around the graveyard, looking for the monster. My muscles relaxed when my gaze settled on the statue of Limbo's king.

Jesus, I was really on edge if I thought he meant the Lord of Bones was here, watching us from somewhere in the bushes.

Then again, after my run-in with him last night under the plum tree, my paranoia couldn't really be blamed.

"So you want me to do what, exactly?" I cocked a skeptical brow at him. Maybe he'd have me get on my knees to worship whatever it was creating that bulge in his pants… "Pray? Sing a hymn?"

"The only hymn I want to hear is the anthem of your cries as I use your body however I want. And right now, I want to punish you."

"Punish me?" I gasped, taking a step back. "For what?"

"For not calling me sooner. I could have helped you with the blood oak."

I rolled my eyes. "I didn't need your help."

"You could have broken your fucking neck." There was a sharper edge to his voice. "I only caught you because you accidentally drew your blood with my silver trying to escape."

"And so what if I had?" My patience with this demon was running thin. If he gave a damn about me dying, he wouldn't leave me in the maze to fend for myself at all. Did the 'damsel in distress' thing do it for him? I wondered if he had a hero complex with a compulsion to swoop in at the last second. "Why do you care so much about what happens to me, anyway?"

His eyes darkened with a dangerous gleam. "Turn around, bend over the statue's base, and pull your dress up."

"And if I don't?" I was being stubborn and I knew it, but the way he stared at me like an animal about to attack its prey was like gasoline to the fire already burning inside me. I wanted to get under his skin. He was sexy as hell when he was annoyed. "Will you take my boots away?"

"No, but you're going to do it anyway," he said, closing the space between us. The way he stared down at me, his eyes radiating sheer power, made my core throb. "Not because I'm forcing you to do this. No, there is a dark part of your soul that *needs* this, isn't there?"

I wasn't going to give him the satisfaction of an answer, even though I could already feel my arousal dripping between my thighs. Yes, I needed this. I needed him to use me the way he did in his bed. I wanted any and every part of him on me, but a flurry of nerves rolled through me at the thought. "Is it going to hurt?"

"Do you want it to hurt?" He moved closer yet, until the fabric of his shirt danced over my exposed chest.

It wasn't really a question. I wanted whatever this demon would give me, however he would give it to me. "Yes."

"That's what I suspected." He gestured toward the statue with a tilt of his horns. "Now, do as I said. Bend over and show me that pretty ass."

I hesitated, my nerves shooting sky-high, but I did as he instructed, pulling my dress up and bending at the waist, my hands on the statue's base. The stone was rough against my palms, the cool breeze licking against my bare backside.

I felt horribly exposed, but I didn't hate it, even with the Lord of Bones' stony eye sockets boring into me from above.

"That's my good girl," Belial praised, his voice rough with something that had goosebumps exploding over my skin.

Sneaking a peek over my shoulder, my heart lurched into my throat when I found him pulling his gloves off. I shouldn't have been this excited about the thought of his bare skin on mine, but I was reeling, my skin prickling with anticipation. I whimpered when he tucked the gloves in his back pocket and bent over me, his hand smoothing over my ass.

"You liked the sting of the wax when I played with you." His tone turned soft in my ear, which had me relaxing into his palm. "Didn't you?"

"Yes..."

"Good, because this is going to sting even more."

"I want it to hurt," I murmured, confirming what I'd already admitted, more to myself than him.

He was right. I didn't just want the pain—I needed it. This pain numbed the rest of the hurt and suffering the labyrinth had already caused me, that the Lord of Bones had caused me.

Belial's punishment was the kind of pain I had the choice to receive, and for a moment, it would drown out everything else.

He was more than the masked stranger who'd saved me from the quicksand, more than the hero who'd whisked me away from the blood oak. He was quickly becoming my painkiller, my lifeline, my phone-a-fucking-friend and hope he picks up the goddamn phone.

I'd been so stubborn not to ask for help. I wasn't used to asking for things from anyone.

Maybe, buried under all that lust and depravity, there was some part of the demon that actually cared about what happened to me.

The first smack to my ass came as a surprise, even though I'd suspected he was going to spank me. It had enough force to knock a whimper from my lips.

"What do you say, Rayven?"

"Go fuck yourself?" I managed through gritted teeth. "Then again, you probably do all the time. Why else would that hand be *so* strong?"

He smacked me again, this time so hard, my hands slipped on the ledge, and I had to catch myself. My skin was hot and stinging, probably with the impression of a very large hand forming across it.

My pussy clenched at the image.

"Let's try that again. What do you say when I make you feel pain?"

He swatted me again—another delicious blow that had my legs shaking.

"T-thank you?" I bit out, my vision blurring with hot tears.

I had every reason to hate this, but I didn't. I was crying from sheer fucking euphoria.

"That's right. Every time your flesh turns red and raw from my abuse, every time I make you forget about all the other bad things, I want to hear those words," he said, his hand trailing over my sensitive skin and tearing a whine from my lips. "When I protect you and save you from everything but me, thank me."

He straightened to his full height, the shadow of his horns falling over the statue above my head. With a kick of his boot against mine, he spread my stance wider. He rubbed my burning flesh, and then his fingers trailed to my center, where he found me dripping.

The shadow of his horns dipped, telling me he was looking down at the little puddle that had formed on the stone between my legs.

"Bleeding Hells, you're fucking perfect," he said on a dark growl as his fingers slipped through my folds. Two fingers sunk inside me, and he spread them, forcing me to stretch around him.

I was shaking so much, it was a miracle my legs still held me up.

"And what do you say when I make you feel pleasure? When I fill you up, and your walls clamp around me, hoping I'll never leave? What do you say?"

"Thank you?" I groaned.

"That's my good girl," he purred, his fingers pushing deeper inside me. It felt so good, a swollen moan curled up from my throat, and I dropped my head, losing myself to the pleasure.

It felt so good, I could cry. I *was* crying.

I wanted more of him inside me. I wanted him to fuck me. I wanted him to never stop. The things I'd give to stay in this moment with him forever...to have him never leave me, to remain in the little safe space I felt whenever I was in his orbit.

"Don't stop... *please* don't stop."

"Hells," he hissed. "The things I want to do to you when you beg me like that. The things I want to give you."

While his one hand pumped into me at a pace that had me close to the edge in seconds, his other raked my raw, red ass cheek. His claw-like nails dragged marks into my flesh, and by the warmth spilling down my thigh, I was sure he'd drawn blood.

"You're the perfect mortal slut—so tight and wet and needy."

His fingers inside me were heaven, and his voice was dark as hell. Just a little longer, and I'd come....

He must have felt the flutter of my walls, the surge of heat deep within, because just when I was about to spill over the edge, he withdrew his fingers.

I whipped around, teeth bared, my cheeks hot with tears. "You can't stop there."

He laughed, the sound brutally sexy. "Actually, I can. You don't get to come yet. You're going to have to call on me again if you want that. For now, you're still worshiping *me*, remember? Now, get on your knees."

"But—"

"On your knees." He pointed at his boots. "*Now*."

My fists clenched at my sides. I thought I hated him at first, but no. What I hated was how addicted I was becoming to this demon, the way he crawled under my skin and pushed all my freaking buttons.

It was a delicious kind of contempt that pooled hot in the pit of my gut, keeping me warm and chasing away the labyrinth's bitter cold.

So, I obeyed and lowered myself to the ground at his feet.

# CHAPTER TWENTY-ONE

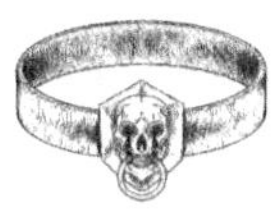

## BELIAL

BLEEDING, *WEEPING* HELLS. SHE looked so beautiful on her knees.

She liked kneeling before me. The fear she exuded was nearly tangible, with its faint sweet taste, but it was barely palpable under her arousal. As her pheromones bled into the air, assaulting my senses, my thoughts raced back to the way she looked in my bed.

Chained to my headboard. Heavy manacles around her dainty wrists. Covered in wax and cum, begging for me to take her. The thought had my cock hard in seconds, straining against my pants.

The desire to take her here, to throw her to the ground and bury myself inside her, was overwhelming. I wanted her tight, warm pussy around my cock as she came undone. I wanted to fill more than just her mouth with my seed.

I wanted to claim her and mark her as my mate, my queen, my pet. My little living treasure.

No, I couldn't—not yet.

If I took her now, I'd drag her from the maze kicking and screaming back to my castle. I'd go back on my word to give her three days to escape, and I'd spend the rest of eternity nestled between her thighs, fucking her into oblivion.

She'd hate me for it.

I couldn't bear any more hatred, not after Catherine. Besides, I had enough self-loathing for the both of us for what I was doing to her, how I was driving her into my arms with lies and deceit.

No matter what, she'd be mine. Before then, though, I need-ed to foster that little flame of desire she had for me, in the hopes I could stoke it into something more...

I tapped my fingers on the chin of my mask, drawing out her anticipation. I'd given much thought to what I wanted, spent countless hours imagining it as I waited for her to summon me.

Now that it was here, I was going to tease it out, leaving her quivering in frustration. I'd brought her to the brink of com-pletion. Once I'd fucked her mouth and left her with nothing but the taste of me at the back of her throat, would she touch herself after I was gone?

Would I stick around to watch?

My gaze dropped to her full lips as she worried the bottom one between her teeth, and my cock twitched at the thought of her tongue on me. That nearly undid me then and there.

"I've tasted you. Now, I want you to taste me," I said, tracing a finger along her jaw and rubbing my thumb across her lips, dragging her saliva with it. "I'm going to fuck your mouth, Rayven, and when I empty every last drop of cum onto that tongue..." My finger slid from her lips to playfully flick her septum piercing. "I want you to swallow every last drop of me. Understood?"

Her eyes widened at the words, and her arousal continued to spill into the air. I could feel it, smell it, *taste* it. It was hard to imagine her wetter than before, when I'd found her soaking from her spanking, but if I lifted her dress, I knew I'd find another puddle on the ground between her legs.

My cock ached with need.

My eyes dropped lower, to the collar—*my* collar—around her throat, marveling at how beautiful it looked against her pale skin.

I couldn't wait to see her naked, wearing nothing but that collar and her crown.

My beautiful slave queen.

My eyes dropped lower still, landing on the damp nightgown clinging to her flesh. It was mostly see-through and shredded now, hardly protection from the elements or my gaze, a stunning sight to behold. I loved the way the fabric molded around her nipple jewelry, how it clung to the curvature of her waist and hips.

Hells, if I could die, my little human would have been the death of me.

It would have been too easy to pull out my dick and palm it, giving it to her willingly, but I knew how bad she wanted this. It might have been a price to pay, but she was eager to fulfill her end of our agreement. There was no hiding it.

If she'd begged for it before, I knew she'd beg for it again, especially if I told her to.

"I want you to beg for it, little human," I growled, my fingers drumming against the laces of my pants.

Her dark eyes burned with curiosity. I wasn't a small male. Oh no, I had one of the biggest cocks in all the nine layers.

I could already imagine the warmth of her mouth, her tongue swirling around me. Would she be able to fit it all?

My dark thoughts turned pitch black; I'd make her fit it all.

How ironic would it be for me to have saved her from the quicksand, only for her to suffocate on my cock?

"Let me hear how badly you want me in your mouth." I was torturing myself by prolonging it, but I was torturing her in return, so I'd suffer willingly.

"Belial," she said softly, my name in her mouth heightening the desire thrumming through me, making my cock hard as my statue behind her. "Please, let me suck your cock. Let me repay you for your help."

Her desperate litany nearly brought me to my knees.

"That's a good girl," I growled out. "Take it out."

She looked up at me hesitantly for a beat, and I nodded to the bulge in my pants. If she wanted it, she'd have to work for it. Understanding registered in her gaze a second later, and she reached for the laces, loosening them and dragging the material down until my cock bobbed free.

I could almost come from her expression alone.

Her eyes widened, her dark lashes fluttering as she found herself face-to-face with what was likely the biggest cock she'd ever seen. It was long and thick, with a complex network of veins wrapping around the shaft.

Then, there was the jewelry.

A silver cuff encircled the base, with a dainty chain connecting it to the prince albert piercing at the tip of my dick.

Her plush lips parted on a winded "*oooh*," and I couldn't fight a confident smirk.

"What do you think?" I asked, cocking an eyebrow she couldn't see.

She nodded, her tongue poking out to run along her top lip. "I think...I think it's the most intense cock I've ever seen. If you had an internet connection down here, you could have a popping Only Fans account."

I barely knew what she was talking about, but it was cute the way she blathered when she was nervous.

I reached up, my thumb grazing her bottom lip. "Do you like it?"

Her mouth softened under my touch. "I like it."

Satisfaction wound through me, and I nodded in approval. "Good. Show me how much you like it."

Her slender fingers wrapped around my shaft, unable to circle it completely as she experimentally pumped her hand up and down. I sucked in a breath at the way the chain tugged on the piercing.

It hurt, and the pain by her hand was fucking delicious.

Her motions were slow and deliberate, her eyes staring up at me as she gauged my reaction. My breaths were raspy, and the heat from her hand quickly spread through me, making my cool skin flush with warmth.

Then she ran her tongue along the slit, lapping up the beads of pre-cum. "You taste so good," she said, humming as she took my head into her mouth.

"Fuck," I groaned. My fingers twisted into her raven hair, and I tilted my hips forward to urge her on. "Take more of me. You can do it."

She worked another few inches inside her mouth, but the ring of her lips were still too far away from the silver cuff adorning my base. I wanted to watch it disappear inside her.

My fingers tightened in her dark locks, and with a savage punch of my hips, I sank my entire length inside.

Her eyes bulged. She sputtered and thrashed, her throat spasming around my cock. Her hands came up to claw at my hips, but I held her head steady as I fucked her throat with reckless abandon.

I drew in a shaky breath, pulling her off my shaft—just long enough for her to fling a curse at me—and driving her back down.

My cock jerked as my cuff disappeared completely inside her. Fuck, she fit all of me. No woman had ever fit me down their throat.

I was going to have so much fun seeing how well her other holes swallowed me.

My pace was relentless, but I couldn't help myself. That dark part of me had come undone, lost to how amazing she felt wrapped around my dick. It took everything in me not to shift and claim her in my true form here and now.

*Not yet.* She couldn't know yet.

Frustration and lust fueled me. Her eyes watered, and I felt the muscles in her throat flex as she gagged.

"Your mouth feels fucking incredible, little human."

I was starting to wonder if she was enjoying this, if maybe I was going a little too hard, when she reached up and cupped my balls. She wasn't gentle. Why would she be when I didn't give her the same courtesy? She squeezed them, her nails scouring my flesh.

The sensation had every muscle in my body tightening, screaming for release.

"Fucking Hells!" I snarled, my voice husky and broken and barely my own. Slamming her down on me until her lips were flush with my pelvis, I held her there until I was pumping hot cum down her throat.

Withdrawing, I left a thick rope of cum from her throat to her lips. It spilled down her chin and dribbled onto her chest.

I was about to tell her to open for me, but she did it anyway, opening her mouth to show me the mess I'd made.

"You're learning to be such a good girl for me," I praised her, my half-hard cock twitching at the sight of her tongue—rubbed raw from the chain—covered in my cum. "Now make your god happy and swallow."

The pleasure on her face had me fully erect again. She loved it when I referred to myself as her god.

If only she knew it wasn't just dirty talk—that I was truly her god.

Her throat flexed against the collar as she swallowed, and she held my gaze as she leaned forward and licked up the last drop of cum clinging to my cock piercing.

*Blood and Darkness.* If I hadn't wanted to leave her side before, I definitely didn't want to walk away from her now.

I wanted to stay and enjoy the rest of her body. I wanted to fill the rest of her holes with every bit of me, and I nearly conceded when she licked her lips again, stirring a warmth in my gut that threatened to sear straight through me.

Reluctantly, I tucked my spent cock back into my pants, tightening the laces. Before I made a very stupid mistake, I turned on my heel to take my leave.

"Wait!"

She lunged to her feet and caught my arm.

Snarling, I whipped around. "We're done here. I've given you what you asked for, and you've paid your debt."

"I need something else. Better clothes." She gestured to her tattered nightgown that left much of her body exposed. "I'm cold at night, and the heads in the brambles, they ogle me."

I snickered. "Let them look. It's not like they can touch you. As for keeping warm at night, you still have the dagger. Call me, and you can wear me as a blanket."

With that, I turned and walked away.

I didn't plan on giving her a single thing more until she summoned me again, but there was something about her desperate pleas that pulled the strings of a heart I hadn't known I had.

"When you get to the Styx, go against the current," I said without turning around. Following it would take her in the right direction, toward the end of the maze, but she'd never be able to find it. "Stay far away from the water. Your soul won't be able to escape once it enters the river."

"Thank you," she said softly, her appreciation weighing in her voice. "Next time, if I need help, I'll call you."

A smile bowed my scarred lips beneath my mask as I rounded a hedge. There was no *if*; it was just a matter of when. The dark plan unfurling in my mind ensured she'd need me sooner rather than later, and when she called, I would drive her right back into my bed.

Next time, my services wouldn't come so cheaply.

# CHAPTER TWENTY-TWO

## BELIAL

One of the perks of being a demon lord was the severe lack of a moral compass.

The first layer of Hell was my realm, Limbo, purgatory, the space where souls remained until I decided where they deserved to spend eternity. I made the rules, defined the difference between what was right and what was unjust.

At the end of the day, though, it didn't matter. I was the king of this realm. My whim was law. I'd never worried about being "evil" because my brothers had always been far worse than me.

Until now.

Until *her*.

What had started out as punishment for what she did to Catherine's remains had morphed into something else entirely, something dark and volatile and dangerously addictive.

My obsession with her was turning into something so much more than what I'd held for Catherine.

I wanted her body *and* her soul. As the King of Limbo, I could have those things if she was dead. They'd become mine by right. Alas... I wanted her alive and breathing, with her beating heart and her flush lips, her flesh raw, red and bloody from my abuse, her lips swollen from my kisses, and not from putrefaction.

To pull that off, I'd have to lie and manipulate and seduce. I'd have to stoop to the lowest levels of depravity, the kind of sin I'd condemned so many other souls for, the ones I'd sent to my most vile brothers for punishment.

I was a fucking hypocrite, but I wanted Rayven to the point where I couldn't even bother to care. That was the kind of drug she was. I'd do damn near anything to get another hit of her—*anything* to have her coursing through my system.

She'd never accept me without the games, without the lies. No, she'd see my scars, the ones on my skin and the ones on my cold, dead heart. She'd see me for what I was. A beast, a monster, inside and out.

So, if the only way I could claim all of her with her heart still beating was through my illusions, my honied half-truths, and my huge cock, then so fucking be it.

I'd play the part of the devil if that's what it took to make her mine.

I should have left the labyrinth. Instead, I lingered, invisible, watching Rayven invisibly from the shadows.

Now that I'd given her a tip on where to find the exit, I expected her to get up and hurry to find the river as I'd instructed. Only, she didn't move—She stared at the spot where she'd last seen me, as if she couldn't believe what had just happened. Her fingers touched her lips, probably recalling what it had felt like to have them wrapped around my shaft.

After a beat, she walked to a headstone and sat down, her back resting against it. Her legs were bent at the knee and spread out, her feet planted firmly on the grave. With a quick look around the graveyard to make sure she was alone, she hiked up her dress and slipped her hand between her thighs.

Every muscle in my body wound tight as I watched her touch herself. I had left my little mortal pet unsatisfied.

I'd hoped she'd put on a show for me, though I hadn't actually thought she'd do it, not when there were so many horrors lurking in my labyrinth who could take her. Not that I'd let them, but she didn't know that.

Her desire must have smothered her fear, because there she was, spread wide for me, her fingers working over her clit atop some unknown demon's grave. I guess she was too worked up to care what kind of monsters could crawl out of the shadows and fuck her. Maybe it was that dark thought that had her stroking her little bud, the sexiest fucking sounds spilling from her lips as her head fell back onto the headstone.

I strode closer, careful to keep up the spell that silenced my footsteps.

When I was just a few feet away from her, I crouched down so I could get a good look at her core. *Fuck.* She looked so beautiful slumped against my old reaper's grave, her face contorted with pleasure as her fingers pumped in and out of her pussy. She was so wet and pink and *perfect.*

My mind went to that dark place for a moment, imagining how she might react if I threw her down, spread her legs open, and plunged myself into her while the invisibility spell was up. The thought made my cock twitch, but I dismissed it a second later. I wouldn't give into the temptation, but there was a wicked little voice in the back of my mind telling me she'd love every fucking second of it if I did.

"Belial," she moaned, her voice husky with need.

My name in her mouth shattered something inside me and monstrous urges clawed at my insides. I wanted her so badly it scared me, and *nothing* fucking scared me.

I'd been numb for so long, just a ghost of the demon I once was. Now, this mortal female lit a flame inside me. It burned so hot, it threatened to burn me and my entire world down, and I didn't even care, as long as I rose from the ashes with her in my arms and her heart still beating.

Gnashing my teeth, I pulled out my cock, already rock hard again, my eyes locked on my little human as she fucked herself at a feverish pace. Every sigh and moan had me racing toward the edge of an orgasm as I pretended it was her I was pumping into instead of my hand. I stroked my flesh until I came, my seed as thick and vicious as my obsession for her.

"I want you inside me, Belial," she whispered to herself as she came, my name on her tongue chased with the sweetest moan as she writhed then slumped against the headstone. "I want you..."

I fell deathly still, my chest heaving in tandem with hers as I stared at her with a thunderstruck expression.

She wouldn't want me if she knew the truth.

Soon, she would. I'd reveal myself to her at the All-Hallows' Eve ball my brother had cornered me into throwing. Then, she'd see the monster beneath the mask. It wouldn't matter if she wanted me at that point. By then it would be too late. By then, I'd own every piece of her.

I watched silently as she bathed in the afterglow for a few more minutes, memorizing every detail of her as though I hadn't already. Her mussed hair, her blushed cheeks, the way her shredded dress barely provided any modesty. It didn't matter how much time I spent watching her, it was never enough, and when she finally got to her feet and chose to follow one of the pathways leading from the graveyard, I followed.

There were a hundred other things I could do, like pass Judgement. The queue was backed up at least a century, and my brothers would throw a fit if they saw just how many souls languished around my castle. Or, I could help Cecil catalog souls I'd already judged and decided to keep for my own collection in eternal rest. I could visit my reapers out in the field, see to the graves of the freshly passed, collect the bones of the truly wicked.

Instead, I stalked Rayven through the labyrinth, watching, waiting for her to take my silver to her flesh and summon me.

She didn't want my help, and that only heightened my curiosity. It made me want her to need me even more.

I knew little of her past. If she was dead, I would have known everything about her, her entire life, everything she'd experienced in the palm of my hand. While her heart still beat, though, her past would remain a mystery unless she told me herself.

She'd experienced loss. She knew death. She had the stench of it on her skin, more than what came from raiding graves. Did she have a family to go home to? Had that pathetic mate of hers been her only connection? I wanted to know, wanted to hear it all from her lips so I could better understand my pet, but there was something I wanted more than knowledge.

I wanted her to call for me, to admit she needed my help, and it infuriated me after a few hours when she still refused to do so.

I'd make her see. If she wouldn't call for me on her own, I'd *make* her need me.

Reluctantly, I pulled myself away, my plan to have her begging for my help unfurling in my mind.

I teleported to one of the deepest corners of my labyrinth—a cave nearly forgotten by time. A bone-deep chill wafted from the cave's mouth, the faintest breeze coming from within stirring the silver draping my horns.

How long had it been since I'd visited this place? I couldn't recall. It was buried so deep within my psyche, time had eroded the memory.

It had been eons since I did my own field work anyway. Most tasks I delegated to my reapers and other, lesser demons, even though none of them dared come here.

This was where I kept the most ancient, corrupted of souls, only to be released for the most insidious purposes. These were creatures that belonged in the deepest, darkest pits of Hell, but I kept them here just in case.

Stepping into the ice-cold cave, my gaze swept around to the various cages of rusted iron. Each one contained a nightmare incarnate, a beast made of bone and pure evil. All I had to do was give the word, and they would tear every shred of flesh from Rayven's bones. If a carnivorous tree didn't terrify her enough to make her call for me, one of these ancient horrors would surely do the trick.

I approached the cage at the back of the cave, my hand trailing over the cell bars as I peered into the darkness. "Answer the call of your king, lost soul. I have a task for you. Do this and I'll release you from your prison."

Something stirred in the shadows and a moment later it slithered into the limited light, obeying my call. A low growl resonated from the creature, and it dipped its angular skull in obedience.

The blood oak was a vicious predator, but nothing compared to this ancient monster. It could move freely through the maze.

It could hunt her. It could chase her, and she wouldn't be able to outrun it.

She'd have no choice but to call and beg me for help.

I'd be watching, waiting, ready to swoop in and save her.

For a price.

# CHAPTER TWENTY-THREE

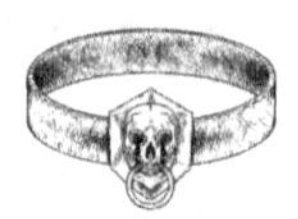

## RAYVEN

*I KNEW HE'D BEEN there, watching me touch myself.*

He'd thought he was being sneaky, but I'd seen the moss on the ground compress under his weight, the faintest outline of his large boots giving him away.

The bastard had left me hanging. He'd gotten to come, and I hadn't—not that I hadn't thoroughly enjoyed his "punishment." I'd been spanked before, but not like that. Mark and the boyfriends before him had given me a couple of light swats during sex.

Belial had violated my flesh, leaving it red and stinging, but the burn had only pushed the pleasure higher. His fingers inside me had been the perfect chaser to the pain. I wanted to tease him for giving me blue balls—or whatever the female equivalent was.

I'd thought he might try to touch me while he was invisible, but he hadn't. Of course not. He got off on hearing me beg.

So I'd come quickly, knowing he was watching, his name on my lips and his marks on my skin. And I'd humored myself with thoughts of his flustered expression as I gathered myself and wandered around until I found the Styx, following it as he suggested.

It was easy to tell which way the river flowed by the bobbing corpses jostling in the current. Following his instructions gave me hope, like I was truly getting somewhere for the first time, like I knew what I was doing.

He didn't have to give me that tip. *But he had…*

At the thought of Belial, my stomach fluttered, and heat scorched my cheeks.

Fuck. I couldn't get that asshole out of my head. He had a way of invading my senses. I needed to keep my mind focused on escape, not cock, but my thoughts kept gravitating toward the latter.

I knew falling for a demon was a terrible idea—probably the worst thing I could do if I was trying to escape purgatory—but I couldn't help it. Something about him was so mystifying. *So goddamn sexy.*

He was cruel but kind, rough yet soft. There was something about him that was forbidden, off limits. I loved breaking rules, and venturing places I didn't belong. It was part of the reason why I raided graves.

Death's ferryman was everything I wanted, and everything I shouldn't have.

Maybe I really was losing my mind in the labyrinth. Why else would thoughts of a demon ferryman turn my knees to jello and kickstart a heartbeat between my thighs?

If I knew what was good for me, I'd stop daydreaming about him. Stop letting our moments together occupy my thoughts and stop wanting to repeat every one of them.

Then again, I wasn't known for making the best decisions in life.

After a while, the ground beneath my feet transformed. The rain-soaked soil was replaced by drier, rockier terrain. Jagged rocks crunched beneath my boots, and the body parts stuck in the brambles were twisted and gnarled with unnatural bones protruding from them.

Torsos with jagged spikes growing out of their chests, heads with extra teeth and bones. Hands with extra fingers, feet with extra toes. They all looked older, more withered, skin peeling and falling off.

Goosebumps crawled over my skin when I realized the whispers had died, no longer a steady ballad drifting around me. Everything was eerily quiet, like the souls trapped in this part of the maze had been here too long, were too tired to bother talking anymore. That, or they couldn't.

My movements felt too loud, every footstep crunching and disturbing the eerie silence. My gut told me I shouldn't be here, that I should turn back, but I refused to follow that instinct.

There was nowhere to go back to, except maybe the castle. Fuck that shit.

I made a right around a corner and found myself on a long, straight path. It seemed to stretch on forever, the longest path I'd seen in the maze so far. My heart leapt into my throat—Did this mean I was getting close to the exit?

It felt dangerous to get my hopes up.

Before I could keep going, a rustling sound made me freeze, icy fear prickling over my skin, making my hair stand on end. That was new. It didn't sound like the hedges shifting or re-growing, a noise I'd committed to memory over the countless hours I'd been trapped.

I swallowed hard, my heart galloping against my ribs as my insides knotted.

"Belial?" I said, afraid to call out. What if it was the Lord of Bones lurking nearby? It wasn't time for him to come again; it hadn't been a day since he marked me last.

*What if it was something else?*

My breath stuttered, and I took a few shaky steps, treading as quietly as possible. The fear had my blood pounding in my ears. After a minute, I started to think maybe I'd imagined it. The solitude and the lack of noise were making me hear things.

Then, I heard it again: a sickening slither. *Oh shit.* Something large was dragging itself along the ground, crunching against the rocks.

I gasped, every muscle in my body tensing as I swiveled my head around, looking for the source of the noise. Up ahead, the brambles shifted, cutting off the long, straight pathway and opening to reveal a new path to the right. My heart bottomed out, and it took every shred of willpower I had to keep walking.

One step after another, I headed for the new path, unaware if I was moving toward or away from the noise. When I reached the new opening, I cautiously peered around the corner, a shaky exhale releasing when I saw the path was empty—aside from the ancient souls caught in the bramble.

I should have found solace in the fact that I was alone, but my chest was still tight with anticipation.

Where the fuck was the noise coming from? What kind of monster was making it? Could anything be worse than the blood oak? My imagination went wild with the kind of horrors that could be wandering the maze, wanting to eat me.

I slipped around the corner, making my way down the next path as quietly as possible, cursing my haggard breath for being so loud. Every move I made, every breath I took, felt like a smoke signal to whatever was creeping through the maze, a beacon that would draw it straight to me.

Other than my breathing, I was managing to stay quiet...until my boot came down on a twig, its snap scaring me so badly, I squeaked.

The noise that followed shook me to my core. It was a demonic hiss, like air escaping ancient lungs after being trapped for hundreds of years, followed by an unholy growl. My stomach somersaulted as my heart lurched, beating so hard I could feel it in my ears. I looked in every direction, trying to find the source.

There was no sign of it, but it was close.

I was terrified to move, afraid I would step around a corner and find the elusive beast lying in wait. Still, it would eventually find me if I stayed rooted to the spot. I needed to put distance between me and whatever it was, the quicker the better.

I took a right and then a left, praying to whatever god would listen that I wasn't going in circles.

Maybe the only god to hear me was the one of this realm, because just then, I rounded the wrong corner and saw it. A serpentine monster, at least fifteen–maybe even twenty–feet long, made entirely of bones.

It had a wide, angular head connected to a chain of enormous vertebrae, but they were spiked, with growth-like ridges shooting out at odd angles. It slithered, curling its way along the ground, its eye sockets filled with red flames. Suddenly, its head whipped in my direction, and it snapped its jaws full of razor-sharp teeth as it hissed, the sound hellishly unnatural.

Fuck. This was bad.

By the time I registered the need to run, the serpentine bone monster had sped up, whipping in my direction. I stumbled over my feet, turning around and sprinting in the opposite direction, praying I was fast enough to outrun it.

I wasn't.

The sound of it slithering along behind me, hissing and snapping its jaws as it drew nearer, rang out into the air and made my heart skip a painful beat.

I needed a plan, because I certainly couldn't kill it in a straight fight. I doubted that creatures down here could die, since pretty much everything was already dead.

I couldn't climb under the hedges. The roots were too thick, the brambles too dense, the body parts caught up in their thorns too numerous to slip through, and finding the exit seemed less likely than me taking the serpent on in a fist fight and winning.

I banked left, my feet beating hard against the ground and my arms pumping furiously at my sides. I was more grateful than ever for my boots—I wouldn't be able to run nearly this fast without them.

Precious seconds ticked by, the monster's sounds drawing closer. I chanced a glance over my shoulder to see the beast gaining on me; a few more yards, and it would catch up.

It had no digestive system to swallow me. Would its teeth rip me to shreds, leaving the Lord of Bones to piece me back together with his magic?

A scream was brewing in my chest, but I swallowed it down. What good would it do? No one but the trapped souls could hear me, and they were useless.

Another right, and I found my path blocked by the River Styx. There was a section of wall on the other side, creating a ledge that stretched several feet over the river. Hope lifted in my heart as I realized there had to be something above that wall, a higher level of the labyrinth maybe.

As soon as my heart soared with hope, it plummeted again as reality set in. I couldn't swim across, and I couldn't turn back. Any chance of escape existed in this singular path, and my odds were looking slimmer by the second.

As the ground between me and the Styx quickly disappeared, my thoughts spun. If I jumped, would I come close to clearing the river at all? It wasn't very wide, but it seemed too risky. If I touched the water, my soul would never leave.

Maybe I could somehow climb across the bramble-covered ledge jutting out over the water. I'd climbed things before—wrought iron fences and rope ladders—so it wasn't anything new to me.

It wasn't a great plan, but I hadn't come this far and fought this hard to die now.

I was so focused on my plan, I failed to notice the shift behind me, the subtle crescendo of noise as the monster closed the distance between us, until it was too late. Something slammed into my back, sending me flying. I skidded across the ground, rocks, sticks, and a thorn or two ripping the front of my dress a white-hot pain seared across my skin.

"Fuck," I gritted out, rolling onto my back as the serpent monster reared up. I only had a second to prepare for its attack, tensing as the giant skeleton lunged at me with gaping jowls.

Thinking fast, I grabbed a handful of dirt and gravel and tossed it into the creature's eye sockets. The flames were extinguished for a moment, and sputtering, trying to flicker back to life. The snake roared in rage, its head lashing back and forth. While it was blinded, I scrambled to my feet in a blink.

Before I had time to get away, the snake's flames fired back to life. It lunged, and I leapt back to dodge its lethal teeth as they snapped at me. I slammed into a hedge, the impact leaving me gasping, the bramble and thorns tearing at my skin and catching on the nightgown.

"Fuck," I hissed at the pain, struggling to regain my footing. I pulled myself out of the hedge, leaving shreds of fabric behind, and dove out of the way as the monster lunged again.

I was almost fast enough, but one of its teeth snagged on my forearm, tearing through the skin before its head slammed into the maze wall. A stream of blood spilled down toward my wrist, dripping off my fingers. A quick glance down had nausea turning my stomach.

I hadn't bled this badly in a while, and I couldn't gauge how deep the cut was, nor did I have time to. I leaped over the monster's body as it fought to dislodge itself from the bramble. I ran for the river, my legs moving as fast as they could.

The snake monster shifted, roaring behind me, and my heart crashed against my ribs. There were only a few feet between me and the river now, and I was running too fast to slow down in time. I'd have to attempt to climb my way along the hedge to cross the river. It was my only option.

My feet left the ground, and I was airborne for a brief moment, the crimson Styx flowing beneath me. I caught my breath, time seeming to slow to a crawl. Then, it sped up again and I slammed into the bramble, grabbing desperately at the knotted branches as pain exploded over every inch of my body.

I cried out, clinging to the hedge as the thorns stabbed into my flesh, the pain so intense, my nerves shorted out for a moment. I had to hold on; getting stabbed a thousand times over was still better than disappearing into the corpse-logged water below with no hope of escape. Still better than getting mauled by a bone monster.

I attempted to climb, reaching for another branch as my grip began to slip. My fingers were numb with pain, my arms already growing weak. I wasn't going to make it...

Suddenly, hands pushed out of the bramble, gripping me by my arms and legs. I started to scream, flashbacks of the oubliette rushing at me as fast as the current blow.

Then, it hit me, the severed limbs weren't greedily groping at my exposed flesh. No, they were holding me up. *They were saving me.*

I looked to the side to see a head inches from me, instructing the limbs to keep me steady.

"You're helping me?" I pushed out, my voice rife with both relief and disbelief.

"You're the Lord's queen-to-be. He wouldn't want you to slip into the Styx where you might drift to devil lords far worse than him."

I didn't have time to dwell on his words before the serpent lunged, its movement flashing in the corner of my eye, and I screamed again. The limbs started passing me down the line of outstretched hands, all pushing out from the long hedge, and the snake's fangs narrowly missed my skin. They snagged on the nightgown, ripping half of it from my body as it fell toward the river below.

The water rippled, jostling the decaying body parts where the snake had disappeared underwater. I expected to see it swimming upstream toward me, or even slithering out of the river to try again. What I saw instead had my mouth falling open.

The floating corpses I'd assumed were mindless and unresponsive had come to life, grabbing for the monster as it attempted to reemerge. It hissed and growled as hands clamped down on every inch of it, dragging it beneath the surface.

It didn't reappear.

I choked on a sob, overcome with relief at escaping the beast, every inch of my body screaming in pain as the adrenaline began to subside.

I'd survived, just barely.

The limbs passed me up over the ledge to a higher level of the labyrinth, allowing me to see all the ground I'd covered.

"You're halfway through," one of the helpful heads told me.

Unlike times before, I believed this one.

I dropped to my knees, overcome with exhaustion and a myriad of emotions. I was bleeding everywhere, tiny cuts decorating my skin like morbid confetti. The gash in my forearm, the arm opposite from the mark the Lord of Bones had given me, had stopped bleeding. It wasn't very deep, but seeing it still made my stomach turn.

*Fuck.*

I was hurt even more than before. I needed a bath. A good meal. Bandages. Company. Nothing that I would find out here in the maze. Not without Belial's help.

I seemed to be heading in the right direction. Maybe I could make it out of here after all.

But that meant I wouldn't get to see him again.

As eager as I was to get the hell out of this place, I wasn't ready to say goodbye. Maybe one night with him wouldn't hurt.

I reached for the dagger earring dangling from my earlobe, thoughts full of all the things I needed right now, thoughts of Belial bringing them to me, making me pay again. Then a branch crunched behind me, the sound of a very large piece of wood cracking under a *very* heavy boot.

My eyes shot upward and my stomach dropped when I registered the hue of the sky. Crimson red. It was nightfall—the end of the second day.

I lifted my wrist to see the mark the Lord of Bones had carved into my skin at the end of day one.

"You look so beautiful, drenched in blood." That deep, gravelly voice rumbled, making the hairs on the back of my neck stand. "Are you ready for my second mark?"

# CHAPTER TWENTY-FOUR

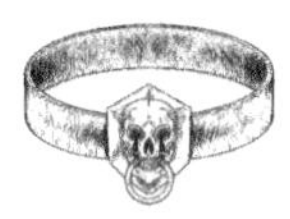

## RAYVEN

I slowly pivoted on my feet to see the Lord of Bones standing at the end of the path, his worn cloak swaying gently around his ankles in the breeze.

I should have been cold, standing there in nothing but rags, but the blue flames in the monster's eyes burned me up from the outside, while molten anger consumed me from within.

The last time I'd seen him, I'd been scared shitless. Now, after everything I'd been through, I'd had enough of being scared. Now, fury ran hot inside me, burning away everything else.

My fists clenched at my sides, and my upper lip peeled in a snarl. "Oh, good. It's the Lord of Assholes."

The King of Limbo looked particularly terrifying today. He was so tall, his animal skull head rising over the hedges. He wore no shirt, exposing the same black and white necros pattern I'd seen in my dream. A single pauldron—which looked to be an entire silver ribcage—sat on his shoulder, held in place by a leather belt strapped across his chest.

The moon was starting to come out; at least, I thought it was the moon. It was a bright red crescent, perfectly framed in the cradle of his curved horns.

A crimson halo for the angel of death.

"It's good to hear you mouthing off, little thief. It means you have more fight in you."

"Don't you want me to give up? Isn't that what you're doing?" My jaw hardened and I perched my hands on my hips. "Trying to wear me down so I give in?"

"No." His tone came out hard and so deep it was almost a perpetual growl. "I'm enjoying watching you try your very hardest."

I swallowed thickly, hating how his voice so easily worked its way inside me. "Because you get off on my suffering."

"Because I get off on making you *feel*, Rayven."

My name in his mouth took me by surprise. It was the first time I'd heard him say it. I didn't remember actually telling him my name. Maybe Holga told him, or even Belial. Even though the masked demon was helping me, I couldn't let myself forget that he worked for the Lord.

"What do you mean, make me feel? All I've felt is pain and suffering in your stupid labyrinth."

He took a step forward, his demeanor radiating power and violence. "But that isn't true, is it? You've felt so much more than pain."

Another step. The closer he came, the more palpable his aura was. It slid over my skin, making me hot and cold all at once.

A fist-sized lump swelled in my throat as I gaped at the monster, a confusing maelstrom of emotions whirling inside me.

*He knew I was messing around with Belial.* Had more than just his likeness watched us in the graveyard? Had he really been there, hiding amongst the shadows?

My stomach churned. "So you *have* been spying on me."

"Spying? No. The king doesn't spy on his own property." The Lord of Bones' voice was sharp, but it softened as he continued. "I've been admiring you. Studying you so closely, that I've seen every shiver that's rattled down your spine, every hair on your nape that's raised in fear. Every cut. Every bruise."

One last stride and he closed the distance between us. I held my ground, glaring up at him as his fingers ghosted down my sternum.

"Every bead of blood that's oozed down your flesh," he continued, his deep timbre turning dark and primal. "Every pearl of cum."

The blood drained from my face all at once, leaving me a little light-headed. He definitely knew about Belial.

"Don't hurt him," I blurted out.

The Lord of Bones seemed to falter, taken aback by my request. "You care for him?"

"Why wouldn't I care about someone who's trying to help me? I don't know what you did to Holga, but she tried to help Catherine, didn't she? She cared about her, and now she can barely stand to speak her name. Whatever you did to her, don't do it to Belial."

A low growl rumbled in the monster's chest. "You should be more worried about what I'm going to do with you when my crown is on your head."

I craned my neck, my mouth going dry at the way he loomed over me, the blood moon suspended ominously between his horns. "What are you going to do to me?"

It was a dangerous question, but one that had all my insides heating.

The monster brushed the back of his knuckles over my cheek. His touch was so soft and reverent—it didn't make sense. This wasn't the cruel monster who had shucked out Mark's spine a few days ago.

It was an act. It had to be. He was trying to get into my head.

His hand smoothed over the dip in my waist, gently pulling me closer until my chest was flush with his abdominal muscles.

Fuck. *And it was working.*

"I'm going to do what I love doing most to you," he said, peering down at me with those flickering flames that burned me up. "I'm going to make you feel..."

His other hand curved over my ass, bringing me snug against him so my exposed flesh pressed flush against his.

His meaning was clear. He was going to make me feel him. *All* of him.

As a loner goth girl who never really had much of a connection with humans, I'd always loved movie monsters and monster romance books, anything dark and gothic and strange. You'd think I'd be jumping at the chance to be the queen of the dead.

This creature, however, was evil, mean. He wanted to hurt me and draw pleasure from my pain.

I shouldn't have wanted that.

The prospect of wanting to be this brutal male's queen in any capacity was way scarier than a carnivorous tree or giant snake monster.

I thrashed as hard as I could in his grip, and he was holding me so gently, I managed to squirm loose. His claws snagged in my dress, and it was so torn, it shredded right off my body. I turned, sprinting away as fast as I could in nothing but my boots.

Behind me, the Lord of Bones' footsteps charged after me as his laugh filled the air. "Go ahead, run. Scurry through my maze like the little mouse you are. Once I catch you, and I will catch you, I'm marking you."

*He was going to cut me again.*

My boots slapped hard against the stone path, falling in sync with my heart as it crashed against my ribcage.

"I've watched you shiver in terror, Rayven," he called out from behind me. "I've watched your body be tattered and torn, your muscles trembling from exhaustion, yet your spirit has grown all the stronger. Your soul is one of the purest I've ever seen, and I will own it."

The faster I ran, the louder his voice became, and it boomed from all around. There was no outrunning the god of this realm.

No sooner had the last thought left my mind, a flash of blue exploded in front of me. A magical doorway opened, revealing the Lord of Bones. I crashed right into him, and he captured my wrist, stretching my arm so high over my head, my toes barely touched the ground.

"Let me go!"

"You will endure me, my beautiful little Rayven." The monster's voice was deep and silken, like smoke and black velvet. "And in time, you shall come to love me."

"Just like Catherine came to love you?" I spat, my voice full of venom.

His fingers tightened around my wrist, squeezing a pained moan from my lips.

"You are nothing like Catherine. She was a fool's hope, a spark of something that never took flame. My lust for life and nothing more." He pulled my wrist closer, though his gaze never left mine. "You are so much more. You will be my mate, my queen. You will know my body as she never did, my love as she never would."

"Why me?" I sobbed, hot tears burning the corners of my eyes.

"When I felt you enter Catherine's tomb, I thought you were nothing but a rat in need of extermination, but in that dusty, old crypt, it was treasure I found."

Treasure. No one in my whole life had ever referred to me as their treasure.

Tears of anger turned into tears of confusion.

Why was he doing this? Why was he making me feel these things? Things I didn't want to feel, things I didn't want to like.

It was just another mind game, another layer to the torture. It had to be.

"Fuck you," I snarled, my tone barely more than a whisper as hot tears rolled down my cheeks.

He held a single claw to my cheek to catch one of my tears, holding it up to examine the salty drop before popping it into his mouth.

Humming in approval at the taste, he chuckled. "You will, my treasure. You will."

He brought the same claw to my outstretched wrist and began to carve a second line to join the first. Hot pain seared up my arm, drawing out a whimper. "You have one more day, my treasure. Try not to exert yourself too much. Tomorrow at midnight, when your time is up, it will be All Hallows' Eve. We'll have many guests. I will greet them all from my throne, and you will be right there with me, sitting so pretty in my lap with my crown on your head."

He stooped, his long black tongue sliding up my inner arm to lap up the blood he'd spilled. Then, he let me go, and I dropped to my knees, staring down at the newest mark adorning my skin.

When I looked up again, he was gone. The only thing I could see was the blood red moon glowing through wisps of clouds overhead, a glaring reminder of the limited time I had left.

Tomorrow night, when the same crimson crescent appeared, my time would run out.

I would officially belong to the Lord of Bones forever.

# CHAPTER TWENTY-FIVE

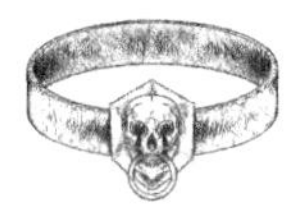

## RAYVEN

I STAYED ON MY knees, right where the Lord of Bones left me, for what felt like an eternity, Belial's dagger earring pinched between my trembling fingers. The adrenaline might have been fading, but I was still in shock, my mind a blur as I tried to process everything.

I needed the masked demon.

It was selfish. I didn't know what the Lord of Bones was going to do now. I was sure he knew Belial was helping me. Would he punish him? Demote him? End his soul like he had those in the dungeon?

I didn't want to care. He was supposed to be my ticket out of here. When in the last couple of days had he become something more?

Something to take the pain away, to make me forget my reality?

I held the blade to my wrist—the opposite one from where the Lord of Bones had cut—but I hesitated for what had to be the dozenth time.

How could I call on him when I wasn't even sure what I needed? The boots had been straightforward, a simple enough request. What I needed now was so much more. I was exhausted, battered, and mentally drained. I needed something to make it all go away.

I needed a bed and strong arms to hold me close. Maybe a stiff drink and more clothes since I had no intention of wandering around the labyrinth on the final day in the buff, as much as Belial would love that.

I needed to feel safe, and I knew seeing Belial would bring me a whisper of comfort and security.

The fact that he was the first thing that came to mind should have scared me, but as I finally dragged the dagger over my skin, soaking the blade in my blood, I realized I didn't care.

There was a flash of blue light, and a moment later, the scent of strawberries and pine permeated the air.

"Rayven," Belial called behind me.

My heart clenched at the concern in his voice.

I looked over my shoulder and saw him hurrying over to kneel beside me. His eyes roved over my exposed skin, assessing the damage.

"Did you get in a fight with a hedge and lose?"

He was joking, probably to lift the mood, but my cheeks instantly flushed with anger. "Are you fucking kidding me? I got chased by a giant snake monster that *you* failed to tell me was in the maze. I could have died."

He was silent for a moment, running his gloved thumb over one of my scratches so the blood smeared across my pale skin. He looked amused, like he'd enjoy using my blood as watercolor paint and creating a masterpiece all over my body.

"But did you?" he asked, his voice kicking up an octave.

I stared daggers through his face.

*The fucking psychopath.* I hated how happy I was to see him.

"I'm sorry," the demon added after registering the irritation in my expression. "But you should have called me. I could have helped—though according to the souls in the hedges, you managed on your own. Apparently, you're quite the badass."

My eyes narrowed on him. "Next time, you could at least warn me, asshole."

He chuckled. "To be fair, I didn't know it had awakened. It's been asleep for so long. It was wise to lure him into the water. He'll be ushered to the next layer of hell, unless the Lord of Bones decides to keep it."

"Would he actually save it?" My eyes widened at the thought of the beast returning.

He paused, the trace of a frown showing through the mouth of his mask. "I doubt it. The Lord doesn't save many."

A beat of silence fell between us, and I became hyper-aware of his hands on me. He was taking his time assessing my wounds, drawing his fingers through my blood, as though it intrigued him. Then again, it probably did; most of the company he kept were probably dead people—souls.

There was no telling how long it had been since he'd seen something bleed.

His touch didn't take the pain away, but it was enough of a drug that I temporarily forgot about it. I shoved everything weighing on me to the back of my mind and focused on Belial.

"Why did you call me?" the demon asked, the softness in his words making my eyes flick up to lock with his. "Because you've proven that you don't really *need* my help."

My chest tightened under his scrutiny. "You're right, I don't need your help. Ever since my dad passed away, and my mom kicked me out of the house at eighteen, I haven't needed anyone. I'm not used to people helping me, but I want your help. If man-eating trees and snake monsters can't kill me, neither will asking for help."

He cocked his head to the side, the jewelry on his horns jingling, another thing to soothe my nerves. His lips pursed beneath the mask, and another moment of silence passed.

"And what is it you're wanting from me?"

I chewed at the corner of my mouth, losing myself in the depth of his gaze. My mind was a muddled mess, conflicted with fear and longing. I wasn't sure of anything aside from the stinging in the corners of my eyes as tears threatened to fall. I didn't want to cry in front of Belial.

The Lord of Bones might have been able to force tears from my eyes, to break me down into a pathetic mess, but Belial was different.

"I'm not really sure..."

He stood and offered me his hand, dragging me to my feet. I wobbled, my legs weak from all the running I'd done, but I froze as his eyes roved over me.

"You look like Hell," he said, sweeping a rogue lock of hair behind my ear. "A Hell far more beautiful than this one."

My cheeks flamed. "You're just saying that to get in my pants."

His eyes gleamed behind the mask. "A feat you'd think would be way easier, considering you're not wearing any."

"You know, you're kind of charming."

"And you're kind of stubborn. I'll tell you what you need." His voice hardened, as did the look in his eyes. "You need rest. You need a bath. Your wounds aren't deep, but they still need tending."

I cocked a singular brow up at him. Why was he baiting me? Was he just trying to give me ideas so he could have my body at his disposal again?

Did he genuinely care that I was hurt? The tenderness in his voice said yes, but... I didn't want to let myself believe that. It tugged at too many heartstrings to think this demon cared what happened to me.

"Yeah," I admitted, my pride crumbling at the mention of a bath. "And food. A massage, a medium rare steak with mashed potatoes, and a bed."

Belial tilted his head to the other side, his eyes glinting with thought. "Alright. Why don't I take you back to the castle–"

"No." I cut him off, panic setting in. "Absolutely the fuck not. I've fought so hard to get away from there. Why the hell would I go back?"

I tried to push him away, but his arms banded around me, holding me close to his hard chest.

"Hey. It's okay. It's not a trick to get you to turn back."

My eyes narrowed into deadly slivers. "It *feels* like a trick."

"What the Hells am I supposed to do?" His voice was sharp as a knife, his eyes dark. "Summon a bed and a bathtub in the middle of the labyrinth? Shall I pull Holga out of thin air and hope she brings bath salts and lotion?"

"I don't know. It's fucking magic."

"I'm not a fairy godmother, Rayven. It has its limits. Besides, sleeping in my bedroom will be more private. You need a break from this place. Let me take you back to the castle. You can bathe, change, and eat."

At the thought of a warm bath and dinner, I nearly sobbed, but I managed to hold it together. It was too good of an offer. There had to be hefty strings attached. Besides, I didn't have time to start all over. My time was running out, and I still hadn't found my way out of the maze.

"I don't have time to waste," I said broken-heartedly. "If I start over, I'll never make it out. I can't risk it. I have to–"

"You won't be starting over," he jumped in. "I'll bring you back to this exact spot in the morning. I swear by my bone."

His promise made my heart flutter, and I fought the smile teasing the corners of my mouth. Now it definitely sounded too good to be true, but I was beyond exhausted, mentally and physically drained.

If I rested a while, I knew I'd be better for it. My reflexes would be faster, my mind sharper.

"In the morning?" I echoed, staring up at him with uncertainty. "Why so long? I only have until midnight tomorrow. And the Lord of Bones...he knows you're helping me. It could be risky taking me back."

His expression shifted at the mention of the Lord. He probably sensed the fear that shot through me at his name, and he reached for my cheek, the cool leather of his glove teasing my jawline.

"He won't," he said. "And if he does, I'll take care of it."

He sounded confident, but his words didn't do much to reassure me.

I wasn't sure if I could trust him. What stunk about that was I wasn't sure if the foreboding sensation hooking in my gut was just my old trust issues rearing their ugly head, or if something was actually off with Belial.

I wanted to believe him.

I decided to believe him. What other option did I have? Wander around naked, starving, cold, and bloody? Be more alone than ever, with nothing but thoughts of what could have been to tease me into insanity?

Yeah, that was gonna be a hard pass from me.

"What's the price? You aren't going to do all that for free."

His arms banded tighter around me, tucking me close to him. My nipples hardened to stiff peaks at the contact, and my pussy throbbed needily.

"I want to take care of you, in whatever way I see fit," he answered.

I inhaled sharply. "That can mean a lot of things."

"I'm not about to give you a list of everything I plan to do to you. We don't have time for that."

"Are you going to hurt me?"

He smirked. "Only in ways you'll like."

I didn't know what to think. I could have everything I'd been deprived of for two days, and he'd get to use and abuse me all night. Heat clawed through my body at the thought.

Was it a terrible idea? Probably, but my desire to be clean, to lie in his bed with his body wrapped around me was overwhelming, trumping every bit of logic I had left. My body begged me, pleaded with me, to concede.

If I didn't know better, he was pleading with me silently too, the conviction in his gaze enough to sway me.

"So... I get a bath, food, and clothes," I started slowly. "And you get the whole night to do whatever you want to me?"

He nodded once. "That's my price."

"And you'll bring me right back here tomorrow morning? Early?"

"Tomorrow morning, early. Right at this spot."

"How can I trust you?" My jaw hardened on the question. "How do I know you won't trap me there until my time is up?"

He lifted one shoulder in a shrug. "You don't."

His honesty made my stomach twist into knots. He'd let me go once before. Could I trust him to do it a second time?

His hand skimmed up my arm, his eyes focusing on his fingers, as if he was transfixed with the mere notion of touching me. "What's your answer? Time is not our friend, little human."

"Okay, it's a deal, but if you backstab me..." I trailed off. I wasn't really sure what I'd do.

He stared at me with amusement banked in his stormy orbs. "You'll, what? Kill me? I can't die."

I twirled his dagger earring between my fingers. "I'll cut your giant dick off and wear it around my neck like a trophy, a warning to all men not to fuck with me."

He blinked. For a second, I thought I'd fucked up, and he'd rescind his invite to help. Thankfully, he threw his head back and laughed. For the first time, it sounded genuine—*happy*.

"If I break my promise, I don't deserve to hang from such a beautiful neck." He leaned back to gesture at my pierced nipples. "Especially if I get to be so close to these on a daily basis."

"You're really fucked up, you know that?" I laughed, but the humor in his eyes was gone. When he spoke again, the bend in his voice turned my blood cold.

"Oh, little human. If I know anything, it's that."

# CHAPTER TWENTY-SIX

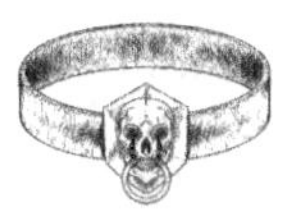

## RAYVEN

"Hold tight," Belial instructed. A tiny squeak left me when he scooped me into his arms, and my own instinctually banded around his neck.

He stared down at my small frame cradled against him, and the blush from my cheeks instantly spread down my chest to my breasts.

The human instinct to cover myself immediately ebbed when I caught the way his eyes danced over my bare body. I was wearing only my boots and a thin layer of my own sweat and blood, but I felt like a goddamn goddess with the way he looked at me.

There was a swirl of blue, glimmering magic whirling around us, bouncing off my skin and blinding me. One second, we were in the middle of the maze, and the next, we were standing in his bedroom.

The familiar castle smell washed over me, along with a wave of relief. I never imagined being so happy to see this place. Then again, a night spent in a luxurious cage was way better than a hellish garden filled with man-eating monsters.

At least, I hoped it would be.

Belial pulled his cloak off, slung it over the chair beside the roaring fire, and strode toward the bathroom. My eyes went to the bed, my breathing short and sharp as memories came surging back.

It really was a beautiful bed, with its elaborately carved posts and the canopy draped over it. Even with the wisps of old spider silk, heavy with dust and clinging to the swathes of fabric, there was no disguising its grandeur.

The sheets were black and silken, and something told me he hadn't changed them since I'd been in them last.

The thought of him smelling me as he slept had my heart clenching.

I sucked my bottom lip between my teeth as my attention landed on the heavy chain still bolted to his headboard, now looped around one of the posts.

"Rayven..."

Belial's voice had my gaze jerking back to the bathroom door.

I swallowed hard when I saw him in the doorway with one arm stretched out, braced against the doorframe. "Come here."

My feet were scrambling to obey before my brain fully caught up, and I followed him inside.

I'd been in here already, but the first time, I'd been so stressed, I'd barely noticed the room. It was beautiful, with stone walls, plants and bone candelabras hanging from the ceiling. All the candles were lit, casting everything in a comforting, amber glow. Jars in varying colors, shapes, and sizes sat on a ledge built into the stone. If I had to guess, they were probably filled with salts, since they were within arm's reach of the clawfoot tub.

I glanced back at Belial, who watched me through the slits of his mask.

Fuck. I wanted to see his face so badly. *What was he hiding?*

"Sit," he instructed, his voice clipped as he pointed to a stool beside the bath. "As beautiful as you look covered in blood, I'll get you cleaned up first. Then, I'll send Holga for food."

I blinked at him, sure I'd heard him wrong. "*You'll* get me cleaned up?"

"I told you to give all of yourself to me, and that includes control, Rayven. Tonight, you won't lift a finger."

I moved to sit down, watching him with curiosity as he leaned over the bath and turned the faucet on, hot steam filling the air.

Belial dumped a glob of purple soap—plum scented, by its aroma and color—into the bath and bubbles exploded beneath the rush of water, quickly filling the tub.

He threw in a couple more handfuls of salts and who knew what else from the various jars on the ledge. Soon, the entire bathroom smelled so sweet, my mouth began to water, and my sore muscles twitched in excitement.

When the demon was satisfied with the bath, he strode over to my chair and dropped to his knees in front of me—*kneeling*.

My heart slammed into the roof of my mouth as I watched his shoulder muscles strain against his black shirt, his slender fingers working to undo my bootlaces. His hand gently cupped my calf while his other pulled the boot off. He gently lowered my foot to the floor, then went to work on the other one.

It was a tender moment, one that caught me completely off guard. He was sharp around the edges, even brutal at times, but it seemed he was capable of being soft, too. There was so much beneath that mask I wanted to see, that went deeper than flesh.

Belial was becoming a very big problem.

How the hell was I supposed to just walk away from him when he did things like this? When he made it so damn hard to get him out of my brain?

When he tossed my boots aside, I expected him to rise to his feet and leave me to bathe. Instead, his hand smoothed over my knee while gently pushing my legs apart.

I sucked in a breath when he brought the lips of his mask to my inner thigh. The material was warm from his lips, but its touch sent a chill through my bones.

What I'd give to feel his bare lips on my skin...

I tried to pull away, but his hands gripped me tight, holding me in place on the stool. "Stay still."

"I should be clean before you touch me."

"Let's get one thing straight. You'll get your bath, but you won't be leaving this room clean."

Before I could say anything else, he hauled me into his arms, held me over the bath, and *dropped* me.

I fell into the tub with a splash, water and suds going everywhere. My head slipped beneath the surface, water gushing up my nose and making my sinuses burn. I fumbled, trying to get my bearings, and lurched up into a sitting position with a gasp. My hands gripped the edge of the tub, and I glared up at Belial who stood over me menacingly, his eyes gleaming with dark amusement.

He rolled his black sleeves up to his elbows, dark veins straining against pale flesh covered in various scars and ink from ancient tattoos so faded they were barely there. "You're so fucking gorgeous when you struggle, little mortal."

How was he so sexy and yet so mean, and why did it turn me on *so* much? It wasn't fair. It didn't make any sense. He was soft one moment, cruel the next. I found myself reeling from the whiplash and burning for more in the same breath.

Crouching, his hands gripped his knees as he got to my eye level. "You can use your safeword. Say black widow, and I take you back to the labyrinth."

He was giving me another out, but by the hint of a smirk behind his mask, he knew I was too stubborn to take it.

"Fuck you." I spit in his face. He didn't even bat an eye as the glob of saliva slid down the black mask and streaked down its lips. He touched the mouth of the mask and held his fingers up, watching the way they glistened with my spit.

"Oh, pet. If I didn't know you to be a glutton for pain along with your pleasure, I'd say you're going to regret that. No, I think you're going to enjoy this quite a bit. Now, hold your breath."

His hand snapped forward, his fingers gripping my throat over the collar. With more force than I could ever hope to fight, he pushed me back into the water.

I screamed, bubbles exploding to the surface. I heard his voice, but it was muffled by the water filling my ears—not that I needed to hear his words to make out their meaning. He was chastising me for wasting air.

My scream turned to a moan as I felt his other hand slip under the water between my thighs.

He was touching me while keeping me under the water. I couldn't breathe, couldn't move. I was forced to take his fingers as they stoked–painfully gently–over my folds. When two fingers dipped inside, the burning in my lungs and the knot of anxiety in my gut somehow pushed the pleasure higher.

It was terrifying and wonderfully intense—delicious, dark, and depraved torment.

The bastard was right. I was enjoying it.

"Come, and I'll let you breathe."

This time, I made out the demon's words as he shouted to be heard.

His fingers picked up their pace. They weren't gentle anymore. Now they worked furiously over my tender flesh, pumping into me so hard, I saw stars.

Each precious second felt like an eternity.

Then, the pressure mounted. His fingers curled inside me, hitting that hidden spot, and I came with a scream, releasing my final vestiges of air. His fingers slipped into my collar, and he wrenched me out of the water.

I gulped down several desperate breaths, then shot him a savage look. "You fucking bastard!"

He laughed, the sound dark and deep, sinking straight to the place still throbbing from his touch.

"Remember what you say to your God when he makes you come?"

"Go to hell!"

"Already there, baby, and I'm pulling you down into the infernal dark with me."

He pushed me back into the water, just as I was able to swallow down another breath. His hand was between my thighs again, this time with a pinky finger sliding into my ass, his thumb on my clit, and three fingers inside.

It was too much and not enough at the same time. It hurt so good that my nerves felt like they were ripping apart, only to fuse back together into something stronger.

I came a second time, but he wasn't letting up, his fingers keeping that same delirious pace...

This was just like with the quicksand, waiting until the last possible moment to pull me out.

Then, why he was so into this clicked. He fetishized my heartbeat, my life—which seemed to be a common kink for demons here. He enjoyed bringing me to the brink of death, just to pull me back out again, to feel my heart race.

He was a creature surrounded by so much death, he craved to feel alive.

A wicked thought bloomed in my mind as the fire in my lungs became unbearable. Before I could decide against it, I was pulling his earring out of my ear and, with all my strength, burying the blade in his arm.

There was a growl, and on the next beat, his hold loosened, allowing me to lurch out of the water.

He was on his feet, wrenching the tiny blade out of his flesh and throwing it to the ground with a snarl. Blood welled from the wound, rolling down his arm and dripping onto the floor. It took me a moment to register the blood's hue.

Black. Belial's blood was as black as ink.

He looked up, his eyes dark and tumultuous behind his mask. "You audacious little slut."

His words were a snarl, but there was no anger in them. If anything, they were charged with wonder, like he couldn't believe I'd gone so far as to stab him.

I sat in the bath, thunderstruck by what had just happened.

I wasn't sure what I'd been expecting. A relaxing bath? Not with this man. I guess I'd known this would turn into another dark game. He'd warned me it would, and I'd still gone with him willingly. He'd given me an out, and I'd denied it.

We both knew I wanted this.

I wanted this as much as he did.

It was like he'd helped awaken something inside me—something dangerous and volatile, something that made me feel powerful, more alive than ever.

"New plan. I don't need a safeword," I said, a cocky smirk lifting my lips. "Cross my boundaries and I'll just stab you. Sound good?"

Belial stared at me. Then, after the most intense seconds of silence of my life, he laughed. He strode back toward the tub and fell to his knees before me.

The demon sat on his heels, completely soaked, his black shirt sticking to his chest and strands of his hair sticking to his temples. "Feel better?"

My mind was reeling. Adrenaline slammed through my veins, the afterglow coursing through me, making my body light and tingly. His cruel ministrations had relieved the pressure inside me, like cuts meant to drain poison.

It was a heady combination of things that had all my aches and pains, my anxiety, and all the other bullshit that had been weighing on me gone in a blink.

"I feel better," I admitted on a rasp, my eyes wide as realization sunk in.

"Good," he said, a smug smile in his voice. "Now that we've had that little warm up..."

He pulled off his shirt, revealing a chiseled torso littered with more scars and faded ink.

"W-what are you doing?"

"Getting in."

He dropped his wet shirt to the floor and as his hands went to the laces on his pants.

"B-but I'm filthy."

He titled his head, the silver hanging from his horns jingling. "And that's supposed to deter me? Move over."

# CHAPTER TWENTY-SEVEN

## RAYVEN

I STARED AT THE demon's naked body, my jaw going slack at the sight of him. Belial was so fucking sexy, my brain stalled out as my hungry eyes wolfed down his every detail.

His pale skin was covered in swathes of ancient ink, old scars, and a fine layer of sweat that shone in the candlelight.

He stripped out of everything except for the silver cuff and chain decorating his cock, the charms and chains dangling from his horns, and of course, the mask.

The mask always stayed on.

I shuffled toward the center of the tub, and he sank into the water behind me.

"You can relax," Belial's delicious, velvety voice said as his arms came up around me, pulling me against his chest. "I'm not going to hurt you."

"I did just stab you…" I murmured, my muscles tensing.

The demon gave a sigh as he reached for one of the bottles on the ledge and dumped some divine smelling soap into his palm. "I probably deserved it."

He began to work the shampoo into my hair, building up a lather. I expected the water to muddy the moment I hit the water, but it stayed pristine, even as I smoothed my hands over my skin, washing the grime loose. Whatever Belial put in the bath, it must have been a spell of sorts to keep the water clean and clear.

As he washed me, my muscles relaxed some, and I settled against him, the ripples of his muscular chest against my back sending a pulse of heat straight to my core.

I knew he planned to make me hurt later, make me ache in a way only he could. This right here, this perfect moment of solace in the middle of a shitstorm, would be worth every second of the pain. It would make the agony oh so sweet.

For a few minutes, we were both silent, our nearly tandem breaths the only sound around us. Then, finally, Belial spoke, his velvety voice echoing off every polished surface in the room. "Is this what you wanted?"

I smirked, trailing my fingers up his thigh, enjoying the way his muscles flexed beneath my touch. "Well, my baths back at home don't usually involve a sexy masked demon, or me almost drowning because said demon has an intense asphyxiation kink. Or me stabbing anyone. Still, this is better... I think."

"You think?"

I settled my head back against his shoulder, shrugging my own. "There's a part of me that feels safe with you."

"But?" he asked, anticipating the next word out of my mouth.

"*But* I'm anticipating the knife in my back."

A soft chuckle tickled the column of my neck, his hand coming up to idly twirl the baby hairs at my nape around his finger. On the next breath, his fingers curved around my throat to clamp over my collar.

"If that's the case, why are you naked in the bath with me? With your back to me..." He leaned forward, his hard chest pressing into my shoulder blades. My breath hitched when his arm banded around my waist under the water and pulled me into his lap. He was *very* hard. "Your ass pressed against my cock. Not exactly a position for you to fend off any potential attacks."

His words had every reason to spike my suspicion, but there was no hiding the amusement in his voice, as if I was telling a joke.

"You know the saying: keep your friends close, your enemies closer. I feel like I can't completely let my guard down around you."

"Smart girl," he chuckled, that smile still in his voice. I'd come to love that smile, even if I'd never seen it beyond the small peek I got every now and again through the slit in his mask.

I turned my head, catching his stormy gaze. "So I'm right not to trust you?"

"I didn't say that," he replied with a bend in his tone I couldn't parse.

"You still haven't taken your mask off for me, even in the bath. What are you hiding?"

His muscles tensed against me. "Scars."

"That's specific," I said with a frustrated sigh. I knew he wasn't lying, but he was being vague as hell. I'd surmised as much—I could see his scarred lips—but I wanted to know what *else* he was hiding.

"I'll let you see other parts of me, Rayven, the parts I don't show anyone else." He brushed my hair back away from my face with his wet fingers, sending tingles down my spine.

"I've already seen your dick." Felt it, too, by the way it was jabbing into my ass—not that I was complaining.

He gave a dark chuckle in my ear, the nose of his mask brushing against the edge of my jaw. "I'm not talking about that. I meant parts of me on the inside, things about me no one else knows."

I blinked, casting him a curious sideways glance. Christ, he was so handsome. The warmth of the bath made his skin slick with sweat, which gleamed in the firelight. "Like what?"

His eyes glazed with thought. "No one else knows about my..." he paused, seeming to choose his words carefully. "Carnal preferences. No one knows how fucked up I am."

"You're kinky. So what?" I said, trying to sound unimpressed, even as my body flushed with heat. "Tell me a secret, something you've never told anyone."

He thought for another moment. "Belphegor, one of the Lord of Bones' brothers, is a shapeshifter, one of his favorite forms is that of a beautiful woman. He once seduced another brother, Asmodeus, the Lord of Lechery."

My brows hiked up close to my hairline. "How do you know that?"

"I know a lot of shit. I travel the Styx and see all sorts of things others don't."

"Well, that's interesting. Also, gross." I giggled. "But that doesn't tell me anything about *you*."

Belial sighed, probably realizing I wasn't giving up so easily. I was determined to find out more about him. "Alright—I wasn't always a demon."

"Really?"

He gave a nod. "I was a human a long, long time ago. One of the first, I think. So long ago I don't remember who I was, or anything about my old life. I died, and as one of the first humans to cross into this realm, I took up the mantle as one of the high-ranking members of this court, to help dictate what would happen to all souls who followed suit."

"The face beneath your mask, is that what you looked like as a human?"

"I think so."

The pain in his voice had me turning around in the tub to face him. My eyes dropped to his scarred lips, barely visible through the slitted mouth of his mask. I wondered if those scars covered his entire face.

"Tell me how you got your scars, and I'll tell you how I got mine."

His eyes narrowed. "I know how you got yours. You are the worst kind of thief: a grave robber. You're lucky you haven't been speared on one of those fences. I've plucked a few souls off those iron spikes over the years."

I pursed my lips at his arrogance. I had plenty of scars from grave robbing, yes, but there were others he didn't know about—some on the surface, and others that ran deeper. "Are your scars from when you were human?"

It was probably stupid to press my luck, since this topic clearly had him shutting down, but I was desperate to connect with him, to know things about him, to break through his defenses. I'd scaled spiked fences, broke through countless crypts, and picked every kind of lock there was. I could crack this demon's emotional armor too.

"From when I died. Don't bother asking how. I don't remember, and I don't care to."

We fell into a moment of silence, and I could tell my line of questioning had stirred up memories—or maybe lack thereof—that weren't so pleasant, things he hadn't thought about in a long time.

Still, I'd gotten what I wanted: a straightforward answer, not one riddled with cryptic bullshit. In a sense, I felt closer to him. It might have been a small crack in his emotional fortress, but it was there. Later, I'd take another stab at bringing the wall down completely.

Eager to lift the vibe of the room, I turned my attention to the chains and charms draped from his horns.

"You're also a fan of jewelry."

My gaze dropped to the water, where a flash of silver could be seen beneath the bubbles.

"I don't wear it for fashion purposes. Each demon lord has their own metal, and all demons under their rule wear it to show loyalty and allegiance to their respective realm. The King of Limbo is silver. The King of Lust is gold. The King of Gluttony's is bronze, and so on."

"So it's kind of like a religious thing?"

"Of sorts."

I smiled at him, and by what I could see of his mouth and the twinkle in his eye, I was sure he was smiling back.

I didn't want to move. I wanted to melt into Belial and forget about what would happen when the morning came, how I'd once again be out in the maze, fighting to escape.

If I somehow managed to escape, if I broke out of this realm of death, I wouldn't see him again. At least, not for a very long time—not until my body gave out and my soul made its way back to purgatory.

Would he still remember me then?

Would he have forgotten about these moments?

I exhaled shakily, chasing the thoughts away. None of it mattered, not right now. I could worry about it when the sun rose, when the countdown to my deal with the Lord of Bones stared me in the face again.

I would escape, and I'd deal with the disappointment then. I didn't want to be disappointed right now. I wanted to sit here with him forever, reveling in the way his chest rose and fell beneath me with every breath, how his rough fingers danced over my skin. I wished the bubbles would disappear so I could admire every inch of him again.

"Are you ready to get out?" he asked, breaking my train of thought.

"And do what?"

He shrugged. "Eat. Sleep. Let me devour every inch of you."

I found myself smiling. "That sounds fucking perfect."

# CHAPTER TWENTY-EIGHT

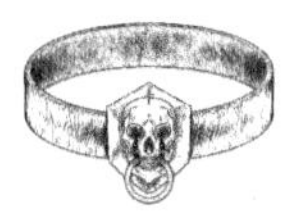

## RAYVEN

Wrapped in a towel, I made my way back into the bedroom to find Belial splayed across the dark sheets of his bed, wearing nothing but a fresh pair of black pants. His hands were tucked behind his head, his pale, muscular chest on full display.

He was sexy and he knew it, the cocky fuck. Still, I drank in every inch of him, wishing once again that he'd abandon his mask and let me see his face.

After our conversation in the bathtub, though, I knew better than to ask about it again.

My gaze caught on a white gown at the end of the bed. It was similar to the first dress I'd worn, long and flowy, but this one had billowing sleeves and ruffles around the hems.

Dainty, delicate. *And fucking white.*

At least he'd offered me clothes.

"Black is more my color, but I guess I shouldn't complain. I'm lucky you're not forcing me to walk around naked," I said, raising a brow at him.

He chuckled. "Naked is certainly my preference. I just thought you might like some modesty when Holga brings dinner."

Heat burned my cheeks, and my mouth went dry, but not at the thought of being naked in front of the maid—she'd already seen everything I had to offer. What left me speechless was the fact that he'd considered my comfort by laying the dress out in the first place.

It was... kind, nicer than anything I expected from him, especially after getting almost drowned in the tub. The change of pace nearly gave me whiplash. With a smile, I walked to the edge of the bed and ran my fingers over the silky fabric of the dress. It was just as sheer as the last one, but maybe tonight, that wasn't such a bad thing.

"What is it with this place and white gowns?" I asked, pursing my lips. "In a place so dark, I'd expect all the clothes to be black or something."

Belial shifted, moving to sit on the edge of the bed and considering me as my eyes bounced between him and the dress. "I like to think they reflect the only spot of light in this dark abyss."

I froze, heart jumping into my throat as his eyes held mine, unable to move or breathe or think. Was he saying what I thought he was saying?

Of course he was. He hadn't stuttered.

"It would look better in black." I grabbed the dress up, dropping my towel to the floor.

"Wait," Belial said, his velvety voice making me freeze. Tipping his chin, he gestured to the floor in front of him. "Come to me first. Leave the dress."

I shifted, tempted to argue, but I knew he'd make me pay for it. Not to mention his sweet disposition had doused some of my natural fire for the moment. I wanted to soak in every second of it before he went back to being an ass.

Silently, I obeyed, laying the dress back on the bed and making my way around the footboard. I stopped in front of him, my stomach knotting as his intense gaze settled on mine, slipping down my body before slowly working its way up again. Water dripped from my hair, trailing down my breasts, before it fell to the floor.

"Turn around," he said.

I spun on the spot to expose my ass. I wasn't sure what to expect, but when his fingers hooked around my hips, dragging me backwards onto his lap, I gasped.

"You're beautiful, Rayven," he whispered, the warmth of his breath on my back making goosebumps race over my skin.

I hated how much I loved his compliments. His words might have made me blush, but I wanted him to keep saying them, wanted him to praise me for being his good girl and obeying his commands. I wanted him to punish me for rebelling, for running my bratty mouth, for stabbing him.

I wanted every sensation he cared to inflict.

I wanted him to drag me onto the bed and crush me into the mattress beneath him.

What would it feel like to have him inside me? The slide of the chain, the kiss of his piercing hitting my deepest parts. Would he even fit? I'd seen that look in his eye when he'd managed to stuff his entire length down my throat, with the cuff around his base disappearing inside me...

"Close your eyes," he said, his voice breathy in my ear. My pussy throbbed at his closeness, but I did as I was told, closing them tight. "If you open them, you can spend the night in the dungeon. Understand?"

I nodded with a shaky breath. I'd seen enough to know he would make good on that promise, and if there was one place in this realm I didn't want to be, it was in the dungeons with the hundreds of unworthy souls the Lord of Bones had killed. I'd rather take my chances naked in the maze.

The demon shifted behind me, making me wonder what he was up to, and I nearly fell out of his lap when his lips pressed against my shoulder. My mouth fell open on a singular, tiny gasp at the sensation. He hummed against my skin at my re-action and swept my hair aside, peppering slow, delicate kisses across my back.

*He'd taken his mask off.*

The heartbeat between my thighs raced as his hands danced their way over my flesh, groping me, cupping my breasts, pluck-ing at my nipple piercings. I wanted him to memorize every inch of me with his mouth, to kiss me from head to toe before making me shatter into pieces, and my heart squeezed at the thought.

I loved how brutal he normally was—the pain, the humiliation, the dark and demented things he did that made me ache for more.

But this... this soft, intimate effort threatened to tear me apart at the seams. It took everything in me not to turn around, despite my promise. Maybe a night in the dungeon wouldn't be so bad if I could just see his face, press my lips against his, to have my tongue tangle with his while my hands fisted his hair and gripped his horns.

Then again, knowing Belial, he'd be too possessive to throw me in with the other souls, especially since he knew what had gone down in the oubliette.

It was more likely that he'd chain me up again and do dark things to me that would have me screaming...

"I know what you're thinking." His breath came out in an electrified whisper that slithered across my skin.

The hairs on my neck stood up. "And what's that?"

"You're wanting to disobey me. Turn around, and you're in for a world of hurt, little human, and not the kind that will have you screaming in pleasure."

His voice was full of warning, a stark contrast to his sweet touch.

One arm slid around me, pulling me hard against him and tearing a ragged breath from my lungs. His lips brushed the shell of my ear, and he tenderly sucked on my earlobe.

I whimpered, and he groaned at the sound.

"You're radiant sin, Rayven. You'll be my complete undoing."

My name on his mouth was like a prayer on the lips of a damned man, begging for salvation. It had every nerve ending in my body flaring to life.

"I shouldn't want you this badly," he admitted, his tone more vulnerable than I'd ever heard it.

I knew what he meant, because I felt it too. He was a demon ferryman in the land of the dead, and I'd made a deal with his lord. He was a cocky asshole with a tendency to inflict pain, and he'd nearly let me die, a couple of times.

I shouldn't want him.

But that didn't mean I couldn't.

When his lips left my skin, I whined, not ready for the moment to end.

"Get dressed now," he said shortly. "Holga will be here soon with your dinner."

By the time I stood and looked back at him, Belial had replaced his mask, but I couldn't scrub the feel of his lips from my mind.

I ran the towel over my dripping hair before pulling on the white dress, his words playing on loop in my head.

*"You'll be my complete undoing."*

I couldn't shake the foreboding sensation that he was right, and that he would be mine too.

# CHAPTER TWENTY-NINE

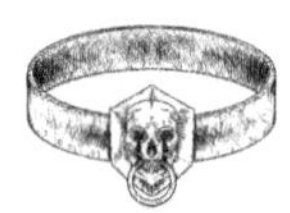

## RAYVEN

I shivered in delight as I pulled on the new nightgown, the fabric dancing over my nipples.

I was desperate for more of Belial's touch. My body ached for more, and even the faintest whisper of sensation had my entire body throbbing.

Belial watched me quietly as I gave a twirl, the garment swaying around my ankles. I felt like one of those damsels in an old romance movie. I internally sighed—if only it was black.

A knock at the door made me jump, and I looked over to see Holga slipping through the doorway with a silver platter clutched in her hands. Today, the skeleton witch's hair was braided over one shoulder, and when her sockets landed on me, she stopped short.

I looked nervously between her and Belial, my heart racing.

Did she know where I'd been for the last two days, fighting my way through the labyrinth of hedges outside? Would she rat Belial out to the Lord of Bones for having me in his bed when I should have been trying to escape, or was she in on the plan?

A million questions and not enough answers, but my stomach growled at the thought of food.

"Place it here, Holga," Belial urged, gesturing to the bedside table.

She moved, setting the tray down. With a wave of her hand, she produced a bottle of wine and set it next to the tray before she offered a shallow bow. "Is there anything else I can do for you, sir?"

"Yes, there is. Fetch Cecil for me," he said, making Holga stop short again.

"T-the librarian?" she asked, clearly surprised. As was I. There were plenty of books on the shelves by the fireplace if he wanted to read. What could Belial possibly want with a librarian?

"Yes. Go now."

I stood by silently, arms wrapped tightly around myself as I watched the interaction between them. I noticed everything from the way she spoke to him to the way she bowed.

The witch was nervous.

Belial's position as the ferryman was obviously one of importance, and I didn't know why that turned me on so much.

Holga threw me another glance that had nerves eating at me from the inside out before turning to leave.

"Let's eat by the fire," Belial said when we were alone again, shoving to his feet. He grabbed the tray, along with the wine bottle, and jerked his horns toward the sitting area.

I followed his lead, crawling up on one end of the couch as he set the food on the low coffee table. He removed the tray cover to reveal a small feast, along with two plates and a pair of silver goblets.

My mouth watered, my stomach twisting painfully with hunger. It was a small feast for two. I reached for a plate, but he scolded me. "I told you already. You're not to lift a finger."

"I broke that rule when I stabbed you," I said, eyeing him carefully as he loaded my plate with meat, fruit, bread, and a delicious looking plum tart.

"Yes," he said with a purring chuckle. "You're lucky I liked that. No more rule breaking."

I nodded as he handed me my plate, a sob hitching in my chest. After suffering for two days in the maze with nothing but a scrap of bread and a few plums to eat, I'd never felt so relieved, spoiled, or *wanted*.

A wave of guilt washed over me, threatening to rob me of my appetite.

Belial was going out of his way to help me, and something as simple as a meal could be what killed him. I wouldn't be able to live with myself if that happened.

He turned to hand me a goblet full of red wine, the look in his eyes pulling me from my troubled thoughts.

"Drink," he urged, taking a seat next to me.

I almost wished he'd tell me to chug the bottle instead. It would be nice to lose myself in the alcohol, too drunk for me to fight the demon as he took his payment for the food and wine.

That rough, possessive side of him made sense to me, even if it was nerve-wracking how he was helping me discover new things about myself.

I wasn't sure. I didn't know how to handle tender Belial.

The metal was cool against my lips, and the wine burned a little on the way down. It was stronger, more bitter than the last one I'd tasted, but the sight of the bottle on the table sent my thoughts careening out of control all the same.

Jesus Christ. I couldn't go a minute without thinking about the things I wanted this demon to do to me. I needed a distraction, and I decided to bring up the first thing my eyes landed on—the bookshelves.

"Do you read a lot?" I asked, popping a grape into my mouth. Tart juice spilled across my tongue as I bit into it.

"Not much anymore," he said. "I've read these particular books so many times I've memorized their words."

"What about the library?" I asked. "Have you read all the books in there too?"

I looked up to see him grinning through his mask.

"There are books there, but not the kind you're familiar with," he said vaguely. "You won't find words or stories written in them. Do you read?"

I almost choked on my grape. What a way to die—not by quicksand or man-eating trees or speared on the cock of the biggest dick in existence, but by choking to death on a grape because someone asked a monster fucker about their reading preferences.

"Um, yeah."

He canted his head, silver chains spilling to the side. "Such as?"

"Um, fantasy, I guess? Romance?"

He stared at me for a beat, picking up on my panicky tone by the amusement in his eyes. "Was that a question?"

"I read monster romance, okay? There. You beat it out of me."

Another knock at the door caught our attention, and Belial pushed to his feet.

"Keep eating." He gestured to my plate.

I took another bite and craned my neck around as Belial padded across the room, his bare feet nearly silent on the floor. When he pulled open the door, I could see a pair of skeletons standing in the hall. One was Holga, her boney arms crossed over her chest as she glared daggers at Belial, and the other was a shorter, more ancient-looking man with withered skin stretched over his skeletal-looking body.

When I registered his eye sockets, I had to suppress a gag. *Were those teeth?*

Snippets of the conversation trickled over, but it wasn't enough to string together its contents.

I couldn't be certain, especially with her lack of facial expressions, but Holga was on edge. She hovered too close to the doorframe, fidgeting with a torn piece of her dress, her sockets bouncing between Belial and the librarian.

Was she worried about what Belial had in store for me? Worried the Lord of Bones would catch Cecil away from his post? I had no idea why she'd be nervous, but it had my anxiety spiking through the roof.

After another moment, the door closed, and Belial joined me on the couch again.

"What was that about?"

"Cecil is going to bring us a book from the library," he said.

It seemed like a lot of trouble to go to, but I fought the smile making its way across my face. He could have just taken me there, sneaking me through the halls, but I knew better. If the Lord of Bones happened across us... I'd rather not think about the outcome.

"Aside from books and ferrying souls to the next layer of hell, what do you spend all your time doing?" I asked, wondering what could possibly keep this place from getting boring very quickly. I was probably the most interesting thing to happen to the place since... Catherine.

To my surprise, he hesitated, his eyes reflecting the light of the fireplace as he stared into it. I took another bite to fill the silence.

"Normally, my duties consume most of my time," he said, his voice soft and deep. "Humans die every day, and they must be ushered to the lower levels of hell to maintain the balance."

"Shouldn't you be working now then?"

He paused again, his throat bobbing with a swallow, and his eyes fell, staring at nothing. "The Lord has slacked on his job over the last century or so. Things are behind. Souls aren't being filtered down to lower levels. It's…"

"A mess?"

His gaze swung in my direction. "A giant one."

"Why?" I asked, popping another grape into my mouth. "Why is he not doing his job?"

I could tell by the way he shifted that Belial didn't want to talk about the Lord of Bones, but it didn't abate my curiosity. If he wasn't doing his job, what did he possibly fill his time with, aside from tormenting me?

Did he just stay holed up in his study all the time? Moping? Jacking off to demented thoughts?

I had no idea, and it was clear I was reaching the end of the ferryman's patience.

He grabbed the bottle of wine, ignoring his untouched goblet on the table, and knocked the bottle back, taking several deep swallows.

"It's impossible to understand the Lord of Bones," he finally said, placing the bottle back on the table. "It's a waste of your time to try."

He was probably right. After all, he'd known the Lord far longer than I had.

"And what about you?" I asked, changing the subject. I didn't miss the way Belial's mouth slipped into a smirk behind his mask. "Is it a waste of time to try and figure you out?"

"Definitely," he said, his fiery gaze catching mine and making my thighs clench. "But I'll enjoy watching you try."

# CHAPTER THIRTY

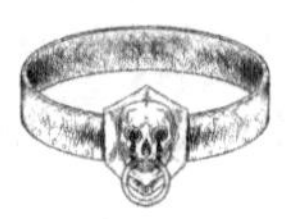

## Belial

My little human seemed to glow, wrapped in a spill of white fabric as the firelight danced over her pale skin. Her midnight hair had dried, hanging in loose waves over her shoulders, but my favorite part was the metal around her throat. The pendant shone, the teardrop eyes sparkling with a sinister twinkle.

Little did she know, the pendant would never come off. It allowed me to track her every move, hear her every heartbeat.

Soon, she'd wear my crown too.

My little pet, my slave queen.

She was beautiful, perfect in every way... save her desire to leave my castle. To leave this realm. *To leave me.*

It wouldn't happen—I'd make sure of that—but knowing she didn't want to stay stirred up old feelings, ones better off dead.

Rayven had a way of unearthing things she shouldn't have. It was her curse, and my blessing.

This time was different, though. I knew it, even if no one else could see it. My little human wasn't Catherine. Even if she didn't want to stay here in Limbo, there was a part of her, however small, that wanted me. The uptick in her heartbeat, that sweet scent between her thighs whenever she saw me, gave her away.

Yes, my little human wanted me.

She never flinched away from my touch, welcoming it instead. The Lord of Bones might have terrified her, but when she looked at me over the rim of her silver goblet, her dark eyes full of genuine curiosity, she wasn't afraid. It was both unexpected and thrilling.

I would soon own and dominate her mind and body. What I'd never imagined possible, though, was the prospect of owning her heart. Her love. That she might willingly give it to me...

*No.* It was a fool's hope.

Tomorrow, she'd discover that Belial and the Lord of Bones were one and the same, and that I'd been manipulating her to drive her into my arms.

That she'd never had a chance of escape to begin with.

Now, I loathed myself more than ever for deceiving her. What I hated most was that there was no going back. I *refused*. That's what she did to me. My obsession for her was like poison, a drug I'd never be able to wean myself from.

And I didn't care.

I'd do anything to have her, no matter how much she resented me in the end.

So tonight, I'd love her all the harder, show her all the ways I could worship her before she shut me out completely.

I tore my gaze away, desperate for a distraction.

Maybe there was a chance to worm my way into her heart.

The soul Cecil was fetching me could be the key.

"Are you full?" I asked, clearing my throat and chasing away my thoughts.

"Yes." She set her plate aside. "Thank you."

I pushed off the couch and offered her my hand. She looked at it, cocking a single eyebrow at the gesture, before threading her fingers through mine.

I led her to the bed, and she crawled across the mattress, sitting with her back against the headboard, looking expectantly at the pillow next to hers.

I was about to join when there was another knock at the door. Damn. Cecil was faster than I'd given him credit for.

"Come in," I called.

The door swung inward, revealing the librarian clutching a thick book in his arms. On his heels was Holga, no doubt to see if Rayven was still alive. She'd always had a bleeding heart, and if I didn't know better, I'd say she'd become fond of Cecil since Asmodeus sent her soul back. That in itself was hilarious; the two had always hated each other.

"As you requested, sir," Cecil said, leading the way across my bedroom and holding it out to me with a shallow bow.

They'd both been instructed to drop my honorifics in this form when Rayven was present. I couldn't risk my plan going to shit because of them. If they ruined this for me, I'd send their souls straight to Belphegor for the rest of their miserable existence.

I watched them, noticing how their hands brushed. Well, at least I would send them together. I was a romantic, after all.

"Thank you, Cecil," I said, opening the front cover of the book and glancing at the first page to ensure it was the right book.

"My pleasure," he said, tugging at the cravat around his neck. "How else can I offer my services?"

"This is all, thank you. You may go."

He bowed again, so deeply his brittle spine made an uncomfortable cracking sound. His gaze flicked to the bed, radiating curiosity when he noticed my guest.

If I wasn't so fond of Cecil, I'd rip apart his eye sockets tooth by tooth for looking too long.

Catching my disapproval, he gave another bow and hurried out the door.

Holga lingered a second longer, cocking her head, looking like she wanted to say something. Then, she turned and hurried to catch up with Cecil, snapping the door closed behind her. I wouldn't be surprised if she was pressed against the door, making sure I didn't harm her mistress.

I smiled to myself. The price of getting Holga back from my brother had been worth it. It didn't matter if she hated me—she cared for Rayven.

My little queen deserved to have someone in her corner that wasn't me, someone far kinder.

My fingers stroked over the book's leather binding. It wasn't old compared to most of the other souls. It was one of the few newer ones that had made it through the queue in the last two decades.

I held it close to my chest, keeping my back turned as I stood at the foot of the bed.

This feeling—this excitement—I couldn't remember when I'd last felt it. It was the simple joy of giving a gift just for the pleasure of seeing the receiver's face light up. It almost made me feel human again.

"What is that?"

I turned to see my raven-haired human eyeing me with more curiosity than ever.

I took a seat beside her on the bed, the book resting on my lap. "A gift."

"What is it?" Rayven asked, reaching into my lap to run her fingers along the book's coarse spine.

"This is a book of the dead. It's a catalog of someone's soul," I explained carefully, knowing it would be a lot for her to wrap her mind around.

What I was about to show her would be a lot for anyone to unpack.

"The Lord of Bones keeps a library of souls he deems worthy of saving from the lower levels of hell. Each soul has its own book, and it records the most special moments from that person's life, the moments most deeply ingrained in their hearts when they died. It's in those special memories where they're most happy that their soul resides."

Her eyes grew big as saucers. "Either your library is fucking huge, or he's really picky about who he deems worthy."

I laughed at her assessment. She wasn't wrong. "A little bit of both."

She pulled herself up on her elbows, a bewildered look wrinkling her perfect features. "So... What about heaven?"

A weighted sigh spun out from me. I'd been expecting this question.

"The Library of Souls is the closest thing to eternal paradise that a mortal can get, though many more meet peace if they request to be simply... put to rest, like dust blowing away in the wind."

Her face paled, the grim reality beginning to sink in.

Mortal souls always came to me, blathering about heaven, claiming they were sent to the wrong place. Little did many of them know, I was their only chance at salvation, their only chance at peace. I could just as easily send them down to my brothers for an eternity of agony.

Such was the duty of the King of Limbo.

"So the god who dictates good people's eternal paradise is the Lord of Bones?" she said after several moments of stewing in the information I gave her. "That's awful. That's cruel."

Her words struck a soft spot, and I resisted the urge to flinch.

I tried my best. Lately, my best had fallen woefully short of even my brothers' expectations, which was the biggest slap in the face of all.

After Catherine's final suicide, I couldn't bring myself to create world's of eternal happiness for other people. So, I stopped Judgement almost all together. I plucked the occasional soul from the queue—usually someone who had obviously been a piece of shit in their waking life—and sent them to the lower layers, just to satisfy my brothers.

The rest sat rotting in my realm, waiting for their final Judgement day.

Maybe part of the reason I was dragging my feet was because I hated the thought of sending most souls to my brothers. If I could, I'd give every half-decent soul their own book within my library.

"The Library of Souls is eternal paradise, or as close as anyone can get to it, anyway."

To my surprise, the ghost of a smile tugged at the corners of her mouth. "It figures heaven is a library."

I gaped at her, her words catching me by surprise. Then, I was smiling; she really was perfect.

"I can take you there. The Lord of Bones doesn't go in there very often these days. We could have the place to ourselves. We can get Holga to distract Cecil…"

My words died off at the tears welling in her eyes.

"You're crying. Why?"

She sat up, pulling her knees to her chest. "Belial, I'm leaving. This is my last night in the castle."

An invisible fist squeezed my heart. I wanted to correct her, but I bit my tongue. She'd find out soon enough how wrong she was.

"Fine. I can at least show you the soul in this book."

Her gaze dropped to the yellowed pages as I opened it. "Do they know they're dead? Do they know they are stuffed into a book, living on a shelf forever?"

"No. They simply go through the happiest moments of their life for all eternity, on repeat. It's their own personal paradise."

"Isn't it kind of sad, though? That they exist only within the pages of a book?"

I found myself smiling again, a melancholy smile I almost wished she could see. "I don't think it's such an awful thing to exist in only a book, Rayven."

She shifted next to me, scooting closer. "Can I ask you a question?"

"Anything, pet."

And I meant it. She could ask me anything in that moment and I would answer, without all the lies and the illusions and the trickery.

"What will happen if I become the Queen of Limbo? Will I die of old age and be shoved into one of these books? If he gets tired of me, will he…" Her throat strained against her collar with a swallow. "Will he send me down to the lower levels when he gets tired of me, pass me off to one of his brothers?"

It took everything in me not to shift right then and throw her down onto my bed to show her just how much I meant it when I said she was mine. Only mine. I would never do anything so heinous as to throw her to my brothers.

As if she wasn't the most important treasure I had.

"You will be made immortal, like a demon. The Lord of Bones has the power to grant life, just as he does to take it away. It's how he…" I sighed. I didn't like talking about this, but she needed to know. "It's how the Lord got Catherine. She was the daughter of some selfish noble who sold her for eternal life."

Horror carved Rayven's features. "He sold his only daughter to death, so he could live forever? What an asshole. See, this is why I raid rich asshole's graves. They have it fucking coming."

"Well, if you somehow managed to find his unmarked grave, you'd find him very much alive."

"No…" Horror morphed into wicked glee. "He gave him eternal life and buried him anyway?"

I didn't expect her to appreciate the ending I'd given Catherine's father, but then again, how could I not? I'd known she'd make a perfect queen for me the moment she first raised a hand against me.

My defiant, stubborn goddess of death.

"Now, are you ready to see into the world of this departed soul? I must warn you, it takes some getting used to," I said, watching the wheels turn behind her eyes. "We'll be immersed in their memories, seeing it as though it's happening, but the dead can't hear you or see you. Neither can anyone else in the memory."

"Like watching TV."

"Something like that."

"Okay," she said with an understanding nod. "Who is the soul?"

I took a deep breath, flipping the book open to the first page where the name was printed, along with the birth and death dates.

"It's your father's."

# CHAPTER THIRTY-ONE

## RAYVEN

EVERYTHING FROZE. TIME. MY breathing. The blood in my veins.

For a moment, nothing existed except the name in the book: John Carver, alongside his birthday and the day of his death that I'd burned into my brain from staring at his headstone almost every day of my youth.

My lungs seized, forbidding air from entering, and all I could do was gape down at the book.

I felt like I was suffocating all over again. If this was another one of his games, it crossed the fucking line.

But... the thing about the demon's games was that he only played ones I enjoyed, at least in some capacity. He administered his cruelty only to bring me pleasure.

If this was a trick, it was just cruel.

I barely knew him, but something told me he wouldn't be this evil. He wouldn't get my hopes up by lying about having my father's soul.

This was real.

I couldn't breathe. It was like I'd been plunged underwater. My lungs burned, like they were going to explode.

"Breathe, Rayven. You're having a panic attack."

A strong, firm hand smoothed over my knee, and the moment he touched me, oxygen siphoned into my lungs.

He sat there with me, the weight of his hand planted on my knee, not demanding anything, just anchoring me there, waiting patiently for me to gather myself.

"Rayven," he said, but his voice sounded a million miles away through the blood pounding in my ears. "Rayven, talk to me if you can."

It took everything in me to come back to reality, to tear my eyes away from the book—the eternal resting place of my father's soul—and look at Belial.

His eyes were narrowed with worry through his mask, and he snapped the cover of the book closed.

"Are you alright? We don't have to do this. I'm sorry."

"I…"

The words wouldn't come. Was I alright?

No. I wasn't fine or well at all. I hadn't been for days. Here I was, prisoner to the literal god of death, with three days to escape or I'd become his queen—which wouldn't sound so bad if he wasn't a horrible fucking monster. He wanted to own me, hurt me, torture me for eternity. He was a murderer, and I was to wear a crown made of my ex's bones.

He literally murdered Mark, and he'd *enjoyed* it.

I'd been cut, bruised, almost eaten alive, drowned, fucked, and now...

Now I was falling in love with a mysterious psychopomp who had so many secrets. I knew better than to trust him, I knew better than to give him my heart.

He was presenting my father's soul, and for what? What did he have to gain? I'd already told him he could have whatever he wanted from me tonight, so it wasn't a ploy to get in my pants.

He was doing this just so I could see my father again. To make me happy. To see me happy.

It made me wonder if demons were capable of emotions that went beyond lust and obsession, because this was starting to feel like something way more significant, and far more dangerous.

I couldn't think straight.

My father had been here the whole time—not in heaven like my mother had told me all these years, floating in the clouds and smiling down on me. He was in a book, living blissfully unaware in his own memories.

This was so much to unload, my brain could barely compute. Was I happy? Sad? Angry that this was how the afterlife worked? That the boss in charge of it all was a major dick?

Then again, by the sounds of it, he wasn't suffering. The Lord of Bones could have sent my dad to the lower layers of Hell, or even let him sit and rot in his realm. But he'd been one of the few safely kept in the Library of Souls.

Maybe the Lord of Bones wasn't the evil asshole I took him for. At least, maybe he hadn't always been. Maybe Catherine's death had broken him.

I'd been too young to remember much of my dad. I only had bits and pieces of memories to hold onto.

Visions of all my trips to his grave came swimming back. I knew the gravesite better than I knew the man himself—the texture of the headstone, the intricate carvings around the edges. I remembered the vibrant blades of grass around it, and even the names on the graves next to his. I'd spent so many hours there, wishing I could be with him again.

The room swam as tears threatened to fall.

There was so much I wanted to say to my father, so many years I wanted to make up for, but this book was the closest I'd ever get to him.

"I'm fine," I said after what had to be several minutes. I released a slow exhale and reached for the book with shaking hands. "I'm ready."

Belial stiffened, worry banked in his eyes, making my heart twist in my chest. "Are you sure?"

I wasn't sure. In fact, I was pretty damn sure I *wasn't* ready. Who the hell would be? But after tonight, I'd never come back to this castle. I wouldn't have a chance like this again.

"I'm sure," I reassured him. "I want to see him."

Belial hesitated, like he didn't believe me. Like he was worried I'd have another panic attack.

"You must think it's pretty weird that I can come close to dying so many times in so many grotesque ways without much more than a blink, but you try to do something nice by showing me a book, and I have a freaking meltdown."

The demon gave a slight shake of his head. "No, Rayven. I think you're fucking beautiful, strong and stupidly stubborn. Inside, you're... hurting. You miss your father. There's nothing weird about that."

He handed the book to me and I held it to my chest for a moment before daring to open it.

"What am I going to find inside? What if he isn't happy? What if he wasn't what I imagined him to be?"

Belial reached up to tug idly on one of the charms dangling from his horns. It was a silver spider, and toying with it nervously had to be a common thing for him by the way its sheen was worn down compared to the others.

"Perhaps you should open the book and find out for yourself."

Tamping down on my nerves, I gave a nod. "Okay... I'm ready."

He patted the bed between us, and I placed the book where he directed.

Belial peeled back the cover and hooked his fingers beneath several pages, sweeping them back. At first, all I saw was a blank page, yellowed and spotted with age, with not so much as a drop of ink.

Then, magic began to bleed out from the crease in the middle, bright, white and blinding.

It grew, spreading to consume the entire book, and I squeezed my eyes closed.

A second later, my feet slammed into hard ground. A hand slipped into mine, our fingers intertwining, and when I opened my eyes, Belial and I were standing in an unfamiliar room.

It was a child's room, model airplanes hanging from the ceiling and superhero posters plastered to the walls. A young boy no older than ten was sprawled out on the floor, drawing in a sketchbook.

The door across the room opened, and a woman poked her head inside. Her curly hair and glasses were familiar. I'd seen them in enough pictures to know she was my grandmother, and she looked a lot like my father when she smiled.

"John," she said in a sing-song voice. "Did you wash all the dishes and put them up?"

His dark eyes popped up from his drawing, and he grinned from ear to ear. "I knew you'd be tired after work, and I didn't want you to have to do them."

"Oh," my grandmother said, a little wobble in her voice. "Oh, I love you, Johnny. I appreciate you more than you'll ever know."

The door clicked shut, and my dad was left staring at the spot my grandmother had been with a twinkle in his eye.

The scene shifted, the child's room replaced by a classroom. Four rows of kids were sitting quietly as a teacher with a bald head and a goatee passed out graded tests. The disappointed murmurs told me nearly everyone had done badly.

When the teacher got to my father's desk, he paused and smirked before placing his paper down.

"Congratulations, Mr. Carver," he said, his smile widening. "Another perfect score."

The glowing pride in my father's eyes warmed my heart. He'd done well in school; that was something I hadn't known before.

More images appeared: my father's first car, his first home run, his high school graduation. I watched them all, drinking in every detail I could, learning about the man I never really knew.

The memory changed again. This time, we were standing in a park. It was summertime, the grass and trees around us vibrant and full of life. The familiarity made me a little homesick. This time, my father was college age, wearing jeans and a collared shirt. He was walking arm in arm down a worn path with a petite, raven-haired woman I recognized as much as my own reflection.

*My mother.*

My father beamed as he looked down at her, happiness exuding from him. He was so content, so in love. She looked like she'd just been swept off her feet by prince charming, her cheeks blushing as she laughed at something he'd said.

They stopped in the middle of the path when my father stooped down to pick up something—a black raven feather. He handed it to my mother, who took it with a smile I'd never seen her wear before.

The corners of my eyes prickled, but I didn't have time to cry before the scene changed again.

Their wedding. Buying a house. Finding out my mother was pregnant.

When a hospital room appeared, my chest clenched, and I gripped Belial's hand to keep from falling over. My mother was asleep in the bed, which had my heart dropping to the pit of my stomach until I saw my father sitting in the chair next to her. He was a few years older now, the stubble on his chin making him look much more like the picture that hung in my mother's living room.

Swaddled in his arms, wrapped tightly in a pink blanket, was a baby. *Me.*

"Dad?" The word escaped automatically as I stared at his familiar face.

He was slowly rocking back and forth, rubbing his fingers over my jet-black hair as I slept, a look of unbridled joy on his face. I stepped closer, dragging Belial along with me, and stopped right in front of him, soaking in the sight. I'd seen pictures hoarded in the bottom of my mom's closet, but this was completely different.

"My little Rayven," he whispered, careful not to wake my mother. "You're the best thing I've done in this life, you know that? I love you so much."

His words hit me, a sucker punch to the gut, and the tears I'd been holding back began to fall.

"We can go when you're ready," Belial's deep voice assured me in my ear.

I shook my head. "Not yet."

My father began to hum, a nursery rhyme that stirred up old memories. My mother had sung the same tune to get me to sleep countless times, but hearing it from him had my heart cracking apart.

I was in every one of the memories that followed: my first word, my first steps, my first birthday. He was happy, *so* happy, in every one of them. The twinkle in his eye and the smile on his face told me this fate, reliving the happiest moments of his life, was his own slice of paradise.

This was his heaven, and I was in it.

By the time we got to my third birthday, I was sobbing into the sleeve of my dress, crushed by unexpected emotions. Belial drew me against his chest, and in a flurry of magic, we were back in his bed, the book laid between us, unopened.

He let me cry, holding me and stroking my hair, which only had me crying harder.

This wasn't how this night was supposed to go.

"Are you sad I showed you this?" he asked after a while, reaching up to wipe the tears from my cheeks.

It was a lot—more emotional than I'd imagined possible, but... cathartic. My father was, and always would be, at peace.

Even though it hurt, knowing I was there to spend forever with him—even in memory—was comforting.

"No," I said, taking a deep breath to abate the tears. "This was the best gift anyone's ever given me. So, thank you. Truly."

He smiled beneath his mask, sinking down with me until my head rested on his chest. His fingers ran through my hair, consoling me.

"Making paradises isn't the Lord's strong suit as a demon, but he tries his best to give good afterlives to good souls," Belial said. "Your father was a good soul."

I nodded against his muscular chest. "He was. I worry I'll never be even half as good as him."

"Oh, little human..." he cooed in that dark, purring rumble that had goosebumps exploding over my skin. His arm came up to curl behind my back, tucking me against his side. "Of all the things you have to worry about, that's not one of them. I can promise you that."

# CHAPTER THIRTY-TWO

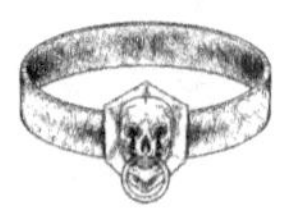

## BELIAL

Watching my little thief's heart shatter and mend itself all in one fell swoop was more than I'd anticipated when I sent for her father's soul. I thought I could show her a lighter side of my realm. That way, she might warm to the idea of staying here. I hadn't expected her to feel so much for a man she never really knew.

I definitely didn't count on feeling so much as I watched her fall apart. I didn't know what to do about the unfamiliar tightness squeezing my chest, or the warmth flooding my blood. All I knew was that this—whatever was happening between us—was right.

*Rayven* was right, and I needed her, more than I was willing to admit.

I stared at her for several minutes, wishing I had the power to manipulate time, so I could freeze this moment and stay like this, with her, forever. Tomorrow, I was going to break her heart.

I would have done anything in my power to ensure tonight never ended.

"You didn't have to do that for me, you know," she said, lifting her face from my chest to pin me with a sharp look. "*Why* did you do that?"

"This realm isn't all that you think it is. There are parts that suck, yes, but there are good parts, too."

The prettiest little smile curved her lips, and I wanted nothing more than to kiss them. "Like you?"

*Blood and Darkness*. The things this little human was doing to me... Making me feel alive again, almost like she had the power to stir life into my long-dead heart.

"Maybe you should get some sleep," I said to her softly, my fingertips brushing over her cheek.

She blinked at me. "You don't want to...." Her cheeks turned that delicious hue of pink, making my dick thicken in my pants. "You know."

"Oh, you can bet your pretty little ass I want to. I want you so badly it scares me," I admitted. "But I figured you wouldn't be in the mood after seeing your dad."

"You showed me his soul knowing there was a chance?"

I tweaked a brow at her, even though she couldn't see it behind the mask. "So?"

"*So*, you could have fucked me first and then showed me the book."

"You seeing your father, knowing he's at peace, is more important than my own carnal desires, Rayven. I may be a monster, but I'm not *that* kind of monster. I told you I wanted you to be open and vulnerable, and that's exactly what I got."

"What is this?" Her voice was laced with suspicion. "What are you playing at?"

"I don't know what you're talking about," I said in an over-dramatized, innocent tone.

"You're being too nice. This bipolar thing you've got going on is confusing me."

My eyes darkened as I reached for her lips, tracing them with the pad of my finger. Fuck, how I loved the way they softened under my touch. When she did that, I couldn't help thinking about when they'd been wrapped around my cock in the cemetery. "I have two very different sides."

"Yeah, I'm starting to see that."

She didn't see it, but she would tomorrow, at the All Hallows' Eve ball. At the stroke of midnight, her time would be up. I'd make my third and final mark.

She'd see me for what I truly was.

"I've had a taste of your brutal side..." She sucked her lower lip between her teeth, chewing it coyly. "Now, I want this side of you."

Hells. How could I say no to that?

I dragged her on top of me, her luscious legs draping over either side of my waist as my hand slipped up to tangle in her hair. Her weight on my cock made it ache with need, and I wanted to sink into her heat, to bury myself inside her and lose myself there.

But I wouldn't. Not yet. Not until her soul belonged to me.

I would, however, savor her in other ways.

My free hand squeezed her ass so hard, she gasped—hard enough that my fingertips would leave bruises on her flesh.

With her face mere inches from mine, both her hands planted on either side of my head, I could taste her breath carrying every moan and whimper as my gaze dropped to her plush lips.

I wanted to see that mouth wrapped around my cock again, but I wanted to show her that soft side she was so convinced I had.

"I'm going to taste you, Rayven," I whispered, my voice hard steel wrapped in downy velvet. "I'm going to taste every goddamn inch of you."

At my words, her heart thrummed hard against my chest, and it was everything I could do to keep myself from rolling over and sheathing all of me inside her with one savage thrust.

No, I was dead set on teasing out every second I had with her.

My hand smoothed down her back and curved over the swell of her ass. "I'm going to be gentle with you this time, but I'm going to be in complete control. Understand?"

"What are you going to do?"

"I'm going to cuff you again, just like the last time you were in this bed. This time, I'm going to blindfold you. I'll be taking my mask off, and I won't have you sneaking a peek at me."

I knew she wouldn't like that last part. As expected, she opened her mouth to protest but before she could get out the words, I rolled us over and pinned her to the bed.

In the same beat, I tugged on the sash of her gown and tweaked her pierced nipples hard enough to knock a delicious whimper from her mouth.

"No arguing, little human. Now. Do. You. Understand. Me?" Each word was gnashed out between rough breaths, punctuated with a growl.

Her skin heated, and her pulse kicked up. "Yes," she finally said on a whisper.

"Good."

Weeping Hells, she looked so good beneath me, with her pale flesh wrapped in firelight—soon to be wrapped in me.

Her nose and nipple piercings gleamed in the room's amber glow. I wondered what metal they were—probably steel. Those would have to come out; steel was Baal's metal. My new queen would look so perfect with her rosy nipples tipped in my silver, perhaps a dainty chain connecting them.

I wondered what emotions bled into my eyes. Whatever it was she saw in them, it had her panting, her breasts pinkening, her arousal seeping into the air.

Wetness soaked my pants, making my cock throb painfully.

She wanted this as badly as I did.

I peeled off my shirt and settled between her thighs. It felt too natural, every inch of her body calling to me like a siren, like no matter what either of us did, this was how things would have ended up.

She would have become mine eventually—everyone did. Still, I found myself thankful that my little thief caught my attention while her heart still beat. My living queen of the dead.

Once again, I felt fear zip through my chest, and I faltered.

Who would have thought the only thing to terrify me to my bones was getting exactly what I wanted?

Tomorrow, if everything fell into place, she'd become mine, but not because she actually loved me. No, it was because I'd tricked her.

Before I could dwell on the anxiety creeping up my spine, I moved us so we were diagonally across the bed. "Put your wrists over your head."

I praised her when she obeyed, her wrists settling around the bedpost, and I leaned back to grab the manacles off the bedside table. I secured them around her delicate wrists, the chain connecting them looped behind the bedpost.

Rayven chewed her bottom lip as I worked, her dark eyes watching me with increasing curiosity. "Is something wrong?"

"Hmm?" Her question jerked me from my deep mire of thoughts, and I realized I was idly stroking the cuts on her wrists. Two on one side where I'd carved the passage of days in her flesh as the Lord of Bones, and one on the other where she'd called me to help her. They were scars she'd wear forever—my own brand on her skin.

"I'm just admiring you," I said truthfully, surprised by the tender bend in my tone. "Cuts and all."

I sat back on my heels, my thighs still clamped around her hips. Thinking. Plotting. I tapped the chin of my mask, grinning beneath its frozen lips. "I want to keep you here forever."

Another truth.

Rayven's muscles stiffened beneath me, but I found no fear or panic in her brown eyes. She probably just wrote it off as meaningless filthy talk. Even if she had no idea how much I meant those words—and the lengths I was going to make them a reality—she was enjoying the fantasy of being mine forever.

It was as plain as the blush on her cheeks.

"What would you do to me, if you kept me here forever?"

"I'd shower you in every luxury possible for a demon of my station." My fingers roved over her thighs, coming close enough to her seam that her breath quickened. I pushed her legs wide, my gaze dropping to her folds.

Hells. I'd barely touched her, and she was already soaking the sheets.

"I've told you before. You are a drug, especially in a place like this," I said, my fingers still exploring her soft skin. "Warm pussy. Beating heart. Perfect, gorgeous skin. Your eyes are filled with fire, your mind churning with beautiful, dark thoughts. You are kind, but you aren't weak. You're stubborn to a fault. If you were mine, I'd spend eternity breathing you in, tasting you, branding every part of you onto my very bones."

Her thunderstruck expression had my cock pulsing hot.

"Now, I'm going to make you come so hard, you'll be begging for me to do just that, little human."

I reached for the white dress she'd been wearing and ripped it out from under her before I tore a long strip of fabric from it. Folding it in half to make it less sheer, I fashioned a decent blindfold.

"Up," I demanded, and she raised her head for me to tie the fabric over her eyes.

Her heart gave a delicious lurch in her chest, and a hint of a smile danced across her lips. She liked not knowing what was coming.

I trailed my fingers over her stomach, up over her chest, playing with the jewelry adorning her nipples. The more I toyed with my mortal pet, the wetter she became, her sweet smell bleeding into the air, making my cock unbearably hard.

"You're a fucking tease, you know that? I don't have all of eternity to wait for you to get on with finally fucking me," she snapped, though the severity of her voice was lost when the words were chased with a moan.

I zeroed in on her bratty little mouth, dark thoughts stirring as I imagined all the fucked-up things I could do with it—the things I *had* done to it.

"Careful, little human..." I leaned over her, bringing my masked face so close to hers that her lips began to quiver under the wash of my breath. "I told you I'd be gentle, but you still have a full night at my mercy. I could keep you chained up, just like this—bring you close to the edge without ever letting you come."

Knowing she couldn't see me, I transformed my tongue into the long black one my monster form bore and ran the tip up her cheek, droplets of saliva peppering her face. I couldn't wait to taste all of her in my other form.

"And when you've passed out from the sheer exhaustion that comes from teetering on the brink of pleasure, I'll use that bratty little mouth as I see fit."

I let go as a shiver worked through her, her blush consuming her entire body like a fever as the pleasure consumed her.

Now that was interesting. I knew Rayven was into some pretty dark kinks—even if she was just coming to discover it for herself—but this one surprised me most of all.

A confession burned at the back of my throat, and before I could bite it back, I decided to see how she'd react. "Don't look at me like that. It's not like I haven't already done it."

My finger traced the seam of her mouth, and when her lips parted at a gasp, I hooked it, tugging her jaw open to get a good look at her tongue. "Seeing you swallow my cum in the labyrinth cemetery was hot as Hell, but it didn't compare to when you were passed out in this very bed, writhing in your sleep as dreams of the Lord of Bones ravaged your mind. You were begging, desperate for a fat cock in your mouth."

My other hand slid up her clavicle, over her throat, and curved over her collar. "And you know I can't resist you when you *beg*."

# CHAPTER THIRTY-THREE

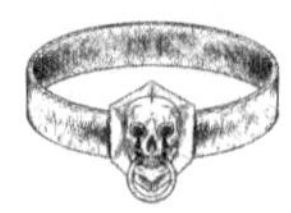

## RAYVEN

THIS DEMON WAS HEAVEN and hell, wrapped up in ink and scars and pretty words, dipped in honey and poison.

His confession turned my blood to ice in one breath, then molten as lava on the next.

What was he doing to me?

I wanted him more than ever. I wanted him to the point of pain, to the point where I was seriously considering making a stupid ass decision just so I could be with him a little longer.

What was wrong with me that I was so head over heels for this fucked up demon? He had me wrapped so tightly around his horns, his confession of using my mouth while I was sleeping only had me wetter.

His obsession with me was rivaling that of his master.

This was dangerous territory.

I was playing with fire, and there was no way I would escape this place without some massive fucking burns—if I escaped at all.

If it wasn't for the monster king who ruled this realm, I might not even want to leave.

It's not like I had anything waiting for me when I got back. A life of crime? A mother who wanted nothing to do with me anymore? None of that was worth going back to.

But I couldn't stay here and be the Lord of Bones' queen.

It was Belial I wanted.

Staying would only put him in danger though. If the Lord of Bones didn't kill him for helping me, he definitely would when he found out my feelings for his ferryman.

I'd been so resistant to the Lord of Bones, and still he'd told me that I'd come to love him.

He was wrong, or at least, he'd been partially wrong.

I'd still fallen in love with a monster.

"I don't care what you've done to me. You've saved my life more than once. I'm still in your debt."

The mattress shifted as Belial seemed to lean back. Suddenly I felt colder—the distance between us was all wrong.

"After tonight, you owe me nothing. That doesn't mean I won't take from you, even if I don't deserve it. I am not a good man, Rayven," he said, his voice suddenly cold and heavy with truth. "Don't ever forget that."

"You *do* deserve it," I argued. "I don't give two fucks if you're not a good person. You're good to me. You didn't have to show me my father's soul. You never had to help me and go against your Lord." My blindfold grew heavier as it absorbed my tears. "I want you. I want you in whatever way you'll give me."

"You think you do. You think you know me..."

"Let me know you then. Let me in, damn it. Take your mask off. Let me see you. "

I wasn't just talking about the mask he wore. Beneath that, he wore another. This gorgeous demon was shrouded in so many secrets. I knew very little about him, but I was still drawn to him. The pull was undeniable, the need to be close to him so strong, it rivaled my need to breathe.

There was so much emotion buzzing between us, so much unknown. Something huge was hanging over our heads, like an invisible ball about to drop. To my dismay, the foreboding and the anticipation only ramped up my desire for him.

"Touch me, Belial. Please." My lips quivered, my voice coming out mewling and pathetic, but I didn't care. I knew he liked it by the way the bulge in his pants twitched against my stomach. "Please."

He hesitated like he sensed it too. This wasn't just sex. We'd broken through some emotional barrier, and if we took this further, if we continued down this path, there'd be no going back to the dynamic we had before.

It would be harder than ever to leave this place without him, but I couldn't think about that right now. I needed a distraction. I needed to get lost in him, to worry about the future later.

So, I begged. I writhed beneath him, my wrists pulling at my cuffs, the rattle of the chain making my pulse push higher. I squirmed and moaned and begged.

This was degrading. Wrong. Sinful. Obscene.

I was eating up every fucking second of it like the good little monster fucker I was.

My desire to be owned and dominated by this demon strangled all that remained of my self-preservation.

"That's right, little human. Beg for me to own your body." He moved lower down my body, settling between my spread thighs. He pressed his thumb to my clit while two fingers sunk inside me. "Beg for me to fill you up with whatever I feel like fucking you with."

"Fill me with whatever you want," I panted, wiggling my hips to urge him on. "Please."

"Beg for me to fuck you with my fingers." The edge of his mask grazed the sensitive skin of my inner thigh, his warm breath rolling over my core.

"Please, Belial, fuck me with your fingers..."

"My tongue."

A whimper left me. "Yes, your tongue..."

"Beg me to stretch out that gorgeous cunt of yours. I want to hear those pretty lips purse around your pathetic whimpers, telling me how much of a little slut you are for demon cock."

"Please. Stretch me open. Fill me up."

"Good girl," he said with a gravelly purr that slid over my skin like sandpaper. "Tell me how badly you want me to fill you with the seed I've been saving for you."

Jesus Christ. The mouth on this demon.

The dark shit he did to me with just a few dirty words and the crook of his finger.

"I want you to fill me with your cum. I want to feel it, warm and hot inside me." More tears flowed, and I felt one slip past the blindfold and roll down my cheek. "Everything else in this realm is so damn cold."

The warble of my voice had him pausing. His fingers pulled out of me, and I cried at the loss.

My mind spun as I tried to make sense of what he was doing. The mattress dipped, and he arched over me, the jingle of his horn jewelry ribboning around my ear as he placed something on the bed beside me.

My heart slammed against my ribs when it struck me. It was his mask.

As soon as I made the connection, his lips were on my cheek, kissing away my tears.

"I want to own every part of you, Rayven. That includes your tears, your scars, and your sadness, too."

His voice was charged with something I couldn't parse, something that sat heavy on my chest, squeezing more tears from me. He kissed away each one before his lips trailed down my thighs, laying a path of kisses that had my skin tingling.

The connection was sweet, and he took his time as his lips traced my scars. His tender kisses might as well have been a whip for how they lashed over me, making me feel more vulnerable than I'd ever felt with anyone else. He was peeling back my layers, exposing parts of me I hadn't known were there.

"Fuck," I panted as his mouth wandered down to my apex, kissing the patch of hair between my legs.

His fingers twirled the coarse hairs, his hot breath spilling down my core with a satisfied hum. "I love the color of your hair here—as black as a raven's back. You know, legend has it that ravens are, in their own way, psychopomps themselves. It's said they carry souls from the land of the living to the land of the dead."

A moan hissed past my clenched teeth as his mouth moved lower, his tongue slipping through my folds. "A-and i-is it true?"

Christ, he *laughed* against me, making my walls clench around his tongue as it dipped in an inch or so before pulling out so he could reply.

"No. Well, not until now," he mused. "You are named Rayven, and you are carrying a soul."

"But I'll be taking my soul back to the land of the living with me," I forced out, my legs beginning to tremble with anticipation. "This isn't a one-way trip."

I expected him to argue, to toss back one of his snarky comments about me not being able to leave. Instead, his lips curved in a smirk against my entrance as his hands came up beneath my thighs, pulling them into the air and spreading them further apart.

His breath had a delicious shiver skipping down my spine, and a moan tore from my throat when his tongue sank back inside. His masculine groan filled the air as my heartbeat drummed against his tongue, and tension coiled in my belly. It was both too much and not enough.

I wanted more. I wanted it to stop.

*Fuck*. I didn't know what I wanted anymore.

It was so good, I never wanted it to end, but I knew it had to. If it didn't, my soul would never make it back to the mortal realm. I'd be stuck here forever, caught between this demon and his king.

My mind was a mess, but through the swirling thoughts, a little voice in the back of my head was loud and clear. *"Would that be so bad?"*

# CHAPTER THIRTY-FOUR

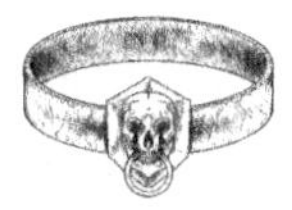

## RAYVEN

BELIAL FUCKED ME WITH his mouth until I was dizzy with pleasure, every part of me screaming for more. When he sucked my clit into his mouth, all my self-composure disintegrated and my eyes rolled into the back of my head.

"I want your cock," I told him on a shaky exhale. "Please. I'm ready for it. I *need* it."

I'd only known him for a few days, but it didn't feel like it. Time passed differently in Limbo, minutes stretching on for hours, hours dragging by like days. It felt like I'd been here for an eon, waiting for Belial to take me for an eternity.

How was that possible? How had I been waiting my entire life to be with someone I'd only just met?

This felt like fate—no, something darker than that. My need for this demon was as palpable and binding as the chains around my wrists and the collar around my throat.

It was a prison sentence, one without parole or bail. Purgatory.

Fitting, considering I was falling in love with a demon of Limbo.

My breath hitched when his hand smoothed over my pussy, his fingers easily sliding through my arousal.

"If you weren't so wet already, I'd prepare you more so you could take all of me." He suddenly flipped me around with ease so I was on my hands and knees. The chain of my handcuffs twisted, the metal biting into my skin.

He planted himself behind me, one hand on my hip, his other working to free the laces of his pants.

"But I don't have the patience for that. Besides…" His voice dropped an octave, making the hairs on the back of my neck rise. "Just in case you don't make it out of the labyrinth, my cock will be good training for you. The Lord of Bones' is much bigger than mine."

I choked on a gasp, a fresh wave of tears stinging my eyes. This time they were bitter and angry.

What the actual fuck?

Why would he say that to me? *Why now?*

Was he trying to hurt me? Or had he expected that saying such a thing would only make me wetter?

Because God-fucking-damn it, it did.

The thought of the Lord of Bones trying to fit his massive monster cock inside me had me frothing at the mouth, which only made me madder. I hated that skull-headed asshole.

The only thing I hated more than the King of Limbo was how much he called to that dark, depraved part of me Belial was so insistent on uncovering. They could both go to Hell.

"I fucking hate you," I snarled in a low voice, which was distorted by a swollen moan as he pushed himself inside me. "I f-fucking...hate...*oh*...you."

He buried more of himself into me, and I stretched to take him. It hurt. *It hurt so fucking good.*

"Oh, little human, even your lies are sweet. They're almost as good as hearing your screams." He punctuated the last word with a punch of his hips, filling me even more.

I screamed as an intense cocktail of pain and pleasure spiked my system. His thrust jerked me forward, my fingers knotting in the sheets. My forehead knocked against the bedpost, and the string of curses pouring from my mouth on the next thrust had him burying the last few inches of himself inside me.

His grip on my hips tightened, his claws elongating and scouring my skin. "Bleeding Hells. You can take all of me."

"You said you were going to be gentle, you bastard."

"I did. I'm sorry."

I blanched at his apology. With the way the words rolled off his tongue, I had a feeling he wasn't used to apologizing to anyone.

"Fuck you, Belial."

A pregnant pause settled between us, the most intense span of awkward silence I'd ever experienced, considering how we were connected.

"I've fucked this up already…" He swore beneath his breath and started to pull out.

"No!" I blurted before I could swallow down the word.

His spine bowed and he draped himself over me, the weight of his muscled body making my arms and legs shake.

"Do you want me to stop or not?" he asked, his mouth in my hair. I turned my head, trying to see him through the blindfold, but I could only make out a vague silhouette through the fabric.

"I don't want you to stop, but it hurts being this close to you…" I admitted.

His lips kissed the patch of skin behind my ear. "Do you like the pain?"

I did. I hated how much I liked it, but that didn't take away from how much I enjoyed every second of it.

"Yes…"

"That's what I thought. I'm trying to be better at the way I inflict it." His lips went to my shoulder, and he painted a lick down my shoulder blade. "I've forgotten what it's like to be human. All these emotions are new to me. *Caring* is new." He paused for a beat, pressing his lips to my skin again. "Sometimes, I can't control my brutal nature. It's what I've been for so long."

His hands went back to my thighs, and he nudged his hips forward, shoving all of himself back inside me. He growled, his fingers flexing painfully into my flesh.

"I'll try to control myself…:"

He was hesitating, struggling to be gentle like he'd promised, but I didn't need that from him. Mark had been gentle. "Don't be."

He tensed behind me. "Are you sure?"

I nodded into the mattress, my fingers clenching the sheets for dear life. "If it's too much, I have my safeword," I reminded him to ease his mind, although I had no plans to use it. "I want to see how badly you want me."

With that, something snapped inside him, all restraint washing away like the breaking of a dam. He pounded into me, each stroke feeling as though it was relieving the mounting pressure between us.

The relief of it had my hips angling up and pushing back to meet each of his frantic thrusts.

"I'm not going to be able to stop until you're dripping with me, Rayven," he growled.

"Will I get pregnant? I'm… not on birth control." I felt silly asking the question. He said himself he was a human who had died eons ago, but he was something different, a new creature entirely now. Maybe one that was capable of breeding.

The thought had me heating.

I'd never thought about having kids before, just because I'd never thought I'd ever find anybody worth doing it with, but with Belial…

I stuffed that thought back down into the deepest part of my mind as soon as it formed. It was too dangerous and complicated, and it would never be possible.

I was going home tomorrow, and this demon wasn't coming with me.

"Demons can't impregnate humans, little Rayven."

Right. Of course. Good.

That should have been a good thing. It *was* a good thing.

So why was there a hot, uncomfortable pang pulling under my gut and burning into my marrow?

"Fuck me harder," I pleaded, wanting to cover the agony with a different kind of pain. "Don't stop. Don't be gentle."

He shoved into me, his pistoning thrusts unforgiving and brutal. Obscene sounds clawed up my throat as the silver chain connecting the piercing in his tip and the cuff gripping his base rubbed my insides.

It hurt. The pain was delicious agony, but it wasn't enough. I needed him closer, deeper. I wanted him to brand himself onto my very soul so I'd never forget him.

"Harder. I won't break," I said, even as I felt myself shattering apart around him.

I screamed my release, the sharp spike of pain drowned out by ecstasy.

"Rayven..." My name in his mouth was a curse and a prayer all in one. A plea. A man at war with himself as he released inside me.

His seed was hot and thick as it gushed inside me in spurts. The combination of my slick and his cum gushed down my thighs, leaving the sheets beneath my knees cold and wet.

Belial reached around, undoing my cuffs. When they fell away, I moved to pull my blindfold off, but before I could, he flipped me around so I was on my back, his hand pinning my wrists over my head.

His free hand pulled my legs apart, and with another thrust, he was inside me again. He was still hard as a rock, and this time, he didn't just fuck me. He made love to me.

It was slow and tender, and it went on for the rest of the night. The hours bled into one another. *We* bled into one another, until I wasn't sure where I ended and he started. It was the closest thing to heaven that existed for me in this realm of the dead. If I died and my soul ended up on a shelf in the castle library, I knew this would be one of the memories I lived out for all eternity.

When sleep finally began to take me, I imagined we'd fall asleep curled up with one another, but he continued to use me, even as the darkness folded in.

# CHAPTER THIRTY-FIVE

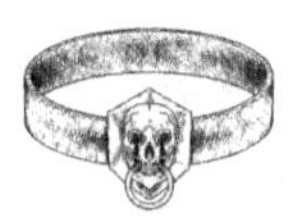

## RAYVEN

I COULDN'T REMEMBER EVER sleeping so peacefully as I did with Belial beside me. Tucked into the crook of his arm, I felt so safe, so comfortable, my head resting on his chest.

My eyes fluttered as exhaustion threatened to pull me back under, but they popped back open when a subtle thumping noise caught my attention. It was a heartbeat, faint, but there, beneath my cheek.

*So he did have a functioning heart.*

Its gentle pitter-patter had my own picking up speed, blood racing through my veins. I never imagined something as simple as a heartbeat could have me feeling more alive in the realm of the dead than I ever had among the living.

I glanced at the heavy curtains covering the floor-to-ceiling windows. Pale light–not red–spilled in through the gap in the fabric.

It was the third day, All Hallows' Eve.

A perfect day to escape Limbo.

It was a bittersweet thought that had my stomach knotting. I couldn't stay here, but the notion of leaving this bed almost brought me physical pain.

Last night was only supposed to be a brief reprieve from the terrifying world I was trapped in, the deadly maze I had to escape from, but it had turned into something much more.

Sitting up, I looked down at Belial's sleeping form and watched as he snored softly. Aside from his mask, he was completely naked—we both were—splayed out over the tousled black sheets. I could have stared at him forever, and I still would have been surprised by how goddamn beautiful he was. He looked like a dark angel, his sleek muscles encased in swathes of faded ink, scars, and the faintest smatter of dark hair.

My attention dropped to the appendage lying limp against his thigh. Electric sparks shot through my system, sinking straight to the place throbbing from his abuse. As I expected, the silver cuff banding around the base of his shaft, along with the chain, had rubbed me raw. Every movement, no matter how small, was a stinging reminder of the night before.

I had a feeling walking around the labyrinth would be extra painful today; I was sure he'd get a lot of satisfaction seeing me limp around the hedge maze, knowing the only monster response for this ache was the one in his pants.

Smug bastard.

My heart clenched again, butterflies whirling in my tummy and turning to hornets at the thought of leaving him. More and more, he was feeling like *my* smug bastard, and it was becoming difficult to imagine telling him goodbye.

My gaze wandered back to his mask, and I tried for the millionth time to imagine the face beneath it. Why was he so secretive about what he looked like?

He knew I was aware of the scars, even if I didn't know how bad they were. He had to know I didn't care. A niggling feeling told me that maybe his reluctance had less to do with me and more to do with the scars beneath his surface—the ones I couldn't see.

I wanted to respect that, but how was I supposed to entertain the possibility of giving more of myself to this demon when he wouldn't even show me his face?

A thought bloomed in my mind, and I toyed with it for a moment. Debating. Weighing the consequences. Before I could write it off as a bad idea—which it was a bad idea, a very bad idea—my hand was reaching for Belial's mask.

My fingers had barely brushed the edge of it at his jawline when his hand snapped up, seizing my wrist.

I yelped in surprise as he lurched up and wrenched me close to his face, his gray eyes burning with rage.

He hadn't been sleeping at all. He'd been faking it.

"Oh, you are in *trouble*," he seethed. "You better watch your-self. Do that one more time and you'll be sorry."

I tried to snatch his mask with my other hand, and he caught that one too. "You're playing with fire, mortal."

"Good," I huffed, trying to pull free from his hold, only to have him scoop me up into his lap. He was hard again, his dick jabbing into my ass. "Maybe I'll burn to ash and be reincarnated as someone who actually gives a shit about your little threats. You don't scare me."

His chest rose and fell in a heavy rhythm as his fingers tight-ened like a vice around my wrist. I choked back a whine, refusing to show any pain, knowing he loved it when I did.

"If I hadn't promised to return you to the labyrinth by the morning, I'd bend you over my knee and spank you so hard, you wouldn't be able to sit until your next life."

"Jokes on you," I spat. "I already can't sit because of your freakishly long dick."

"I don't remember you complaining about that last night." His voice turned soft and sultry, and he fell back onto the pile of pillows, pulling me down with him.

"Belial, I have to go," I whined, weakly pushing against his chest, hoping he'd hold me tighter. He did.

"You don't have to," he said, his fingers running through my hair. "You can stay here a bit longer."

"I only have until midnight. Then my time is up." An icy chill rolled down my spine at the words, my impending fate looming overhead like a thundercloud. "I'll have to accept becoming the queen of the dead."

"Haven't you always felt more at home with the dead anyway? Surely you haven't spent most of your life in cemeteries just to stick it to dead rich people."

I blinked rapidly at the demon, not believing what he was saying. "Is this pro-Lord of Bones propaganda I'm hearing? Or do I still have mud from the labyrinth clogging my ears?"

Belial rolled his eyes behind his mask. "He *is* my Lord, Rayven."

I shoved off his chest, breaking from his arms and stumbling out of the bed. My legs were like jelly—they buckled, and my hand whipped out to grab onto one of the bed posts.

Belial was on his feet and moving to catch me before I found purchase, but I snarled in his direction, hackles raised. "Don't touch me!"

"What have I done now?" He threw his hands out to his sides. "Explain your emotions so I can understand."

This was what I got for falling for a morally gray demon. He really didn't get why I was pissed, and when I'd explain, it was a crap shoot as to whether he'd care or not.

"Take me back to the labyrinth."

"Rayven—"

"You fucking promised! You had your fun. Now, just take me back." My eyes started to leak bitter tears. "Please."

His shoulders fell, that secondary mask snapping into place. "Fine. You'll find a change of clothes in the armoire, something more to your taste."

He began to pull his clothes back on as I stomped to the large wardrobe in the corner of the room. My heart clenched at what I found hanging inside.

A long sleeve turtleneck, thick enough to keep me warm outside, with a little heart cut out in the chest to show a peak of my cleavage There was a pleated canvas mini-skirt with leggings to go underneath, and my boots.

The best part was that it was all black.

"You didn't have to do this," I forced out as I pulled the clothes on, unable to turn and look him in the eye.

"Do what? Give you clothes?" he said with a scoff. "Fine. Wander around naked. You won't get any complaints from me."

When I was fully dressed, I whipped around to glare at him. "Give me clothes I've been begging for since the second I got here. *Black* clothes because I feel comfortable in them. You know that. It's just like with the book. You go out of your way to make me feel comfortable, safe, *loved*, and then you go and do something shitty."

He was shirtless still, with only his pants on, still cinching up the laces when he stormed across the room. "I told you, I'm not a good person. You like pain? Good. That's what I can bring you. That's what I'm good at. As a demon I'm fascinated, by your human emotions. They're like ghosts to me, whispers of distant memories I can only hope to remember. Seeing you react to them, seeing you cry, seeing you blush and heat, scream and yell? It's all beautiful to me."

He finished lacing up his pants and dropped to a crouch to lace up my boots.

I stared down at him, a complicated ball of emotions I couldn't even begin to untangle lodging in my throat.

I swear, these demons and their obsession with making me *feel*... They'd be the end of me if I didn't get out of here.

"Take me back, Belial. I want to go home."

He stood to his full height, glaring down at me through the holes in his mask. "And what's waiting for you there?"

Fucking nothing, except for a normal life away from evil demon lords and their bipolar sidekicks.

When I said nothing, he expelled a conceding sigh and held his hand out for me to take. I stared at him, noting he'd left the gloves...and his shirt.

He wanted me to stay. *Didn't he?* The ferryman had mentioned last night that he wanted to tie me up and use me for all eternity. I'd chalked that up to dirty talk, but maybe he was trying to tempt me to stay. It was a ludicrous thought, a fantasy that could never be reality. The Lord of Bones wouldn't allow it.

If anything, leaving him would keep him safe from his Lord's wrath.

Magic exploded around us, and when it fizzled away, we were left standing exactly where he'd plucked me from the labyrinth last night, just as he'd promised.

I wrenched my hand out of his and turned my back to him, scanning the network of hedges that seemed to go on forever. "Just point me in the right direction, and you can go."

Silence settled between us. I spun around to face him, waiting for him to answer. He just stood in the middle of the path, stoic, shirtless, and beautiful, his black hair and silver chains rustling in the faint breeze. "I'm not telling you."

I glared. "Why not?"

"That wasn't our deal, was it? I promised to give you a bath, a bed to sleep in, a meal. I gave you a few more things I didn't have to, so you're welcome. I got what I wanted, so our transaction is complete."

"*Transaction?*" I walked toward him, my insides burning with rage. "Is that what this was to you?"

His jaw set. "No, but clearly that's all it was to you. So we can be done here, if that's what you want."

*What I want.* If he only knew what I wanted. Hell, if only I knew what I wanted.

Maybe I did know. Maybe I was just too scared to admit it.

"What am I supposed to do, Belial?" I stopped in front of him, crossing my arms tightly over my chest to abate the dull ache forming there. "I have to find the exit to this place, or I become the Queen of Limbo. I'll be forced to wear a crown of bones made from my fucking ex."

"Did you love him?"

"What?" I blanched.

"Did you love your ex-mate?"

"No." The answer came too quickly, but it was true. I had never loved Mark. "He was boring, but that doesn't mean I wanted him to die."

"Humans die all the time." Belial shrugged one bare shoulder. "If you go back to the human realm, you'll eventually die, and then you'll end up back here anyway. Why fight the inevitable?"

"At least I'd have a life there! It might be a shit life, but it's still a life. I'd be free." My cheeks flamed, my voice raising unintentionally. "I wouldn't be the pet of an evil monster."

"Then give yourself to me instead."

I froze, my heart shooting into my throat at his words. "W-what?"

"He can't claim your soul if I own it first." The emotion in his voice was thick and raw, unexpected. It made my stomach flutter and my skin tingle, and I pleaded with him silently to explain what he meant before my heart shattered in suspense. "That's demon law. As a ferryman, I'm not supposed to claim souls for myself but... I can. Yours will be the only one I own, the only one I'll ever need."

I took several steps back, shaking my head slowly. Was I hearing him right? Was he really making a play for my soul?

"He'll kill you," I whispered, my bottom lip threatening to wobble.

"He won't."

"How can you be so sure?"

"There are a lot of things about this world you still don't understand, a lot of things about *me* you don't understand," he said.

"You're right." I took another step back, looking him up and down. "I don't get you at all. I haven't even seen your face, and I'm supposed to sell my soul to you?"

"Not sell," he said in a charged whisper that sent a thrill of electricity through my bloodstream. He took several long-legged strides toward me, the distance between us shrinking as his domineering presence wrapped around me. "Give it to me because you want to. Admit it. You don't want to leave."

Another step forward, and he was right in front of me, a kiss away from his mask's lips. "What you want is to be mine, isn't it? You want to be mine forever."

He was voicing everything I was too scared to say myself. At the words, the invisible bond pulling me toward him intensified, hooking in my chest, beckoning me into his arms.

Was I really considering giving my soul to a demon? It wasn't logical, but the way my heart sped up at the thought gave me my answer.

Maybe this was the solution to my problem after all...

If I gave Belial my soul, it meant I would stay out of the Lord of Bones' claws. He couldn't own me, and I wouldn't have to wear his crown.

That thought alone had my mind spinning.

"What will happen to me?" I asked. "Will I be your thrall or something? I'm not interested in being a slave."

"You'll be mine." His hand came up to cup my chin, his fingertips sending sparks skittering across my skin. "I'll take care of you. I'll treasure you. I'll make you happy."

I hesitated, the weight of silence threatening to crush me. It was a huge decision, one I probably should have considered more, but my time was running out. I only had a few precious hours left before the Lord of Bones came to make his third mark, and my heart was all but screaming for me to take Belial up on his offer.

It was what I wanted.

*He* was what I wanted.

I just needed to be brave enough to accept.

"I'll do it," I said, the words rushing out. "But I have one condition."

The relief in his eyes was obvious, and I didn't miss the tiny sigh that followed. "Name it."

"Take off your mask and show me your face."

# CHAPTER THIRTY-SIX

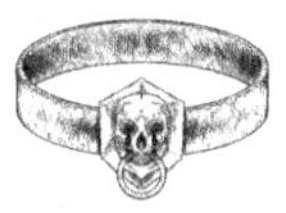

## BELIAL

*THIS WAS IT.*

My plan to claim all of Rayven was working, the pieces falling into place.

This was the moment I would be able to claim her soul—all I had to do was remove my mask and show her my scars. I'd been so ashamed of them ever since Catherine had looked upon them and slit her throat—the first of many times—just to escape me.

I rarely ventured around my castle in my lesser form now, as it brought back haunting memories. The scars were a constant reminder of my solitude, of the way Catherine had sworn no one could ever love a beast like me. Those words had cut deep, and because of them, no one had seen my face without a mask since her.

At the same time, it was such a simple thing for my little treasure to ask for.

Of all the things she could have demanded in exchange for her soul, her most precious possession, even if she didn't realize the magnitude of its importance, all she wanted was for me to remove my mask.

*To see my face.*

I never deserved her, and I probably never would.

Forcing her to be my queen would have been easy. I could have shoved a crown on her head, kept my collar welded around her neck forever. I could have locked up my realm so she could never go back to the mortal one, but she wouldn't be mine by the laws of the Old Ways. Not until she died and her bones, and the soul within passed to me. The only way to own her soul while her heart still beat was if she gave it willingly.

Manipulating her with my lesser form had all been so I could make her truly mine. Her bones. Her flesh. Her blood. Her tears. Her very soul.

All mine.

My careful planning, mind tricks, twisted words, sex games...all of it had been orchestrated to lead to this very moment.

Yet, I found myself... hesitating.

Over these past few days, my obsession had morphed beyond recognition, turned into something more. Even though I didn't have much to compare it to, I knew what it was: *love*.

I loved her.

I loved her more than I'd ever loved anything before, to the point where, after all the careful plotting, lies, tricks, and pining, I would let her go on a whim.

"You're making this too easy for me," I sighed, my hands falling away from her face, putting distance between us with several backwards strides.

Her brows contorted with confusion. "What are you talking about?"

"You shouldn't be making this deal like you're trading away something frivolous. I'm a fucking demon, Rayven. You're going to trade your soul just for a look at my face?"

Confusion quickly became rage as her eyes narrowed and her lips pursed. "Let me get this straight. You're upset because I'm willing to give you what you're asking for?"

"Yes," I said before I could make sense of it. Her soul was exactly what I wanted—all I'd wanted since I first laid eyes on her—but I expected to have to fight for it, to wear her down, to break her for it. Yet here she was, giving it to me freely. "I care about you."

"And I care about y–"

I held a hand up to silence her, shaking my head as my emotions warred within me. "You don't understand. I want you to stay purely out of my own interests. I'm a selfish bastard, Rayven." I paused, caught off guard by the way my chest tightened at the admission. "But now, I also want what's best for you, because I give a damn about you, and what's best for you isn't me."

She lifted her chin, a challenging look in her dark eyes. "So what am I supposed to do?"

Without thinking—if I stopped to think, I wouldn't go through with it—I surged forward, snatching her by the arm.

Ignoring her protests, I waved a hand, and a magical doorway appeared. I stepped through the archway, dragging her behind me.

"Where are we—" Her question immediately cut off when we came through on the other side, stepping out onto a desolate cliffside. It overlooked the sea on one side, with the labyrinth far below on the other. On the very edge of the cliff sat a wooden door, built into the ruins of a stone wall that had crumbled over time.

Rayven turned to see my castle grounds, which looked like miniatures from where we stood. The castle was at least an entire day's walk from this point. Even if she'd found the door leading out of my garden, even if she'd had a map to lead her straight here, she never would have made it in time.

She spun around, her eyes bouncing between the door and the castle as understanding set in. "Is that...?"

"The way back to your world, yes."

Her eyes went wild and glossy with tears of fury. "That *fucker.* I never had a chance."

We stood there for several minutes, and I watched her stare out at the castle, arms wrapped around herself. She was shivering, and I had a feeling it had nothing to do with the cold.

"Why are you showing me the door now?" She turned, her raven hair lashing around her shoulders in the breeze.

Weeping Hells. She was so beautiful.

"You want to go home," I forced out.

Her head tilted to the side. "Do you want me to leave?"

"No, but it would be objectively stupid for you not to. I want you to stay, but as I've told you, I'm not a good man."

"You can't be all that bad if you're defying your lord and showing me the way home." She pointed at the door. "You're giving me a way out. You're saving me, yet again."

"Don't do that." I shook my head adamantly. "I'm not a hero. That first night, when I told you I was your only shot at salvation? That was the first of many lies I've told you. I'm not your savior. I'm your damnation."

Her lips parted as she stared at me, her gaze heavy as her mind worked. It didn't matter what I said—she'd still try to make me out to be the good guy. Meanwhile, I'd been the villain all along.

"Can I ask you one question?" she said, breaking my train of thought. "And give me your word that the answer I get will be the truth."

I tensed. "Yes."

She approached me, the breeze blowing harder, making the dead grass dance and her hair thrash around her like a dark halo. "Do you love me, Belial? Can a demon even love?"

My heart fluttered curiously at her question, and I swallowed as she came to stand in front of me, my eyes sparkling at the mere inches between us. "When I died, I forgot how to feel most human emotions, but love was not among them."

A smile as dark as my infernal magic bowed her lips. "Then I'll stay."

I reached for her, desperate to feel her skin against mine, but I only allowed my fingers to graze her cheek. "If you stay, and you give me your soul... it's going to hurt. I *will* hurt you."

"I thought we established how much I like the pain you bring me."

"Rayven—"

"I'm not going," she said in a firm voice that told me she would argue. "I'm giving you my soul..." She pressed her hands against my hard chest, her smile canting into a mischievous smirk. "And you're going to take it like a good little demon."

I gaped, my jaw falling slack in disbelief. I'd given her an out. Even if I hadn't told her the full truth of what she was getting herself into, my conscience was relieved, at least enough for me to do what I was about to do.

"This is your last chance," I warned, my hand dropping to her shoulder and then to her waist. "You can return to your normal, human life. No one would blame you for walking away."

Her gaze flitted back to the door, then straight back to me. "Or I could stay."

"Or you can stay here with me and be my mate." I nodded. "Come hell or high water, you'll be mine forever."

"The funny thing is, forever doesn't seem like such a long time anymore. You can have my soul. You can have my everything, so long as you take your mask off. I want to know what you look like." She paused, chewing her lip. "What my mate looks like."

I took her hands in mine and guided them to my face. She sucked in a breath, her fingers trembling as they curled underneath the mask and slowly lifted it off.

She released the breath she'd been holding,I watched her face with an uneasy feeling hooking in my gut, but as the seconds passed the feeling was replaced with something warmer.

The mask slipped from her fingers, falling to the grass at her feet. Her stunned lips parted on the tiniest little *"Oh..."*

"Say something," I urged.

Her eyes frantically flitted over scars that ran deep into my flesh. The deepest one was the gash that ran diagonally across my face from my temple, over my nose, down to the edge of my jaw. I couldn't remember how I got the wound exactly, but I vaguely recalled that it involved a halberd.

"You're fucking beautiful," she said, her awestruck expression making my faint heartbeat thrum harder than it had since I was mortal.

*Beautiful.* How could she say that when these same scars had driven Catherine to madness?

"Can I touch them?"

I gave a nod, and her fingertips ghosted over my face, tracing the jagged flesh. I was stunned by the way she looked at me, like my face was better than whatever image she'd formed in her mind.

The pad of her index finger stroked down the hooked ridge of my nose. "This is sexy."

I grabbed her head in my hands before I brought my lips crashing down over hers in a bruising kiss. I poured myself into her, her lips softening against mine.

When I pulled back, a glowing silhouette of her visage—her soul in its purest form—emerged from her body like a shining ghost, still kissing me.

After a beat, I broke the kiss, and all the color drained from Rayven's face when she noticed the brand of my lips upon her soul. When the ghostly silhouette slipped back inside her, her eyelids drifted shut, and I caught her in my arms as she fainted.

For several minutes, I stood there on the cliffside, holding my raven-haired human close to my chest. Her body was limp in my embrace, her head slumped against my shoulder, her hair whipping against my cheek in the breeze.

I could feel her pulse against my skin, and I tapped its beat between her shoulder blades as I stared out over the ink-black ocean.

Tonight was the All Hallow's Eve ball and, at the stroke of midnight, she'd discover my twisted secret. Then, every part of her would belong to me.

I hauled her up into my arms, cradling her close and reveling in the feel of her body against mine as I stamped a kiss to her forehead, gazing down at her with dark reverence.

"You'll be mine forever. Even as the world falls down, little human."

## THE END OF BOOK 1

Find out what happens next to Rayven and Belial in *Queen of Carrion: Death Bound Duet Book 2*